DEATH ISN'T ENOUGH

Death Trilogy Book 1

MARIËTTE WHITCOMB

ISBN Paperback: 978-1-991202-93-2
ISBN eBook: 978-1-991202-94-9

If someone has ever harassed, persecuted, or repeatedly followed you, whether online or in person, I dedicate this book to you.

Prologue

Abducting a woman isn't easy. Not at first. But as with everything else in life – practice makes perfect. Once I started taking women no one cares about, my experiments became rather straightforward. Although, a tad more boring. The thrill just isn't the same.

Unlike the others, this one put up a fight. She fought back like a badger high on bath salts. Earning my respect, but not enough to change my mind and let her go.

That's the risk when you take a woman who has lived a hard life. They're survivors. Unlike most of the women I've met over the years, such as those who won't open a jar if it meant they need to put in effort. Sure, they'll spend hours in the gym, but when it comes down to a life-and-death situation, they'd rather die than break a nail. Vanity has kept no one from death's clutches. Or mine.

The badger's chest rises and falls as the effect of the sedative wears off. She isn't as beautiful or flawless as you are. *Nothing a box of hair dye can't fix.* And once she serves her purpose, she'll join the others.

This one is the last practise session.

It's time for us to be together. Every cell in my body aches for you. Years later, and your taste still lingers on my lips.

You're my drug and I will kill for my next fix.

My laughter fills the cabin. The woman stirs, her ugly pale blue eyes remain hidden behind her eyelids. The fake lashes are long gone. It appears crying isn't good for the glue. But what do I know about female things? Nothing except everything about you. Her eyes aren't yours. I've tried coloured contact lenses, but none of them replicate the exquisiteness of the golden flecks in your emerald eyes.

I'm grateful this one is feistier. Even though she looks nothing like you, she has the same spirit – a fighter. I must break her. Just as I will have to break you.

One of the many benefits of being a part of your life is knowing everything about you. Not even your bitch of a mother can break you. You're perfection, my love.

It pains me to think about the lengths I need to go to in order to have you all to myself.

It will be worth it. Because you're worth it.

"I'm not Emily. Stop calling me that," she whispers through clenched teeth.

My head moves from side to side. The back of my hand connects with her cheek, sending blood spraying onto the bed. "No one is." The others had accepted their new name without question. This little slut is a tough nut.

"How long before you kill me? Just do what you want and get it over and done with. Jokes on you clown-man – I've survived it all."

Rage boils inside me. Her defiance and confidence remind me of a child I watched in a restaurant last week. Do all six-year-olds backchat their parents that much? It's another reason I won't have children. And I refuse to share you, even with our potential offspring.

We'd make beautiful babies. With your eyes, hair, mouth, and exquisite body, combined with my impeccable breeding – perfection. My social standing, attractiveness, and higher-than-average intelligence have taken me far in life.

But not far enough.

Not until I have you.

This week's visitor scoots backwards on her bare ass until her back presses against the side of the bed. Despite the splinters sticking up from the floorboards, she doesn't flinch.

"We're somewhere remote because you didn't gag me. I can scream for days and no one will hear me. I can smell the wet dirt seeping through the cracks in the walls. We're in the forest. A deserted cabin? Or based on your shoes, you own it."

Laughter fills the room. This time, it isn't mine.

If I'm honest, which I rarely am, I'm rather fond of this one. Will it spare her from having her face bashed in? No.

It's the most fun I have with them. Why deny myself the only pleasure I get from conducting these experiments?

"Thank you for rescuing me from my hellish life. Also, thanks for putting an end to it. I didn't expect to last this long on the streets." She raises her bound wrists, trying to show me her palms. "I'm not trying to get you to like me. We both know you didn't bring me here for shits and giggles. I'm just chatty, haven't spent this much time with another person in years."

I walk to the other side of the musty room and sink down on the dust-covered floor. Perhaps I should make this one clean up the place. Not that I have enough time to keep an eye on her. I need to get to my day job. I stare at my designer shoes; the slut has a point. After making a quick mental note to buy a pair of cheap shoes, or steal some from a homeless person, I return my focus to her bruised face. Blood drips from the cut on her lip, landing on her bare chest.

The badger stares at me. "I'm not scared of clowns. Why wear a mask when you're going to kill me? Who am I going to tell? Or don't you want me to recognise you when you join me in hell? Your time will come; death is never late."

I'm taken aback by her lack of fear. Either she isn't afraid of dying or has the best poker face I've ever seen.

The scar tissue I saw on her back earlier tells its own story. I doubt working the streets is a dream job. Not that I know the first thing about pursuing your dreams; Mother and Father had decided for me. All I can dream about is you, and waking up next to you. I get hard just thinking about what it will feel like to be inside you.

"Get on the bed," I say, pushing to my feet.

She does as she's told. "I've been wondering why you haven't raped me yet."

Rape. What a horrible word. A heinous act. I'm not a rapist. She laughs when I tell her this.

"Then why am I here? Why am I naked? Clearly, the problem isn't you getting it up." Her blue eyes stare at my crotch.

I don't have time for this. Before she can react, I jab the needle into her leg and hold her down until the fight drains out of her. The leather straps will keep her in place until I return.

If a whore doesn't fear being sexually assaulted, I wonder if you do. You've opened your legs for so many men that you've admitted to losing count. It no longer matters, as you've been giving yourself to one man for far too long. And he isn't me. Not yet.

At least he's the reason you're back home.

My apologies, but the first thing I'm going to break?

Your heart.

The badger has given me a lot to think about. Driving back to the city offered the perfect time to mull over my plan. The others were easy to manipulate, and ending their sad lives was a blessing. To them and me.

Your life hasn't been easy. The woman who birthed you is the reason you travelled the world for five excruciatingly long years. She is to blame for all the time we've lost.

With patience, I'll mould you into what I need, leaving no trace of the old you.

Rape is a coward's way to break a woman, but I don't know if I can do that to you. No matter how much I ache to be inside you.

None of them matched you in physical strength. The day you graduated as a biokineticist was one of the proudest days of my life.

The biggest obstacle in my way is your mind. You and I are more alike than you realise. Not that you know who I am, other than what I allow you to see.

My Love, the truth is – we both take what we want from others without giving their feelings any thought. You sleep with men who don't deserve to even be in the same room as you. If only it was as easy as getting you drunk, but you're not twenty-two anymore.

Now, as for your boyfriend, getting him out of your life is child's play. He will spend the rest of his life in a state of utter hell. The same torturous suffering I endure every day without you in my bed.

The key is to destroy your identity.

"Sir, there is a police detective who wants to speak to you."

Of the long list of words I want to yell at my assistant, allowing the detective to steal my precious time is the only option. "Of course, please send him in. Bring us coffee."

I straighten my tie, rising from behind the desk to greet the unwanted guest. After getting through the pleasantries of introductions and the usual small talk about the weather, I ask the detective to take a seat. Instead of sitting, I rest my forearms on the black leather chair that gets to touch my sculpted butt. Five days a week, I spend hours in the gym, transforming my body into a machine. You'd be surprised at how much a corpse weighs.

After glancing around my sparsely decorated office, the detective gets to the point of his intrusion. "Where were you on Friday night?"

"The thirteenth?" The detective nods. "I assume you're asking in relation to some crime? Care to tell me what this is about so that I can decide whether my attorney should be present? I doubt it's necessary to waste his time. Detective, I assure you, I haven't committed a crime."

"That may be, but as I mentioned, I'm with the missing persons unit. Every second counts in a situation like this."

I decide to humour the detective and change my approach, taking a seat behind the glass desk. "Today is Tuesday. Correct me if I'm wrong, but isn't the first forty-eight hours the most vital in a missing person's investigation?"

Detective DC Reynolds thanks my assistant for the coffee without as much as glancing in her direction. Fair enough, I didn't hire Gloria for any reason other than her impeccable work ethic. The office is not the place for distractions; besides, I have a reputation to uphold. And a mask to wear.

"Monica Carter wasn't reported as missing until Sunday night when she failed to show up for family dinner." Detective Reynolds raises the mug to his lips without breaking eye contact.

It takes all of my concentration not to laugh at the irony – the police questioning me about the one disappearance I'm not responsible for. "Detective, I've known the Carters my entire life. Her brother and I attended school together and our families are close. I ran into Monica at Page on Friday night. You know the club? Monica struggled to stand without assistance. So, I took to her to her apartment, and I went straight home. A club is the last place a young woman – beautiful or not – who is too drunk to form coherent sentences should be. I'm familiar with the statistics, Detective. Who knows what might've happened to Monica, had I not done the right thing?"

"That's just it. *Something* happened to her." Detective Reynolds returns the mug to the silver tray.

My shoulders lift on their own as I shake my head. "I don't know what Monica did after I dropped her off. The apartment complex has security cameras in the lobby and outside on the street. If you haven't checked them yet, perhaps you should. I'm telling you the truth, Detective. I had nothing to do with Monica's disappearance. She might've gone to another club after I drove off. You know how spontaneous women her age are."

After typing on his phone, Detective Reynolds asks, "How do you know about the security cameras?"

I laugh without malice. "I oversaw the construction of the complex. There isn't a thing I don't know about that building, including the layout of the plumbing. If that will be all, I need to get back to work."

"The security camera footage showed us something very interesting. Before Monica got out of your car, you kissed."

I nod. "What you saw was Monica kissing me. She always said the day she turns eighteen she's going to get me in bed. Countless times I've reminded her I'm not interested. Monica is like a sister to me."

The truth? I wanted to hear Monica scream my name. Nothing tastes better than innocence. Sure, I wouldn't have been her first, but there's something about the way young women taste.

It's not your taste. No, yours is unique.

I have craved you ever since that one night. The night I blew it. In more ways than one. You've never looked at me the same, and I'm to blame.

A grave mistake I'll fix.

With no pressing work issues to attend to, I inform Gloria I'm taking the rest of the day off. The fact that a young woman is missing – one I've known since childhood – is reason enough to take a mental health day. Too much irony in one day. *Mental health.*

At a young age, I already knew I was different. Different is good. People will tell you it isn't, but people are idiots.

Conform. Comply. Blend in. Toe the line. Be less you.

The words are thrown around like confetti, yet parents, teachers, psychologists, and everyone else refuse to see the reality – we're unique. You, me, and a handful of others.

We're kindred spirits in a world too focused on following the narrative to realise they are boring little sheep. Oxygen thieves. Below us. As for you and me? When we want it, we take it.

My Love, if only you could comprehend what an unstoppable force we can be together. I allowed you the freedom to experience the world. Much as I have in your absence. Although, I doubt you've experienced the joy of bashing someone's face in. If you haven't, I'll show you. You can even choose your first piñata. That is how much I love you.

If there was any other way of stripping away the layers until nothing remained but your authentic self, believe me, I wouldn't do what I'm going to.

The City of Marcel has three sides. One reserved for the 'one percent' and middle-class. The second is where people who live from hand to mouth along with the homeless and destitute. And the third is where very few of us ever venture, similar to the dark web.

Because of the bitch who gave birth to you, you're oblivious to its existence. The evil queen deems herself above it all. But we've bumped into each other on more than one occasion deep down in the darkest corners of the beast's belly.

Without having had time for breakfast earlier, I treat myself to lunch at my favourite restaurant. The head waiter is *my guy*. Everyone has one, be it for cars, yachts, or real estate. I don't even know what my guy's name is, because it isn't the one on his name tag. He knows who I am. Everyone in this city does, thanks to my parents. The lack of anonymity is a heavy burden to carry.

Sometimes I wish the two of us could leave it all behind and start afresh in a small town. A place so far away from Marcel, no one would even think to look for us there.

Picture it, My Love. We can change our names, our professions, and you can be my wife. Perhaps we'd get married after I chisel away every piece of doubt and self-hatred your *mother* had plastered to you throughout the years.

Without opening the menu, I order the ribeye. Nothing beats the taste of high-quality meat. A text message from my burner phone is delivered to my guy's burner phone, listing the things I need to satisfy a different craving.

While waiting for both orders, I indulge myself and scroll through your social media photos. I sip the Leopard's Leap cabernet sauvignon merlot, almost choking when I land on your most recent post. If I hadn't visited the wine farm in South Africa, I'd spit it out.

This can't be happening.

It isn't part of the plan.

The words keep repeating in my head. Something spreads through me. Is this fear? Frustration? I'm not sure.

All I can think about is stabbing a fork into the nearest person's neck.

I don't. Instead, I savour the full-bodied delicious wine. Time to perfect my skills. Now.

Typical of you for not informing me in person. How is it possible that I want to make love to you and strangle you at the same time? You might even enjoy that more than I would.

Before I can find your number in the call registry, my phone rings. Your exquisite face fills the screen.

"It would've been nice not to find out on social media." I skip formalities. We've never been big on it.

"I'm sorry, sweetie. It all happened so fast. I left him." Your beautiful voice makes me hard. I don't hide the smirk.

The waiter places a plate on the table and nods. "I trust you'll find *everything* to your liking," he says before turning to tend to other customers.

"I'm sorry. Is this a bad time? I'm not thinking straight. I'm sorry."

I wish it were possible to erase 'I'm sorry' from your vocabulary. That bitch mother of yours needs to be taught a lesson. One day, I'll make her regret everything she did to you.

"I always have time for you, but I'm waiting for a prospective client who should arrive any minute. Tell me what happened. Do you want me to come over?" I stare at the piece of dead cow on the plate. Poor, delicious, dead creature.

It hits me then – not even your mother tastes like you. You're half her and yet there's nothing of her in you. Despite what the world may think, I'll never know how your father tastes.

In the background, *he* calls your name.

"I thought you said you ended things with him? What happened?" I reach for the wine glass and take another sip.

"He cheated on me. I go away for one night and come back to find another woman's underwear in *our* bedroom. The asshole didn't even get rid of the condom."

"I didn't cheat on you! I don't know what happened. Please. You have to believe me." I relish in his distraught, wishing you'd put your phone on speaker.

"Just get out while I pack. I don't want to see your face." Acid drips from your words.

That's my girl. You're in control. Nothing in your tone except rage. If I were him, I'd get out. *Run, little loser.*

The wine has never tasted better. I signal the waiter, asking him to pack my lunch in a takeaway box. Not standard practice for this fine establishment. "I'm on my way. You're coming to stay with me. Pack your stuff. I'll be there in thirty minutes."

It won't take more than fifteen, but this is just the first step in destroying you.

First your life.

Then your soul.

You refuse my help. I'm supposed to be your best friend. An idiot, that's what I am. I want to come to your rescue, so be grateful. Who else has stuck with you? Name one other person who knows as much about you as I do.

I'm a clown. You've already booked a room at The Marcella and contacted the cruise company you used to work for, before calling me.

In two weeks, you plan to leave me. That's what you think. I'm not losing you again. Not after everything I've done. If you leave, you'll open your legs for the first man who looks in your direction.

I deserve you! You ungrateful little whore. No one will get to taste you, but me.

Blisters cover my perfect hands from all the work I've been doing to renovate my parents' country home. I couldn't ask the construction crew to get rid of the bodies. No matter how much father paid them.

The smell of wet concrete remains in my nostrils. I've inhaled paint fumes, mineral turpentine, and other horrible working-class smells. And now you want to leave me? Again.

I slam the Range Rover's steering wheel as I race through the city, heading straight to the cabin. It's not where we will spend time together.

"Make your little plans. You're not going anywhere. You belong to me!" The primal and guttural sound is foreign to me. I never raise my voice.

Inside the Range Rover's boot is everything needed to break the woman tied to the bed. And you. She will help to perfect my skills. Maybe she's more deserving of my attention than you are.

A muscle in my back has pulled into a knot and my jaw is tight. Is this what anger feels like? Whatever it is, I hate it.

"Honey, I'm home." I step into the cabin, not bothering to close the door. The place needs fresh air. She requires sustenance to last long enough for me to determine what it will take to break you. Hopefully, the ribeye nourishes her. The food cupboard is empty. I never asked if she's a vegan. *I'm a terrible host.*

Thanks to you, there are less than two weeks to perfect my methods. I hope she's as arachnophobic as you are. If not, the snakes won't remain caged much longer. After their starring role in the next experiment, they'll be free to slither around the forest. I'm not that cruel.

Darwin had been way off the mark. If humans had truly evolved, then they wouldn't fear irrational things like heights, clowns or even creatures that can be killed by stepping on them. This is the one difference between us — your fears are ridiculous.

I fear nothing. Except losing you.

"My apologies, Emily, for not offering you anything to eat since you arrived. I trust this will make up for the lack of hospitality." Dull blue eyes glare at me as I untie the leather straps, rubbing the bruises for her.

"*Willow.* That's my name. The least you can do is call me by my name before beating me to death." The courageous little badger stares at the dark splatters on the wooden planks on the walls, floor, and ceiling.

I can't help it; I smile. "It's sad that our time together will end. You're unlike the others. *Willow.*"

"What did you bring? It smells delicious."

In my experience, people refuse to accept they're going to die even when they submit to me. Willow is different. She hasn't submitted and claims death will be better than her miserable life. A part of me wants to keep her around long enough to see if she's like us.

I leave Willow to eat what was supposed to be my lunch. Rather rudely, I expect her to eat with her hands, like an animal. But my little badger doesn't seem to mind. With her legs bound at her delicate ankles, I head back to the Rover to retrieve some of the items *my guy* left in the boot. Another perk of making use of their valet parking.

The rest of it will be for use in a different cabin. A special place, just for you. With an indoor shower, two bedrooms and a living area, it's much more comfortable. Not that you'll get to enjoy all the renovations. You will spend the days confined to a bedroom. At least that bed has a new mattress, unlike the piece of ancient sponge in this cabin.

Willow finishes the meal. "What's next? And remove the damn mask. You're going to kill me, so what if I see your face?" There are no visible signs of distress on her face.

The thing is itchy; nothing talcum powder won't take care of. "You have beautiful skin for someone who lives a hard life."

Willow's bony shoulders move up, then down. "I get it from my mom. Are you going to remove my skin and wear it while dancing in the moonlight?"

"Don't be absurd. I'm not insane. Please make yourself

comfortable, arms at your side. You know the drill."

Without a word, she does as I ask. No flicker of resignation in her eyes.

It dawns on me that you'll recognise my voice. *There's a solution to every problem.*

In her own way, Willow has crept under my skin. You, on the other hand, are my soul. How can I destroy my soul?

Silence. Fear. Complete control. Not so hard, now that I think about it.

Willow will sleep for a while and wake up wondering whether it had been a lie when I'd said I'm not a rapist. What I'm about to do borders on it. But the poor thing will never know the truth. Something to ponder until I clobber her face.

She doesn't squirm when I step closer to the bed with a syringe in my right hand. In my left is a box containing eleven condoms. Not twelve, as it had held until last night when I'd shown it to her.

"Playtime is over, Willow. I have a deadline."

In the end, Willow the badger, begged for mercy. I didn't show her any. Not even once in the six days it took to break her. You'll last longer than that, My Love.

Willow's feistiness has taught me a lot about the lengths I can go to in order to destroy someone.

I won't apologise for the things I'm going to do to you.

Enjoy the last day of thinking you're in control of your life.

May you smile when the sunlight warms your skin and the city air pollutes your lungs. Today is the end of your line.

No matter how long it takes, I will destroy your physical strength, determination, stubbornness, and survival instinct.

Tonight, I'm taking what is mine – you.

Chapter 1

Thursday, 17 June

My Love,

For 916 excruciating days I've waited for you to break free from the chrysalis you've constructed around yourself. After all this time, you found your strength again. I can't wait to see the beauty and zest of the woman I fell in love with. You will be you again. Emily.

I long for the days we spent together, just the two of us, in our special place. For forty glorious days you were mine, as you were always meant to be. MINE.

I remember the warmth of your skin under my fingers. The goose bumps rippling across your body when I touched you. Your sweet taste still lingers on my lips and tongue.

I'm waiting for you, and my patience will pay off. You're becoming more adventurous, more of who you once were. Of course, all within the freedom I give you. You don't see it yet, but my gifts to you are endless. My love, your life is mine. Your body, your very essence, belongs to me.

The first time I saw you, I knew there would only ever be you.
We will be together again. Soon.

This time, and forevermore, you will say the only words I ever need to hear.

Remember, My Love – You're mine.

Chapter 2

Doctor Benjamin Clarke settled his hands on the notebook resting on his lap. In over twenty years as a clinical psychologist, he'd never met anyone who intrigued him more than the woman sitting across from him. "Tell me again why Emily had to die?"

"It was the only way for me to be free." Noa Morgan crossed her arms over her chest.

"You're not free. You killed her, but you still live in fear."

Noa's back stiffened, meeting his stare. "For the past year, I have lived on my own. I work outside my house. And I've made friends."

"Yes, you've made significant progress since you moved here, but you continue to avoid intimate relationships with men. Not once have you travelled, something which gave you great pleasure before. You steer clear of men." He raised a hand and shook his head. "Before you remind me about the two dates you've been on, they don't count. You dismissed both men after only one date. I asked you this before – do you feel safe?"

"I don't *avoid* men. My best friend is a man and so is my boss at the gym. I even have male clients."

"Stop avoiding my question."

"No, and I don't think I will ever feel safe being intimate with a man. You know what happened. The things I don't remember and the few I do."

15

Doctor Clarke leaned forward in his chair. "Noa, you should reconsider our previous discussion regarding a sex surrogate. Using one has helped many of my other patients to regain confidence. You're a young, beautiful woman and your sexuality is a big part of who you are. Emily enjoyed sex."

Noa sighed. "Why are we talking in circles today? I'm not open to the idea of a sex surrogate, no matter how many times you tell me it's therapy and not prostitution."

"As I explained to you before, I'll be right there with you when you meet with the sex surrogate. At least until you feel confident to see him on your own."

"No, for so many reasons. *No.* I'm not open to the idea and you said the first time you came to see me in hospital that we never have to discuss anything I'm not comfortable with. This is me telling you, it's not an option. I don't have to have sex to reclaim control of my life. I do it every day I get out of bed, leave the house and interact with people."

"Once you allow yourself to feel safe with someone, it will change."

"Feel safe?" Noa laughed. "I set my alarm every time I enter or leave the house. King goes with me whenever I leave the house, when not for work. I will *never* feel safe. When Emily died, I thought I would. This isn't the life I envisioned for myself."

"You can have the life you had before. What did you love most about Emily?"

Noa rose and walked to the window. "We've discussed this."

Beyond the glass lie the quaint town of River Valley. Winter had settled in; soon the rain would come.

"I know. Humour me." The good doctor admired Noa's sculpted physique, as he often did during their sessions. The instant she had rung the door bell, his body reacted.

"Emily was fearless. No obstacle ever phased her. She did what she wanted to do, without apology." A hint of a smile appeared on Noa's face. "She had too much confidence, and she *lived*. I can tell you one thing, she wasn't afraid of men. In hindsight I would call her promiscuous, but she had a plan and stuck to it."

"Take every part of her you loved and make it part of who *you* are. Don't allow him to control her, even in death. Emily is dead. Her death gave you a second chance, and you owe it to her to live. Your homework for the week is to say *yes*. Next time someone asks you to do something, say *yes*. Push yourself out of your comfort zone. Go to dinner by yourself and remember every time you want to say no, you owe it to Emily to live."

"I will try."

"There is no try." At his reference to Yoda, Noa laughed. The sound stirred a feeling deep in his core. Not for the first time, Benjamin Clarke wished he could reach out and, with the gentlest of touches, remind her what a captivating creature she was.

Just as he did every week, Benjamin watched Noa drive off in her Jeep and picked up his phone, finding his intended caller in the call-log. These days, he had few people to call and even fewer who called him.

"Hello, it's me. Our girl is doing well. I think she's on the brink of assuming more of Emily's persona. She stood up to me today. After two-and-a-half years we're getting somewhere."

"Thank you very much for your call. I am not interested in taking out another credit card. Goodbye." The person on the other end hung up.

Doctor Clarke grinned down at the phone.

Friday, 18 June, 5:04 p.m.

Noa wiped the sweat from her brow and reached for her water bottle. With unsteady hands, she unscrewed the cap and brought the bottle to her lips. Her friends did the same. All four of them were covered in sweat, breathing hard, spending time together. *My friends. Not Emily's.*

After leaving Doctor Clarke's office, Noa had thought about what they discussed. She was proud of the life she had created and grateful for Doctor Clarke's patience. It dawned on her the only time she experienced fear was when she spoke to him about the events which had led to her seeing him. Cautious to a fault she would always be, but Noa wanted to honour what Emily had stood for and live.

Pounding the punching bag with gloved fists; she struck at the memories of *him*. At the control he still had over her life, two-and-a-half years after being rescued from *him*. Whoever *he* was.

"I'm heading home. It's my first night off in more than a week and I need to spend time with my husband," Jamie Edwards said, grabbing her backpack and heading for the door.

Kim stared after Jamie. "I want that."

"To be a police officer who works shifts?"

"You know what I mean. A husband to go home to. Jamie and Spencer are as much in love as they were when they first started dating. How you see them now is how they were ten years ago."

Noa watched as Kim tied her natural golden hair in to a ponytail. She touched her own hair, no longer remembering what she looked like with her natural colour.

Eric cleared his throat and threw a muscular arm around Noa's shoulders. "You could go blonde. It's said they have more fun. But looking at Kim's track record, it's hard to believe there's any truth in that saying. And I like your hair. In the right light it complements the flecks of green in your eyes."

"We can't all be perfect," Kim snapped.

"Oh sweetie, you can at least try. What are you ladies up to tonight? I have a date with a man you could only dream about. Another fitness model."

"Of course he is. When do you ever date a man who doesn't meet your ridiculous standards? I can't believe there are men who do. Have fun. I'm going home to the only male I need."

Noa grabbed her backpack and turned towards the door.

"Noa, wait. I want to ask you to come with us tonight to Rapids. There is a battle of the cover bands thing and I know how much you love music."

Noa exhaled hard and turned to face her friend, seeing the hopefulness on Kim's face. "What time?" she asked, even though every part of her screamed *no*.

"Are you serious? You'll come with?"

Say yes. "Okay, I'll play third wheel."

"You won't. Matthew's best friend moved back to town this week. It's the first time I'm meeting him, I need one of my friends to go with me. Thanks, Noa, I'll give you free lattes for a week."

"But I leave when I want to. No begging me to stay and none of your other tricks."

"I love you." Kim grabbed Noa and hugged her hard. "I'll meet you at Rapids at eight. Thank you."

Eric crossed his arms across his broad chest. "*You*, Noa Morgan, are going out for a night in this little town?"

Noa stared up at him, lifting her chin into the air. "Yes, I am."

"Well, good for you little-miss-social-life. Remember, yoga pants are not proper attire when going to a bar. Rummage through your closet and find something suitable to wear. You don't want people to look at you with pity. If you want, I'll go with, safety in numbers and all that."

"No. Go on your date with the model and I will see you tomorrow night, unless your date turns into a weekend thing. Kim, I'll be there at eight o'clock and I promise to dress the part."

Noa headed for her Jeep, trying to figure out what she was going to wear. She hadn't been to a bar since the night which resulted in Emily's death. Leaning against her Jeep, Noa waited for her breathing to calm and the tremble in her hands to subside. If only King was with her.

Breathe, what's the worst thing that can happen?

Chapter 3

Rapids was filled with locals and people from neighbouring towns who had braced the cold. Nothing noteworthy ever happened in the small towns, which made up the surrounding area. The locals referred to it as 'Wine Country'.

Luke Taylor scanned the crowd for his best friend. At a head taller than most men, his height came in handy when looking for a familiar or wanted face. Luke's friend saw him first and waved from a booth facing the stage, yet was far enough away from the speakers. *We're getting old.*

Coming to Rapids wasn't his idea, but Luke had decided to make the most of his first night out. River Valley had been his home once. It took Luke five minutes to make his way to where Matthew sat with two women. A blonde woman sat next to Matthew, the dark-haired one across from them. Small town living had its advantages and the familiar faces reminded Luke why he'd moved back.

As he approached the table, the dark-haired woman turned in his direction, her eyes focused on his. There was a familiarity to her face which struck him, but he couldn't recall ever meeting her.

Matthew shifted out of the booth and grabbed Luke by the shoulders. "It's so good to see you." Matthew pulled his oldest friend in for a bro hug.

"Owning a gym is good for you. You finally filled out."

"I filled out years ago. As much as I want to discuss why you haven't been home in over a decade, tonight isn't the time.

I'd like to introduce you to my girlfriend, Kim. And the best personal trainer in the country, Noa, who happens to work for me. Perhaps she can give you a few pointers on how not to look like you're on the juice."

Luke shook his head at Matthew's reference to steroids. If only Matthew knew the real reason Luke had spent countless hours in the gym over the preceding months.

Kim rose as much as the table in front of her allowed and reached out to shake Luke's hand. "It's a pleasure to meet you, Luke. I've heard so many good things about you." She turned to Matthew. "Your girlfriend?"

"Yes. What did you think you are?"

Kim reached for him and, as he settled next to her, she kissed him.

Luke and Noa looked at each other, rather than the two people whose PDA could rival that of hormone-fuelled teenagers.

"Do you mind if I sit?" he asked.

"No." Noa butt-shuffled to move further into the booth.

"So, you're to thank for his transformation?" he asked, taking a seat next to her.

Noa took a sip of her virgin margarita. "Matthew did the hard work. I was just there to give him support."

"You're being modest. Getting people to do what you tell them isn't an easy job. When did you move to River Valley?" Luke waited for Noa to swallow another sip of her drink, taking the time to admire her delicate features. *I know her face.*

"Two years ago. You?"

"This week, but I grew up here. Went to university in Shadow Bay; I've spent the greater part of my life in Wine Country. Where did you study?"

"Luke!"

He jerked around. Luke's youngest sister stood next to him

Not for the first time that day did it strike him how much Madison had grown in the years since he'd left town. "What's wrong, Maddie?"

Luke shifted further into the booth to make room for Madison to sit, and then put his right arm around her. As much as Luke was aware of his sister next to him, he couldn't ignore the warmth of the body pressed against his other side.

"I'm screwed." Madison lowered her head onto her arms, sending her blonde curls cascading onto the table.

"What happened?"

"Our drummer hasn't pitched and I can't get hold of him. We're supposed to go on stage in thirty minutes. Dammit."

"Hey, Noa, didn't you tell me you used to be a drummer in a band?" Kim asked.

"No." Noa shook her head, avoiding the interested stares of the people around the table.

"Yes, you did. Remember our margarita night? We got pretty tipsy, and you mentioned playing in a band."

Madison lifted her head and reached past Luke to grab Noa's hand, her eyes pleading. "Please, I will forever be in your debt. We're doing a cover of Slay. Are you familiar with their songs?"

Noa nodded. "I haven't played in years. I doubt I'll be any good."

Luke smiled, knowing Noa would end up on stage. His youngest sister never took no for an answer.

"But you know Slay?" Madison asked.

"Yes; that's not the point. I haven't played in years, don't want to make you look bad."

"Worse than we will without a drummer? Please, Noa. I never beg, but this is me *begging* you. Please." Madison placed both hands on Noa's arm.

"Okay, but I'm not dressed for this. I need a tank top or something that allows better range of motion than this jersey."

"I'm on it! Thank you." Madison focused on Luke. "She's a keeper. Leave it to you to have the hottest woman in town next to on your first night out."

Luke's gaze followed Madison as she pushed through the crowd towards the stage, wishing she hadn't grown up without him. For her to get to know him and not from the stories she had been told.

A hand rubbed his thigh; Luke glanced at the owner. Noa yanked her hand back and pressed it against her darkening cheek.

"You don't have to do this," he said next to Noa's ear, noticing her faint scent. *Why do I know your face?*

"I do."

Friday, 18 June, 9:12 p.m.

With unsteady legs, Noa returned to the booth. To be on stage was a high she had long forgotten. The drumsticks had once again become extensions of her own body as the beat pulsed through her veins.

As she walked closer to where the others sat, they rose to applaud her. Noa's cheeks heated; the smile came without effort.

"What the hell was that?" Kim grabbed Noa's hands.

"Nothing, just making music." Noa pushed past Kim and asked Luke if she could retake her seat next to the wall.

"You were amazing. Marc Barclay can learn a thing from you," Luke said, sitting down.

Noa pushed herself back into the seat, keeping her eyes on the table. Luke shifted, using his body to block her view of the crowd.

Noa's shoulders sagged; she glanced at him with a smile. "Thank you, but I'm no Marc. I just like to beat on stuff."

"Is that why you love kickboxing?" Luke watched her over the rim of the beer glass.

Noa turned to Kim and Matthew. "What did you guys talk about while I was backstage?"

"You, among other things." Luke lowered the glass back to the coaster.

Noa found his honesty refreshing and the rest of the night

she made a point of keeping the conversation to topics that wouldn't lead him to ask any more questions. Something about Luke made her feel uneasy. Being this aware of another person's presence, his smile, and the faint lines at the corners of his eyes when he laughed.

As Noa watched the other three in their group talk and laugh, she remembered how confident Emily had been socially. Not until that moment had she realised how much she had missed being on stage. Or how much fun it was being surrounded by people, laughing and listening to good music.

Friday, 18 June, 10:30 p.m.

Kim and Matthew excused themselves and headed home. Whose home they were heading for neither Luke nor Noa knew, neither did they care – too engrossed in their own conversation. Luke told her he'd been a detective, but decided to get out after his partner died.

"Why did you move back?"

"I've only told my parents, but I couldn't take it anymore. Seeing the bodies of victims who could've protected themselves, if only they'd known how. I'm going to offer free self-defence classes at Matthew's gym and I'm busy talking to other venues in and around the area to hold similar classes. I'm also opening a shooting range. Being comfortable with a weapon is key to self-defence. Too many people lock their guns in a safe and don't have it when they need it most. If people are comfortable with their weapon, they'll carry it twenty-four-seven."

"It's a brilliant idea. You need to contact the University of Shadow Bay and arrange classes for the students, and at the high schools. Bullying is becoming a major problem, not only in our area. I don't condone violence, but if people are confident in their own physical capabilities, they benefit psychologically. My opinion." Noa didn't mention, that sometimes, no matter how well you're prepared for an attack, a stranger can walk up behind you and incapacitate you with a stun gun.

Luke's fingers tapped against the empty beer glass. "Why do you have so much knowledge on the subject?"

"I read a lot, and I hear what's going on when I'm at work. People talk to me, their personal trainer, as if I'm also their therapist." Noa glanced at her mobile phone. "I need to leave and get some sleep. Tomorrow is an early day."

As they exited the bar, Noa reached for the keys inside her purse, wrapping her fingers around the can of pepper spray which served as a key chain.

Luke insisted on walking with to her Jeep; his presence a welcome relief. "Did I hear you correct in there? Did you say Pilates is *the* best workout?"

"Don't shoot it down until you've tried one of my classes, Taylor."

"I'm game. When is your next class? If it isn't *the* best workout, you owe me dinner."

Noa's heart raced at the idea of seeing Luke again. She swallowed hard. "Tomorrow morning, at eight."

"I'll be there. Here is an even better idea for you. After class, you and I are having breakfast at Kim's coffee shop. If, and I say this with great doubt, it is *the* best workout, I'll pay for breakfast. If not, then you need to pay. Deal?" Luke stopped walking and held his hand out towards her.

The ringing in Noa's ears eased, and she realised how quiet the nights were in this picturesque town. In the distance people laughed as they stumbled out of Rapids and onto the street.

Say yes. "Deal. Wear comfortable clothes because I'm going to have you in some very difficult positions."

Noa placed her hand in his; Luke bit the corner of his bottom lip. "I can't tell you how much I'm counting on you doing just that."

Noa turned on her heels and headed for her Jeep, Luke's grip still firm on her hand. "This is my ride."

"Not what I expected you to drive."

"Sorry to disappoint you." Curiosity got the better of her.

"What did you expect?"

"A small three-door hatch back or something more girly. And, for the record, I doubt you will ever disappoint me."

Noa let out a deep breath. "Do you ever not say the first thing that enters your mind?"

Luke reached for her face and pushed a strand of hair behind her ear. "I used to, but life is too short. I enjoyed getting to know the tiny parts of yourself you shared with me. And I look forward to seeing you tomorrow morning."

As he stepped closer, Noa's grip tightened on the can. Luke glanced at her hand, but didn't remove his from her face.

It had been years since someone last touched her, except for the occasional hug from a friend. Noa fought the urge to lean into Luke's palm, instead reminding herself she had no right to savour a moment with a man she didn't know.

"I'm not trying to kiss you on the mouth. I was aiming for your cheek."

"Oh ... uhm ... sorry, I thought ... I should've known, seeing as you kissed Kim goodnight." Noa stared at the kerb.

"Noa, I'll never force you to do anything you don't want to do. I assume you're not as gracious with your clients? Considering Matthew's transformation." Luke smiled. "When you decide to kiss me, I'm right here. Just because I won't kiss you doesn't mean I didn't think about it more than once tonight. Just so there aren't any misunderstandings, I don't see you as a potential friend. I'm attracted to you and find you too intriguing to put you in the friend zone." Luke closed the remaining distance between them.

Noa's eyes lifted to his; adrenaline pumping through her. An ear-splitting sound tore through the quiet of the night. She lost her footing and fell forward.

Luke closed his arms around her. One hand on her lower back, the other in Noa's hair. Over her head, Luke scanned the street.

The squeal of tyres deafening. A black sedan made a U-turn, speeding off in the opposite direction.

"It's okay, I've got you. Just some stupid kids with an air horn." Noa's body trembled against his, her breathing faint yet frantic. "Sit down."

Luke pulled Noa down onto the pavement, keeping his arms around her. Noa pressed her face into his chest as he stroked her back and kept offering her comfort. Protection. Despite the frigid weather, they sat until Noa's breathing calmed.

"I'm sorry, Luke. So much for not wanting to friend zone me. Women having panic attacks are such an aphrodisiac."

"I've had one or two myself, and I've seen my fair share of people getting them over the years. It's nothing to be ashamed of. Let me follow you home and ensure you get home safe. I don't want you to walk into an empty house this late at night."

"No, thank you, I'm fine. My boy is waiting, probably wondering where I am this late."

"You have a son?"

"King is my dog. Prettiest damn pit bull in the world and the best."

Luke eased away from her, cupping Noa's face in his palms. "You do kickboxing. Carry pepper spray on your key chain. Own a pit bull. And you have a gun holstered in your bra. I felt it when you fell against me, occupational hazard, not a pervert." He held his hands up. "Who are you, Noa Morgan, other than being my idea of the perfect woman?"

"Once a detective, always a detective? Goodnight, Luke, I'll see you tomorrow."

Chapter 4

Friday, 18 June

Emily,

You disappoint me. Your first night out on the town and you're already falling into a man's arms. Literally. You're still the same whore you always were. Being onstage must have reminded you of how easy you are. You used to love the way men watched you and how they threw themselves at you.

Tonight, I saw them staring at you, but none of them lusted after you as he did. I will ensure he never even thinks about you again. The next time his skin touches yours will be his last. You don't know what I'm capable of. The things I did to make you mine.

No, the first man who smiles at you, the first to make you laugh so hard you spit your drink out, he is the one you allow to walk you to your Jeep. This might be on me. I can't fault you for not leaving a bar on your own. You experienced first-hand what happens to pretty little sluts like you when you do. But no, I don't think for one second you didn't consider that he might kiss you. You wanted him to. WHORE. Just like you opened your legs for countless men before I claimed you. I ensured that you won't do it again. No other man will get to taste you. EVER.

The air horn was a tad dramatic, my most sincere apologies for the flashback I know you experienced. I couldn't sit back and let him kiss you. You're not his to kiss. I didn't allow you to reclaim so much of your life for you to fall for the first man who comes along. No. YOU'RE MINE!

Soon you will say the words I've been waiting for. This time you will say them.

Chapter 5

Luke rolled up the pink yoga mat, waiting for Noa to finish talking to a group of women he remembered from high school. He wondered if Noa had intended for him to end up with the pink mat. Not that he cared if it meant he had to buy his own pink mat to see Noa bend like that again. *Without clothes.*

The previous night he had lain awake thinking about Noa and tried to place her face. She avoided personal questions, much like career criminals did during interrogation. Noa Morgan was a puzzle Luke intended to solve.

As she walked towards him, he stared in wonder. Never before did muscle definition look so good on a woman without taking away her femininity.

"And?" Noa asked, positioning a blue yoga mat over her shoulder.

"Was that supposed to be 'the best workout'?"

"Okay, come to my ninety-minute class on Wednesday morning. Our breakfast bet can carry over. See you Wednesday."

"Not so fast. You said *this* was going to be *the* best. A deal is a deal. However, being the gentleman I am, breakfast is on me."

Noa bit her bottom lip and Luke wondered how it would feel to have that very lip between his teeth. "Head out of the gutter, Noa. You know what I mean."

She shook her head. "I thought nothing close to what you're insinuating."

29

"If not, then why were you biting your lip?"

"My lips are dry." Noa bit her lip again for effect.

"No, they're not. Perfect, in my opinion. Good job trying to dodge the obvious."

"Listen, Taylor, I'm hungry. If you don't want it to turn in to full-blown hangry, you better get food in me right now."

As they made their way through the gym to Kim's adjoining coffee shop, Koffee, Luke had a gut feeling they were being watched. He scanned around and noticed a few people looking their way. Some even waved or called out to Noa. Yet, Luke still had a sinking feeling in the pit of his stomach. Behind a pair of staring eyes, a predator lurked. *Occupational hazard.*

Saturday, 19 June, 9:15 a.m.

He watched Emily walk through the gym with the same muscle monkey from the night before. How could she spend more time with *him*? Why did she want to?

He'd given Emily too much freedom; she forgot his teachings. Time she remembered the truth he had told her the moment she opened her eyes in the cabin. *You will always be mine.*

The muscle monkey's watchful gaze bothered him. He needed to know who this stranger was and how big a threat he posed. The gym junkie strode with the same confidence he had seen police officers walk with. The very detectives who visited Emily while she had been in hospital. The men who asked her about him, and the wonderful time they had spent together.

The muscle monkey needed to go. He would see to it, just as he had to everyone else who stood between him and Emily.

It's time. Emily needs to know.

***

Saturday, 19 June, 9:25 a.m.

Noa handed the menu to the newest waiter on Kim's staff and waited for their food while sipping her free latte. Across the table, Luke alternated between looking at her and behind her. Noa wondered if Luke was waiting for someone or found her company boring.

"We don't have to do breakfast today, not if you're waiting for someone or need to be somewhere else." She drained the last of the latte, burning her tongue and throat.

"I'm sorry. I don't mean to be rude. I had this strange feeling someone watched us as we walked here from the studio."

"Yes, people were looking us. Some even greeted both of us. Joys of living in a small town." Noa kept it to herself that she thought people were wondering what such a handsome, rugged man was doing with her.

She never cared as much about her appearance as Emily had. As a young girl, her mother had said she looked like Snow White, but with green eyes, and not nearly as pretty.

Luke's mouth opened his; a phone's ringtone cut him off. "Hello Maddie," he said, looking at Noa.

With a mere smile, his face transformed from handsome to devastating. Noa's stomach did a slow roll. Perhaps it would be for the best if they didn't see each other again.

She had spent most of the way home the previous night thinking about Luke, his smile, the physical response she'd had sitting so close to him. The feel of his muscular thigh under her palm. His scent. Noa wondered how he'd known she didn't want people looking at her when she'd returned to the booth after the last set. The safe and warm cocoon Luke had created with his arms and chest; his patience during the panic attack. Never before had anyone held her during an attack. Luke Taylor was unlike anyone she had ever met. Noa wanted to spend more time with him and even considered sharing titbits of her own life, as there was much she still wanted to know about him.

After years of half-truths and full lies, her soul ached. The mere thought of being honest brought on another panic attack. Petting King had helped calm her, but in the darkness of her bedroom Noa admitted to King, none had ever passed as quick as when Luke held her.

"No, I don't have Noa's number, a problem I'll fix, but if you want to talk to her, I'm looking at Noa's beautiful face right now."

Noa's cheeks heated.

"No, Maddie, we didn't spend the night together. Do you want to ask her or shall I hang up?" Luke's head moved from side to side. His laughter filled Koffee. "You'd better be at dinner tonight or Mom's going to skin you. You know how important it is to her to have *all* of us there."

Luke held the phone towards Noa, still shaking his head.

"Good morning, Madison."

"I need another favour, Noa. Please, I'm begging again. And you want to do this. You really do."

"How can I if you haven't told me what *this* is?"

"Pete, our drummer, is in hospital with pneumonia and we have a gig tomorrow afternoon. We're playing at Lamont Wine Estate for their family fun day. Before you say anything, we'll tone it down for the kids and *old* people. Maybe a few of Slay's earlier songs, if you're familiar with them?"

"Why don't you write your own songs?" Noa asked, thanking the waiter for the food with a smile and a nod.

"Because my songs suck. Will you save me again, Noa? Please. I will do anything, give you anything, even my brother if you want him."

Noa failed to suppress her laughter.

"Is that a yes? Come on, Noa, you know you want to. You're the best drummer I've ever played with. Okay, I've only played with two, but you are so talented and—"

"Stop. Breathe. I'll be there tomorrow, but this is the last time, Maddie."

"You like me. Only my friends and family call me Maddie."

"I'm sorry. Madison."

"No, call me Maddie. As I said, my friends and family do, and you're going to be both."

Noa's eyes lifted to the ceiling. "What the hell is it with you Taylors voicing every single thing that comes to mind?"

"That's why you like us. We're good, honest people. You'll never doubt where you stand with us. I don't think my brother has standing in mind when it comes to you, maybe in the shower—"

"Please stop!" Noa's cheeks heated. "I will see you tomorrow. I'll get your number from Luke and you can send me the details. Last time, Madison Taylor. Last time." Noa ended the call without giving Madison an opportunity to say another word.

"Welcome to the roller-coaster we call – Madison Taylor."

"Your brutal honesty is a family affliction. Your sister is something else."

Luke grinned. "What did Maddie say to make you blush?"

"You don't want to know. I think she needs to get laid." Noa pursed her lips.

"Don't ever say my sister needs to have sex. Maddie's my baby sister. How would you like it if I said something like that about one of your siblings?"

"I'm an only child, so I don't understand this whole dynamic. What did you get up to at her age?"

Luke leaned back in the chair and studied Noa, realising yet again how good she was at changing the subject. "Nothing I want someone to do to my sister. How about you?"

"Nothing I want anyone to do to your sister." The corners of Noa's mouth lifted. She give the untouched food on the plate her full attention.

Neither of them said a word until they finished eating and Luke paid the bill.

Noa pushed the chair back. "I don't understand how you think Pilates isn't the best workout ever. Perhaps tomorrow when you're so stiff you struggle to walk, and realise you used muscles you might never have used before, you'll reconsider."

"Do you want to make me stiff, Noa?" Mischief flashed in his eyes.

Focusing on the backpack on the floor, Noa tried to hide her smile, and give herself time to respond because she wanted to say *yes*, in the way he'd implied. "Yes, stiff like a corpse. Isn't that what you detectives call a dead body?"

"Have lunch with me tomorrow after your gig with Maddie?"

Picking up the backpack, Noa swung the yoga mat over her shoulder as she came to her feet. "What's the wager for lunch?"

"No wager. I want to have lunch with you for our second date. I enjoy spending time with you and want to see if I can make you blush as much as you did when Maddie said whatever she did."

"Doubt it." *Second date?*

"Is that a dare, Miss Morgan?"

"No," Noa said over her shoulder, heading towards the front door. "I need to get home, take King for a run, and do some work."

"What work?" Luke asked.

"I'm an online health coach slash personal trainer. And a trainer slash instructor here." Noa considered keeping her other work to herself, but at times the weight of all the secrets became too heavy.

In the parking lot, she turned and Luke almost bumped into her. "I'm active in an online support group for victims of bullying and other forms of abuse. The group is aimed towards teenage girls and young women, think university age."

Luke nodded. "We need to discuss how you can get involved with my self-defence classes. Maybe you can give me pointers on how to approach the schools?"

Noa held a hand out to him. "Okay, but only if you'll consider helping me to moderate a group for boys and young men of the same age groups. They're not comfortable with a woman. I'm struggling to get them to open up."

They shook hands before continuing to Noa's Jeep. The canister was, again, clutched in her hand.

"What's on your windshield?"

Noa stopped in her tracks. "Luke, did you do this?" She stared up at him, her jaw tight.

"No. I'll never give you anything dead."

Noa removed the rose and threw it onto the tar, crushing it under her right trainer.

"It appears I have competition for your attention." The fury in her stare vanquished Luke's grin.

An alarm tone sounded from her backpack. Noa removed her phone and headed for the Jeep's driver side door. "I need to go."

Luke grabbed her arm. "What's wrong?"

"Something triggered the silent alarm at my house. I have to go!"

"I'm coming with you." Noa opened her mouth, but Luke held up his free hand. "This isn't a negotiation. I won't let you walk in on something or someone by yourself."

"You don't need to. I'll be fine." Noa yanked free from his grip.

"I'm not asking for your permission, Noa. Do you have your gun with you?"

"Always." She patted the backpack.

"That's my girl. Do you carry it one-up?"

A hint of a smile tugged at the corners of Noa's mouth. "Always."

Chapter 6

Noa drove as if the devil himself was chasing her. Luke ran around the side of the house with her. Noa whistled, waiting for King to come to her. She deactivated the silent alarm and waited for the app on her phone to show the entry and exit points. The app didn't indicate any.

Luke held his non-gun-carrying-hand out to Noa's dog. King sniffed the stranger and allowed Luke to stroke his head. Standing there, seeing the controlled fear in the woman next to him, Luke realised he could never distance himself from the badge. To serve and protect was ingrained in him. Through nurture, not nature. For thirty years, Luke had lived with the guilt of failing to protect the one person who'd loved him more than anything.

Luke took lead as they entered the house, clearing every room before returning to the living room where he had instructed Noa to wait. King, he had told to stay.

"Does anything look out of place?" he asked, even though Noa's home was a carbon copy of a show house.

"Not that I can see. I'm sorry, Luke. I'll phone the alarm company and ask for a technician to come do a system check." Noa reached into the cupboard, removed a treat for King, but handed it to Luke.

"On top of everything I mentioned last night, you have a state-of-the-art alarm system and burglar bars in front of every single window, as well as security gates in front of all the doors. You realise the crime rate is low in River Valley?" After giving King the treat, Luke sat down on the tiled floor and scratched the dog's belly.

The sincere smile on Noa's face didn't go unnoticed. "What's so funny?" Luke glanced up at her, still rubbing King.

Noa's shoulders moved up then down. "Nothing. You stormed into my house, gun drawn, ready to take out an intruder, with such a serious expression on your face and now you're sitting on the floor playing with King." Noa didn't add that it was the sexiest thing she had ever seen. "Do you want coffee? It's the least I can do after taking up more of your time."

"You will never take up my time, Noa. If you need me, I'll be here."

"You don't even know me."

"That's not the point."

"Once a copper, cop, popo, whatever, always one? A friend of mine is a police officer and lives two blocks from here. I won't bug you again with my faulty alarm system." Noa turned to switch on the kettle. "Thank you for coming with me."

Luke walked closer and touched Noa's shoulder. "I'll stay until the technician arrives. Contact them while I make coffee. And Noa, don't ever think you can't call me. Your friend might be on shift or might be sleeping off a forty-eight-hour one."

"Thank you, but you can't stay. You have dinner with your family and my friend, Eric is coming over tonight. As you can see, King is the best guard dog. He accepts no one as fast as he did you, even before I handed you the treat to give him." Noa turned and looked up at him.

Luke trailed Noa's jaw with his thumb, sending a pulse echoing through her. "Dogs and Noa Morgans' like me." He shrugged.

"I can't fault them." The kettle stopped boiling and her heart attempted the same as his thumb brushed her bottom lip. Noa swallowed hard and tried to turn, to get away from the heat radiating in his stare. Luke held her chin.

The rhythmic tick of the wall clock filled the silence.

King nudged Luke's leg. He gave a short bark when neither human responded. Luke shook his head, taking a step back.

Noa reached for mugs and poured water from the kettle, spilling most of the water onto the counter. Luke reached past her to grab a towel.

He braced himself on the counter, his hands on either side of her, caging Noa in with his arms. His body not touching hers. Leaning forward to wipe the water in front of Noa, he pressed his mouth to her ear. "Next time, King stays outside."

The warmth of his breath made Noa shiver. Without thinking, she stepped back, his hard chest behind her.

Luke wrapped his arms around her. "Do I need to be worried about this Eric?"

Noa laughed. Luke became aware of the rhythmic movement of her breasts on top of his arms.

"No, Taylor. Eric is gay."

"Okay, but I'll still phone you tonight to make sure you're okay. If you feel unsafe, for even a second, you phone me. I don't care what time it is, or even if you tell yourself it's a neighbour's cat going through your trash."

"Yes sir." Noa's eyes burned. Never in her life had anyone worried about her safety.

Saturday, 19 June, 11:30 a.m.

Fists pushed in his sides, he paced the length of the coffee table. Amid a slew of swear words, he stopped and stared at the laptop's screen. Emily remained in the muscle monkey's arms. "Why aren't you pushing him away?"

Rage pulsed through him. His entire body trembled. He grabbed the glass standing next to the laptop and sent it crashing against the nearest wall.

"You'll pay for this, you sonofabitch. You won't take her away from me. Emily is mine!"

A sneer consumed his face at the thought of all the things

he planned to do to his Emily. "Tonight, my love, I will come to you."

Still another man held Emily. "Soon *you* will die."

Chapter 7

Saturday, 19 June, 6:00 p.m.

Most of Luke's family members were seated in his parents' living room. Even Maddie had managed to be there on time. He hated being late.

The hours had raced by as he searched online. Apart from a website for her online health coaching and personal training services, Noa Morgan had no presence in cyberspace. No social media accounts. Her name wasn't listed as part of the alumni on any tertiary institutions' websites. Luke considered contacting an old friend in Marcel, but he drew the line at involving the police. *Stalker alert.*

After spending time in Noa's house he was more intrigued than ever. Devoid of any personal items, even photos. The only items which offered a glimpse into her world were the bookshelves lined with novels and the couch, which would be perfect for cuddling and watching a series on a rainy winter's day in front of the fireplace – and taking his time exploring every part of Noa. *Slow down, Taylor.*

Luke strode towards the only sibling he hadn't seen since returning home. Jamie sat next to her husband, Spencer. "I missed you, Jamie."

"I find it difficult to believe, seeing as you didn't keep in touch much for the past … decade."

"Jamie, stop it," their father said. Aaron Taylor was a gentle giant, but didn't take any nonsense from his children. Not when he knew what having them all under the same roof meant to his wife, and to him.

"I'm just stating facts, Dad." Jamie let out a laboured breath. "I'll go see if Mom needs any help with dinner." She pushed to her feet.

"Sit down and talk to your brother. I'll go help your mom." Spencer pulled her down on to the couch as he rose.

Madison ran into the room and jumped into Luke's arms. "Have I told you, you're the best brother in the world?"

"Not today." Luke held her at arm's length. "What did you say to her? She blushed redder than the shade of lipstick you're wearing."

"That's between us girls."

Aaron cleared his throat and swirled the golden liquid in the tumbler. "Who are you talking about?"

"Luke's girlfriend."

Jamie shook her head. "You're back in town a week and already some poor, unsuspecting woman is pining for you? Typical Luke."

"Jamie, I won't warn you again to stop it with your snide remarks."

Madison hugged Luke's waist and stared daggers at Jamie. "She isn't his girlfriend. Not yet, but soon Noa will be."

Jamie leaned forward. "Noa Morgan?"

From the kitchen, Laura called her youngest child's name and Madison headed towards their mother's voice.

"Noa Morgan?" Jamie asked again.

"Yes, James." Luke poured himself and Jamie a bourbon. As he held it out to her, she shook her head and pursed her lips. She hated being called James.

"Isn't it enough that you destroyed one of my friends' lives? Now you're going to do it again."

"I didn't realise she's your friend, I swear. And for the record, I have no intention of destroying her life. I like her and I want to pursue this *interest* between us."

"I can tell you exactly how this will end – her car wrapped around a tree."

"Enough!" Aaron roared.

"No, Dad. Luke needs to hear this. He wasn't here to live with the consequences of his actions. He left and carried on with his life as if she never existed. The rest of us have had to live through the aftermath of her death. I won't let him do it to another friend of mine. I'll tell Noa the truth."

Luke dropped his head in his hands and exhaled hard, pushing his fingers through his hair.

Aaron watched the colour drain from his son's face. "Luke, it's time you tell Jamie the truth. All of it. Your mother and I can't bear to see this rift between you two. Now that you're back, it's time you bury the hatchet and be best friends like you were all your lives. Before that woman came in to your lives."

"*That woman?* Dad, you've never spoken of Amber like that." Jamie turned to Aaron.

"Son, if you don't tell Jamie, I will. And I promise, I *will* speak ill of the dead. It's high time people heard the truth about Amber." Aaron lifted the glass to his lips.

"Luke, what is Dad talking about?" Jamie asked.

Luke couldn't look at his sister. He took a deep breath and told her. Jamie listened without interrupting as Luke shared the truth about what had happened during the weeks before he left River Valley.

At first, Jamie didn't believe him, until the detective in her started remembering things Amber had said and done.

Before Luke finished talking, Jamie sat next to him with her arms around him, tears streaming down her face. "Why didn't you say something?"

"Because Amber was your friend, and she died. It was easier to have you angry at me than a lifelong friend you couldn't confront. I didn't want you to suffer the pain of losing your friend and mourning the person you'd thought Amber was. It wouldn't have changed anything."

"Like hell it wouldn't have. For the past ten years, I thought you were a heartless bastard. I hated you for leaving and carrying on with your life. For two years, I didn't hear a single word from you, my brother. My *twin* brother." Jamie nudged

Luke with her shoulder; they both smiled. "Just do me a favour, don't tell Noa you're my brother until you are one-thousand percent sure you're serious about her. Please be patient with her. I'm not sure why, but I suspect something horrific happened to Noa before she moved to River Valley. She never speaks of her life before arriving here. When something does come up, she changes the subject."

Luke nodded. "I noticed the same thing and I've known Noa for less than a day."

Madison walked in and settled on the arm rest of Aaron's chair. "I'm glad you two made up. So, Jamie, does he have your blessing to pursue the pants off of your friend?"

"Maddie, I swear you're ageing me by the second." Aaron affectionately punched her shoulder.

"It's true, Dad. I saw the way they were looking at each other and how Luke walked with her out the door. He had his hand on Noa's lower back and everything. That right there, lady and gentlemen, is true love. No guy has ever done that to me."

"Yes, Mads, because you date boys. It's time you date men, or at least boys who know how to treat a woman and not use you as a sex toy."

Aaron dragged a hand down his beard. "Dammit, Jamie, don't you start as well. I swear you children want to give me a heart attack."

A muscle twitched in Luke's jaw. "Madison, did you play a prank last night and blow an air horn?"

"No. Why would you think that?"

"Because it's exactly the kind of childish thing your friends might get up to."

"I swear I didn't, and neither did they. I saw you and Noa leave Rapids and I left an hour or so later."

"What happened, big brother?" Jamie asked.

Luke told her about the air horn and the rose that had been left on Noa's windshield. He also mentioned the gut feeling he had that they were being watched not only in the gym, but while they'd had breakfast. "Have you ever noticed she loathes flowers?" Luke asked.

"No, I haven't."

Spencer returned and wrapped an arm around Jamie's waist. "Don't you remember honey, last year at your birthday dinner? Noa came over and froze the second she noticed the bouquet of white roses I bought for you."

"I don't remember that." Jamie rubbed Spencer's arm. A deep line appeared between her eyes.

"Noa spent the rest of the night stroking King, even at the dinner table. I always got the idea he's more for therapy than a guard dog. Not that he allows anyone close to Noa, took King some time to get used to us."

"He was great with me today. Maybe I should get a dog to keep me company."

"Don't do that," Maddie said.

"Why not? I like dogs and living alone isn't as much fun as you think."

"You won't be living alone for long. Mark my words, before Christmas, you and Noa will sleep in the same bed. Every. Night."

Laughter filled the room.

Aaron cleared his throat. "I'm grateful you said sleep and not something else. Let's eat. It's good to have all of you home. And Luke, next family dinner, invite Noa. I want to find out for myself if she's worthy of my son."

Every time Aaron called him *son,* it reminded Luke how lucky he was to call Aaron, Dad.

Chapter 8

King scratched at the front door, alerting Noa to Eric's arrival. She grabbed her Glock 43 and headed for the door. Noa peered through the window, rolling her shoulders. After Luke had left, she cried on her couch, with King and her Glock on either side of her. *Nothing like a stupid white rose to upset a woman.*

She opened the door for Eric and took his umbrella, leaving it on the porch.

"What's with the gun, Rambo?" Eric kissed her cheek as he walked past her.

"It's been one of those days." Noa took the bag from his hand and carried it to the kitchen.

"Sweetie, look at me." Noa turned and looked at the handsome face of her oldest friend. Kim and Jamie often joked that Eric being gay was womanhood's loss and manhood's gain. "What's going on?" he asked.

"Nothing. Just a bad day." She focused on the Chinese food, removed the containers from the paper bags and dished up for both of them.

"Okay. Do you want to hear about my night with the fitness model?" Eric grinned.

"Does he not have a name?"

"Of course, but it doesn't matter. I deleted his number from my phone as I headed out the door."

"That bad?" Noa reached for a bottle of Lamont Merlot and handed it to Eric to uncork; their domestic dance perfected after having lived together for a year.

"No. That *good*."

"You're such a slut. One day Karma will find you."

"I will sleep with Karma too."

Noa laughed, almost dropping the wine glasses.

"How was your night, little-miss-social-life?"

The corners of her mouth lifted at the memory of being in Luke's arms, but she steeled her face before turning to face Eric. "Good. Fun. You know Kim, she's a magnet for it."

"Tell me about Matthew's friend."

"Luke's nice." *Sexy, strong, caring, and tempting.*

"Is he the gladiator meets Neanderthal who was with you in the gym today?"

Noa handed him the wine glasses. "Yes, why didn't you come say hello before you left? I could've introduced you."

"I was busy chatting up a guy and didn't want people to see me with your Neanderthal. My reputation needs to remain unscathed."

"Luke isn't a Neanderthal. He's just rugged. It suits him."

"Sweetie, Neanderthal, is me being nice. That man desperately needs a shave a and haircut." Eric placed the wine glasses on the counter and crossed his arms over his chest. "Hold on, do you like him?"

"No, Superman."

"Then why were you having breakfast with him?"

"We made a bet last night about Pilates and, as Matthew's best friend, Luke's going to be part of our circle of friends. I might as well get to know him."

Eric stared down at Noa. "No romantic feelings?"

"No." Not a complete lie. *Interested? Very.*

"Good. You're not capable of giving him what he wants."

"How do you know what he wants?"

"I don't have to be straight to see the way he admired your derriere."

Noa felt her cheeks heat and busied herself in the fridge.

"You need to tell him you're not interested. It's not like you can have sex with him. Cut the ties and move on."

Her breath caught. *I am interested.*

"My honest opinion, he only zoned in on you because Kim and Matthew forced you on him. An attractive guy like him will never be interested in you. Sorry, sweetie, I just don't want you to get your heart broken."

Noa didn't look at her friend. "So much for him being a Neanderthal."

"As I said, a shave and a haircut and women will line up for the gladiator. Sweetie, I love you, but you're not his type. Trust me, I'm a guy, we can sense when another man is bad news."

Never pretty enough. Never clever enough. Never anything enough, Noa thought. The exact words her mother had said to her for years.

"Take the plates, I'll bring the wine." Eric gave her a pouty smile and carried the wine and glasses to the dining room table.

King pawed at Noa's leg and she bent down to hug him. "We won't tell him the truth," she whispered into King's ear, kissing his head before straightening her legs.

As she took a seat across from Eric, she studied his profile. Some days, he reminded her more of her mother than the person who had opened his house to her when she first moved to the area.

"How did your meeting go on Friday?" she asked, wrapping udon noodles around her fork and lifting it to her mouth.

Eric smiled. "Good. We're breaking ground on Monday."

"I'm so proud of you. Your first hotel and on the waterfront. How do you think it will feel to stand there, on the official opening day? To think it all started with your idea and drawing."

Eric shrugged. "It's just another building. But I guess I'm erecting monuments and people will remember me as the visionary behind them. As long as my buildings stand, a part of me is immortal."

Noa reached across the table and placed her hand on his. "I'm proud of you. You're living your dream."

"Are you?" Eric squeezed Noa's hand.

"I'm getting there. Had a good and productive session with Doctor Clarke on Friday. He said some valuable things, which I agree with for a change."

Eric released her hand and stared at her. "Are you considering the sex surrogate?"

Noa laughed. "Oh, hell no. I told him it's never happening."

"You need to stop seeing him. The guy is a pervert and I swear he sits there with a hard-on every week listening to you. Why else does he always tell you, he'll sit in on your session with the sex surrogate? He wants to watch you. Pervert."

Noa pointed at the Merlot. "Do you want more wine?"

"No, thank you. I need to be up at the ass crack of noon to pack. Leaving early on Monday and I didn't get any sleep last night."

Noa's stomach clenched. "Where are you going?"

"I'm going to stay in Shadow Bay for the duration of the project, but I'll be back and forth and will be here every other weekend. If you miss me, you can always come visit. Ask Jamie to take King and come stay with me. We can go clubbing. You don't have to be my beard."

A yawn crept up on Noa and she pushed her chair back, ready to pack the dirty dishes in the dishwasher and head to bed.

"What's wrong with you? I know my company isn't boring you."

"I'm tired, not used to being out as late as last night and I didn't sleep well."

Eric pushed to his feet. "Then I guess it's my cue to leave. What are you doing tomorrow?"

"Nothing much. I plan on finishing the novel I'm reading and spend time with King. Usual Sunday."

At the front door, Eric stopped, stroked King's head and took Noa's face in his hands. She yawned again. "Straight to bed with you, missy. You're getting old."

She kissed his cheek. "Goodnight. Call me when you get settled in Shadow Bay."

After Eric left, Noa set the alarm and checked her phone. Luke had sent her another message.

Luke: Do you want me to come over?

Noa: I'm going to bed, but thank you.

Luke: Invitation?

Noa laughed and shook her head. Memories of the scent of his leather jacket filled her head. Her stomach flipped.

Noa: Not tonight...

Luke: Tomorrow night?

Noa: Goodnight, you insufferable man.

Luke: Sweet dreams gorgeous. Can't wait to see you tomorrow. I have a surprise for you. Call me if you need me. I'm going to be up late thinking about you ... in bed.

With a smile Noa climbed into bed, switched off the light, and pulled the duvet to her neck. In the corner of the room, King snored in his bed.

On the pillow next to her wasn't the head of the man she fell asleep thinking about, but her Glock 43.

Sunday, 20 June, 00:15 a.m.

In the darkness of her backyard, he waited. The idea of the warm, sleeping body waiting for him made him hard. He rubbed a hand over his erection and wished it was Emily's expert hand. *Soon it will be.*

While he bided his time he, again, watched Emily lie to her friend about what she had planned for Sunday. Nothing she did, or said, inside her house was a mystery to him. He knew when she woke up, that Emily washed her hair before she washed her body. How frequently she shaved her legs, and when wasn't a good time for his nocturnal visits. *Biology is a bitch.*

Slipping the phone into his coat pocket, he thought of his plans for Emily tonight. The warmth of her bare skin under him. The perfect colour of her nipples. Her taste.

"You're mine, Emily. All mine," he whispered, disarming the alarm.

Chapter 9

Noa awoke to the message alert tone of her mobile phone. King jumped on the bed and this morning she didn't scold him. She pulled him closer, hugging his grey body to her chest.

"Good morning, my man," she said with a yawn and reached for the phone.

Matthew had sent a message informing her a parcel had been delivered to the gym, addressed to her. Noa replied and thanked him, saying she would pick it up later.

Luke had sent a message a few minutes after midnight. She read it; a smile filled her face as she stretched her body. A long, lazy stretch, still smiling.

Luke: Noa, get out of my head. I can't sleep.

How had she not woken up? Noa contemplated how tired she'd been the night before while heading to the kitchen for much needed coffee. Noa disarmed the alarm and opened the back door for King. He rushed out, and she realised how late it was when she glanced at the clock above her oven.

Waiting for the kettle to boil, Noa removed her phone from the robe's pocket and reread Luke's message. She had dreamt of him, touching her, his mouth everywhere. Her body reacted as she recalled the dream. *I'm not broken.*

Her nipples pushed against the tank top. "You didn't break me, you bastard," she said aloud.

She replied to Luke's message.

Noa: Your revenge for not being able to sleep was to invade my dreams? Thank you, Freddie.

She finished making coffee as King ran into the kitchen. Noa looked at him. A scream echoed through the house. "King, release!"

He obeyed.

Bile rose in her throat as Noa grabbed the dustpan and brush.

Sunday, 20 June, 11:30 a.m.

The sight of her getting out of her Jeep left him breathless. Her dark jeans showcased every perfect curve, her black top left little to his imagination. *Beautiful.* If only he could remove her jacket and, by planned accident, brush against the roundness of her breasts. He shifted uncomfortably and thought of his grandparents. A trick he had learned years ago.

As Noa closed the distance between them, he wished he could feel her lips against his. "Good morning, you ready to rock?"

"Rock, Taylor? That's your opening line?" Noa stood on tiptoes and pressed her lips to his cheek. "What happened to your bushy beard?"

"My mother thought I needed to be more presentable for our date." He blushed, sending Noa's heart into a frenzy.

"You take dating advice from your mother?"

"When you meet her, you'll understand. You should see Maddie."

"Where is she?"

"Over there, by the stage." Luke jerked his head back.

Noa looked past him; the colour drained from her face.

"What's wrong? It looks like you've seen a ghost."

Noa opened her mouth but lost the ability to form coherent words.

"Are you okay?"

She nodded and swallowed hard. "Madison reminds me of someone I used to know."

"She wanted to emulate her musical idol – Slay's lead singer."

"Maddie looks so much like her." Noa breathed deep and smiled up at Luke. "What's your plan for lunch? We're going to get drenched any second." She lifted her eyes towards the dark grey sky.

"Don't worry, I took every scenario into account."

"Why do I get the feeling I need to be worried?"

He took her hands in his, threading their fingers together. Noa winced. Luke looked at their joined hands and frowned. He brought her hands to his chest and looked her dead in the eye. "Noa, what happened to your hands?"

"You should see the other guy." She tried to pull her hands from his, but Luke kept his grip firm without hurting her.

"I'm serious."

"Calm down detective, I went to the gym this morning and got into it with a punching bag."

"Why didn't you wear gloves?"

Noa shrugged. "I did."

The warmth of his mouth against her palms made her breath catch. "What happened?"

"King brought me a gift this morning. A rabbit's head."

"Where did he find a rabbit?" Luke brought her palms to his mouth again, smiling as her lips parted.

"I don't know. Haven't seen any rabbits in the area, but I live close to the foot of the mountain, so anything is possible. Or maybe one of my neighbours has – had – a pet rabbit."

Madison rushed towards them, shouting at them to get out of the rain. As they hurried towards the restaurant, Luke put his arm around Noa's shoulder.

"I can't believe it's raining. I was looking forward to playing with you again." Madison pulled Noa out of Luke's reach.

"You look beautiful. The black compliments your eyes and complexion." Noa forced a smile and sincerity into her voice.

"Thank you. My mother almost fainted when I asked her to help me." Madison ran her fingers through her hair. "Then I told her about you and your date with Luke. Mom forgot all about my hair and we only spoke of you. By the way, she's dying to meet you."

Noa looked at Luke, who smiled down at her. "My parents want you to come over for dinner."

Noa shook her head and stared at the floor. "I'm not good with parents."

"You'll be great with ours. They aren't like other parents."

"Did you inherit the honesty gene from them?" Noa's eyes darted between brother and sister, wondering why there was such a big age difference between them.

"Yes," they both said.

"Crap," Noa muttered.

"Over breakfast my mother asked why Luke's been smiling since yesterday."

Noa directed her question at Luke. "You live with your parents?"

"Sort of. Not really." He looked at his shoes.

"Which is it?"

Luke cleared his throat. "I live in my house, on my farm, which happens to be next to theirs. I'm refurbishing the kitchen so I have a few, okay most, meals with them. Is that weird?"

"Depends."

"On what?" Madison asked.

"We'll see."

Chapter 10

Sunday, 20 June

My Darling Emily,

I have done nothing but love you for as long as I have known you. Did I not promise you I would never hurt you? Not once did I lift my hand towards you, I never cut you, I never did anything to deserve what you did to me you cu—My apologies, I shouldn't swear at you, my love. It took every ounce of my self-control not to wrap my hands around your throat and squeeze the life out of you.

I thought I would be calmer after my nap, but rage is still festering deep inside me. How could you do this to me? To me? The person who loves you more than anything. All the things I have done for us to be together. This is how you repay me!

I hope you liked the gift I left you... More will follow...

I know you won't remember what you did, so I'll tell you. Honesty is a crucial part of a healthy relationship. You, my Emily, said HIS name, while I touched you.

Perhaps next time I'll leave his head for King to find.

Chapter 11

Huddled together under the umbrella they made their way down the footpath. Noa took in the scenery, but didn't smell the rain, the wet earth, none of the nature surrounding them. Only Luke.

He had placed his arm around her again as soon as they exited the restaurant and she snuggled into his warmth, wrapping an arm around his waist. Her finger tips ached to explore the muscles in his back.

How had this been so easy for Emily, but not for her? Noa sighed inaudible, she wanted to breathe again, to see if Luke would shiver under her touch. She fought the urge to find out. *Still surviving, never alive.*

Why did *this* man make her feel safe, after knowing Luke less than forty-eight hours?

On the river bank a rustic wooden gazebo came into view as they descended the steps. Luke led her up the gazebo where Noa halted. At her feet was a blanket, a picnic basket to the left and next to it was a silver bucket containing a bottle of champagne.

Noa turned to Luke and found him studying her. For the third time, in less than an hour, she thought he couldn't be more handsome. *Gladiator, never Neanderthal.*

"Is this for me?" She searched his eyes.

Luke wrapped her in his arms and whispered, "Yes."

"No one has ever done anything like this for me. Never Luke. You don't know..." She shut her eyes.

56

"This is just the beginning, Noa Morgan."

He cupped her face in his hands and brought her mouth to his. "Will you shoot me if I kiss you?"

Noa shook her head, pressing her mouth to his. With each brush of his lips, each tease of his tongue, her heart raced, yet an unknown calm washed over her. Luke increased his hold on her when her legs failed.

Against her stomach his body's response to the kiss became clear as Luke pulled her closer. She wasn't repulsed, she didn't pull away. Instead, Noa wrapped her arms around his neck and pushed her body harder against his.

Luke eased back from her and they stood staring at each other, trying to regain control of their breathing, smiling.

Noa thought of something to say but she couldn't construct even the simplest of sentences. Luke led her further under the gazebo and she settled next to him on the blanket.

"This view is spectacular. Can you imagine waking up to this?" she asked.

"I wake up to it every day. This is why I came back and I've never been happier that I did." He brought her hand to his mouth, careful of the broken skin on her knuckles.

"Is this your property?"

"No mine is about a kilometre down the river." He indicated to the left of where they sat.

"How did you organise this?" Noa scanned her immediate surroundings. Lanterns had been placed around them. Fairy lights draped from the roof.

"I know the owners."

"How is it possible you're still single?" Noa pursed her lips.

"I see my brutal honesty is transferable." Luke laughed, fine lines appearing at the corners of his eyes. *Gladiator.* He shrugged. "I've never met anyone I wanted to have a picnic with. This would have been better in summer, but this area is used for weddings during the warmer months so our timing is perfect, except for the rain."

Noa shook her head. "The rain makes it perfect."

Luke drew her closer to his side and ran his fingers through her hair. "I've wanted to kiss you since Friday night."

"Do you want my opinion on the matter?" *Don't let him control you in death.*

Noa got to her knees, swung one leg over Luke's legs and straddled him. With her fingertips Noa traced his jaw line, and brought his mouth to hers. Luke ran his hands down her back and settled his big hands on her bum.

Luke pulled away. "Please stop wiggling your butt around, you're torturing me."

"Sorry ... I'm trying not to, uhm ..." Noa tried to push out of his arms.

"Where do you think you're going? I didn't say stop kissing me, just stop torturing me." Luke gripped her hamstrings and brought her closer.

Sunday, 20 June, 7:28 p.m.

He clicked through the live feed from the multiple cameras inside and outside of her house. "Where are you, Emily?" The moment he reached for the laptop screen, intending to slam it shut, her Jeep pulled into the garage; a smile visible on her face.

"Is this the time to get home? I know each of your smiles. Your *I just got laid* smile, your smile when you walk off the stage, your graduation smile, every last one of them. This one is new. I hate it."

He stared at her face, touching her through the screen, every muscle in his body tensing. "I guess you haven't opened the gift I left for you at the gym yet."

***

Monday, 21 June, 11:02 a.m.

Seated on doctor Clarke's too familiar couch, Noa wondered why he always kept a notebook on his lap, yet never wrote anything down. She considered the possibility of what Eric had said during dinner on Saturday night.

"Tell me about your weekend. You seem less tense than you did on Friday." Benjamin shifted in the chair.

"I met someone." Noa averted his eyes. Instead, she focused on the abstract painting on the wall to her left. Sixty-nine individual brush strokes made up what some people might call art. She had spent a considerable amount of time staring at the painting when doctor Clarke tried to engage her in discussing the events at the cabin.

"Do you not consider it might be too soon?"

Noa leaned forward, resting her elbows on her knees, her stare locked on his. "Wait, a minute. You told me on Friday I needed to get out, meet people, say *yes* to everything that came my way."

"Did you say yes to *him*?" Doctor Clarke's head tilted to the right, a move which, not only got her hackles up, but sent them into orbit.

"I think it's time for us to end our sessions. It has been over two-and-a-half years since the *incident*. I've moved on, and have put it behind me."

"Why are you avoiding my question, Noa?" He tilted his head to the left.

"Because it's none of your business whether I had sex. It's best if I leave." She snatched her handbag from the floor and pushed to her feet.

"Noa, please don't go. I'm merely trying to determine whether you have regained control of this aspect of your life. I don't mean to intrude on your privacy, I'm asking in regard to your recovery."

"My recovery?" Noa laughed, wrapping her arms around her waist. "You don't recover from what I went through. You survive it and carry on as best you can. It will forever be part of who I am. But I choose to no longer give him power. I refuse to continue living in fear. I choose to live, just like I did before, on my terms."

"Who was being held in that cabin ... you or Emily?"

Noa answered the question with a vacant stare; her jaw tight.

"The fact you refuse to answer me is more proof you aren't ready for us to end our sessions. Tell me about this man you met?"

"I'd prefer if we don't discuss him."

"You brought him up, Noa. And you know this is a safe space. In order for me to help you, I need to be privy to *every* part of your life."

"You are not privy to information about him. End of discussion."

"We will circle back to him."

Like hell we will.

"When last did you have a panic attack?"

"Not since the last one I told you about. When was it, maybe three months ago?"

"Noa, this only works if you're honest with me. You met someone this weekend and you want me to believe in no possible scenarios, were there any triggers?"

"Yes. And we're not discussing him."

"Why are you so hostile today?" He tilted his head to the right again.

Noa's nails dug into her sides, her arms still tight around her. "I'm not. I just want these sessions to end. This is the only place I'm reminded of what happened. I don't want to relive it anymore. I want to move forward."

"You're not paying for these sessions, Noa. They were part of the conditions when you moved to River Valley." He laid a hand over the right pocket of his pants. "Please excuse me for a second, I need to go take care of something."

Doctor Clarke stood and made his way across the room.

Noa glanced at his crotch, but didn't see a visible bulge. *Teeny-weeny or Eric is blowing smoke out of his ass.*

Noa retrieved her phone from her handbag. Luke had sent another message, reminding her that he was thinking about her. She looked at the time display and calculated the hours until she would see him again. A self-depreciating smile spread across her face. Noa didn't care that it was childish to count the hours. The time had come for her to make bold strides in moving forward. All the other boxes on her 'becoming-Noa-Morgan-list' had been ticked.

Noa glanced at her phone again, wondering what was keeping doctor Clarke. Five minutes had passed since he left. She decided to do the same. No point in staying when she didn't intend to ever set foot in this office again. *This ends now.*

"I'm sorry, can we please reschedule? I'm not myself today." Doctor Clarke stood in the doorway, his face pale. His hands trembled as he held the door open for her.

What the hell is up with him all of a sudden? "Goodbye, Doctor Clarke. Hope you feel better soon." *And I never have to sit in this office with you again.*

Chapter 12

After a productive meeting with Matthew at Koffee, Luke strolled down River Valley's main street, towards his SUV. On the sidewalk he stopped and took in the sights of the idyllic town. So much, and yet so little, had changed during his absence. The wife of his high school rugby coach still owned the bakery. Now the former coach yelled at their staff and Luke doubted they were keen on huddles.

Down the street, the corner store had made way for a supermarket which carried the logo of a national chain. People knew each other and watered each other's gardens or walked each other's dogs while they were away. This was home.

Luke noticed Noa's red Jeep heading down the street into oncoming traffic. Hooters blared.

Luke ran.

The Jeep crashed into an oak tree. The driver's door opened. Noa fell onto the road.

The second she hit the tar Noa scooted back and away from her vehicle.

Traffic and time stopped as Luke closed the distance to Noa and fell to the ground beside her.

"Noa?" He cupped her face and forced her to meet his eyes.

Tears streamed down her cheeks. She tried to speak; her breathing too erratic.

"Where are you hurt?" He looked her over, pressing Noa's face to his chest in an attempt to still the violent tremble of her body.

"No. Get. Away. In. There." Noa tried to lift her right arm towards the Jeep.

Matthew came running out of Koffee; Luke asked him to search the Jeep's interior.

A violent curse bellowed out of Matthew. He slammed the door shut with another curse. Luke stared up at him, cradling Noa's head to his chest.

"Spiders. Big ass spiders." Matthew's whole body shivered.

"Noa, look at me." As soon as Noa did, he kissed her forehead, cheeks and mouth. Luke held her mouth to his until her violent shaking ceased.

"I need to look and see if they bit you." Noa nodded. "Matthew, I need you to catch one so we can take it to the hospital with us."

"Don't need to dude, not venomous. You forget I grew up with an entomologist."

"Phone your mom. Send her a photo. I need to know Noa isn't in any danger."

She reached for his face. "Please. My legs and neck."

Luke pressed his mouth to her hair. As he started looking at her neck, tyres screeched behind them.

"Noa!" a voice thundered.

Luke turned in the direction from where the shout came.

A man rushed up to them, grabbing Noa's shoulders from behind and made a frivolous attempt to remove her from Luke's grip.

Luke studied the stranger, his back going rigid. "Who the hell are you?"

"Eric Foster. Her best friend, you idiot."

Noa turned towards Eric but held on to Luke. "I'm okay."

"Hey dumb-ass, you were in an accident. You're *not* okay. Come, I'll take you home and arrange for your Jeep to be towed."

Luke's nostrils flared as his hands drew into fists clenching Noa's back. Her whimper forced him to release his hold. "Eric, please stand back. I need to make sure she wasn't bitten and get her to the hospital. Matthew will make the arrangements for the Jeep to be towed." Luke glanced at Matthew and his request was granted with a nod.

"Bitten?"

"Yes. Spider bites."

Eric shook his head. "Noa, look at me. Right now." When she did, he asked, "Spiders?"

Noa nodded and started rocking in the space Luke's arms allowed. Luke stroked her hair, placed his mouth next to her ear and whispered. He kept his lips against Noa's forehead until the she stopped rocking. Noa took a deep breath and opened her eyes.

"Thank you, Eric, but I'm fine. I just want Luke to check that I wasn't bitten and take me to hospital to have my neck checked out for whiplash."

"We need to have you checked for a concussion. I'm your best friend. He whispers in your ear and now I don't exist."

Luke pushed to his feet with Noa in his arms and carried her to his SUV.

Eric was a storm on Luke's heels. "I'm not letting a stranger take care of you."

"Eric, stop." Noa tried to lift her hand when he opened his mouth. "You need to go to Shadow Bay, you have work to do. When you're here over a weekend the three of us will have dinner."

She lifted her eyes to Luke's and breathed through the nausea. "Please ignore what I'm about to say. Eric, Luke isn't a complete stranger. We're unclassified, but I want him to take me. Now …" Noa shook her head, the movement barely noticeable. "… to hospital."

Luke smiled down at her. "Unless you want to go catch one of those eight-legged-demons and bring it to the hospital?"

Eric stepped back. "No, thank you. I don't do spiders. I'll phone you later." He turned his focus on Luke. "If you hurt her, you're a dead man."

Luke grinned and helped Noa into the SUV. As he rounded

the front Matthew ran up to him.

"Spoke to my mom. She said it's wolf spiders and they're not common to this area. Needless to say, four of them in one vehicle isn't normal. You know what this means."

Luke's hands tightened so much his fingernails bit into his palms. "Yes."

Monday, 21 June, 1:48 p.m.

Benjamin Clarke sat in his office staring at the spot where Noa always sat. At the moment her seat was occupied by someone who didn't belong, not in this world. He loathed no one as much as he did his uninvited guest. From the first day they had met he saw through his guest's mask. He would've been the worst psychologist in the world had he not. If someone held a gun to his head, Benjamin might have acknowledged his true feelings about his guest.

"What did you do to her?" Benjamin asked.

"I gave her a gift. A flashback, as you shrinks call it."

"Why spiders?"

"That's a rather personal question, Doc. I'll throw you a bone – the spiders are a reminder of a happier time. But I'm not here to discuss my best days. I'm here to discuss what you didn't do. Your failures."

"For the past two-and-a-half years I've done everything you asked. I even moved to this backward little town. And what do I get in return?" Benjamin knew he was poking a dragon, but he was tired of the games he was being forced to play with Noa. Never being able to play the ones he wanted.

His guest laughed; the sound pure evil. "Don't be coy, Doctor. You got your willies off every time she left. Must be strange for you to do it yourself and not have a patient do it for you. Tsk, tsk, tsk. Your tiny dick got you into this deal."

The devil sneered. "Don't deny it. You have a hidden camera in this room, as do I."

"What do you want? She ended our sessions. I'm done."

"You're done? Oh, that's precious. No, Benjamin, you're done when I say you're done. I ordered you to get Emily over her infatuation with that man. Did you do it? No. You ended your session and sent her on her merry way – well hairy-arachnid-way. You fucked up my entire plan."

"I didn't—"

"Shut up, Benjamin. You know damn well how this relationship works. Need I remind you I'm privy to your little perversion? Do I need to show you, again?" The devil paced across the room, dragging a finger across Benjamin's neck with each passing. "You were supposed to mould her into my creation, not turn her into Emily. Emily was strong, too strong even for me. I'm better prepared now. This time I will *break* her."

Benjamin grabbed at his neck; fire spread through his veins.

Darkness swirled with the devil's laughter and swallowed him.

Chapter 13

Monday, 21 June, 6:05 p.m.

Noa's eyes followed Luke as he moved around her kitchen. It might've been sheer luck that he had been in the vicinity of where she'd crashed into the tree, but she couldn't have imagined getting through the previous few hours without him by her side.

Luke had doted on her. And he had Noa's back when she'd refused to be kept overnight for observation.

Noa hated hospitals and, as it turned out, learned did he. Luke had told her as much as he'd walked her into her house and ensured she had everything she needed within arm's reach.

King hadn't left her side except when Luke had taken him for a run. Noa suspected that they'd only walked down her driveway and stayed there. Her two guardians.

Luke glanced at her and smiled. "Am I warming your soup wrong?"

"Why is the most beautiful man in the world, and believe me I have travelled across the world so I say this with authority, in my kitchen?"

Luke's laughter filled her mind, her heart, her core. "The painkillers are kicking in."

"No, Lucas, I want to know. Not that I'm not appreciative of the view."

"Lucas? My name isn't Lucas. Painkillers." He laughed again and returned his attention to their dinner.

"Dammit, Luke, not the painkillers. Come here, please." Noa patted the spot on the couch next to her. On the coffee table her phone buzzed. "Dammit, not Foster again."

"Let me talk to him. I'll tell him you're asleep." Luke took the phone and answered the call. "Hello, Eric. Noa is sleeping. I'll ask her to call you tomorrow morning."

"Where is she?"

"At home. As Noa told you herself, she's okay. No bites and no whiplash. Just normal pain associated with being in a car accident. If she'd been driving faster, it could've been much worse."

"Thank you, Doctor Luke. Please be a lamb and tell Noa I'll put my life on hold and come nurse her back to health."

"That won't be necessary, but I'll tell her you called to check up on her. Tomorrow morning."

"Are you staying with her?"

"Yes." Luke sighed and looked at King for help. King sighed and sneaked his grey body closer to Noa.

"What qualifies you to be Noa's bodyguard? Three days of knowing her?"

"Your passive aggressiveness might hurt her, but it has no effect on me."

"Well, I never, Doctor Luke has a spine. Probably all those muscles keeping it rigid. My, my aren't you full of surprises."

"*Detective* Luke Taylor. Goodnight Eric. Noa will give you a call when she is up to it." Luke ended the call and returned the phone to the coffee table.

Noa whispered to King, and he obeyed, making his way out the back door.

Taking Luke's hand, she pulled him down onto the couch beside her. "Detective Luke Taylor sounds sexy and dangerous. When did you join the local department?" She ran her fingers through Luke's hair and grinned as he leaned into the caress. "You're my hero Detective Luke – not Lucas – Taylor."

Luke pressed his lips to her palm, and pulled Noa against his chest. "I'm no hero."

"I don't care how you, or the rest of the world, sees you. You're my hero. Mine."

"I didn't do anything." He pressed his lips to her hair and breathed in her scent. *She called me hers.*

"I'm going to tell you a secret. If you ever tell anyone I'll go all 'I never had sexual relations' on you." Noa snickered. "No one has ever taken care of me. Except my grandparents, but they don't count as I was thrust onto them by the bitch birth-giver. They only took care of me for the first three years of my life, then they died. Not at the same time but dead, dead, dead."

"Let me fetch you some soup. The painkillers you snuck on an empty stomach are catching up with you." Luke eased his hold on her but Noa grabbed a fist full of his shirt.

"Thank you, Luke. Thank you for being there today, for getting me through it. For being here, now. For protecting and serving me."

With his thumb he wiped at the tears streaming down her face. "I'm not here because I see you as a victim. I'm here because I care about you and I'll keep caring about you for as long as you let me, even after that. But before either of us say something we're not ready to, let me fetch your dinner, and after you finish eating I want to hold you. Noa, I *need* to hold you."

She smiled up at him and brought his hand to her mouth.

Noa watched Luke walking to the kitchen. He bent down to give King a quick scratch behind his ear, giving her the perfect view of his spectacular rear-end. She saw him lock the back door, set the alarm and his hand touch the gun holstered at his side. She smelled the soup warming on the stove. She heard the voices from the television. For the first time in Noa's life, she felt herself falling in love.

Chapter 14

Tuesday, 22 June

My darling Emily,
Here I sit, watching as you lay asleep, in another man's arms. It makes me yearn for the nights I held you, when every part of you lay bare to me. Do you still not realise how deep my love is for you?

From the day we met, there was no denying it – you're my soul mate. We're so much alike, it's as if we were cut from the same piece of cloth and time had sewn us back together. Forever you and I will be one.

You disappoint me. If you found comfort in one of your friends' arms, I may have been able to forgive you, but not for this stranger. A man you thanked for being there for you when he has done none of the things I have.

Will he kill for you? Will he devote his life to you and only you?

I researched him and it seems he left the police force, a decorated detective. Has he told you he lived in Marcel the same time we did? I'm sorry to tell you this, but he's not the hero he pretends to be. He hasn't been honest with you and I've had enough of him coming between us.

I will take you from him. I promised myself a long time ago to never again do what I did to you years ago. You getting hurt was never my intention. But you're a stubborn bitch who refuses to listen! Why is it so difficult for you to admit the truth? You could've spared yourself a lot of discomfort had you admitted the truth.

You leave me no choice.

What I am about to do, you brought on yourself. The spiders were just the beginning.

If only you opened the gift I left for you on Sunday...

Chapter 15

Luke awoke with a warm body nestled in his arms. During the night, Noa had turned and snuggled her head under his chin. For hours he simply held her, breathing her in and wondering what was going on in her life. Who hated her enough to put four wolf spiders in her Jeep? She could've killed someone, or herself. *Not like Amber.*

The thought of Noa dead sent his pulse racing. Luke drew her closer, resting a hand on her lower back. Next to him Noa was a complete woman and if this had been any other morning, he might've explored the softness and warmth of her skin. The roundness of the breasts which had taunted him from the moment she fell into his arms on Friday night.

Luke's body ached after spending hours laying in the same position, but every kink and spasm was worth having Noa in his arms. He had slept in far worse places than on this beautiful woman's oversized couch. *I need to get one of these for my house, for when she visits, and hopefully spends the night.*

As he listened to her rhythmic breathing, he knew he wanted her. Not for one night and not for a month. No matter the truth behind her panic attacks, or her vigilance when it came to her safety. He wanted her. Never before had Luke Taylor wanted a woman. Usually, the moment they'd start talking about their pasts, he was out the door. Talking led to questions; ones Luke never wanted to answer. Not until he woke up to the woman next to him. *Maybe Noa won't run.*

Noa stirred in his arms, making Luke become painfully aware of his body's reaction to her.

"Good morning. How are you feeling?" Luke pressed his lips to her forehead.

Noa's body stiffened, and he heard the quick intake of her breath. Without warning, she pushed against his chest and fell to the floor, terror visible in her eyes. Noa propelled herself away from him, using her hands and bum, without breaking eye contact.

King rushed through the doggy-door and climbed on top of her lap. With her eyes still on Luke she hugged King to her so hard the dog yelped.

"Noa, it's me. Luke. You're safe. Breathe for me, honey." Luke sat up and kept himself in place even though every cell in his body screamed to go to Noa and hold her.

"What are you doing here?" She looked around franticly. Her eyes came to rest on her Glock on the coffee table between them.

"You were in an accident yesterday. I stayed to take care of you and ensure you were okay during the night. Doctor's orders. We slept together because you asked me to hold you after I helped you to eat some soup. You fell asleep and I drifted off, I didn't want to wake you." Luke got to his hands and knees and crawled closer. "Please tell me who hurt you?"

Noa buried her face in King's neck.

"Nothing happened, Noa. I promise I didn't lay a hand on you. I will *never* take advantage of you, not when you are high on painkillers, or drunk, or emotional, or vulnerable. Never. You should know this much about me by now." Luke eased closer to her.

"Painkillers?" Noa closed her eyes. She rubbed her hands over her face and opened her eyes. "I was on those painkillers years ago. They had no effects on me apart from numbing the pain."

"Did you take anything else after we got home?"

"No, just my multivitamin and pill. But I take them every

day and neither should've had an adverse reaction to the painkillers. I don't remember anything apart from you standing in the kitchen heating soup."

"What *other* pill did you take?"

She turned her focus on the fireplace, resting her head on King's. "*The* pill. I've been on it for years and not because I'm sleeping around or anything."

"No explanation necessary. I would like to talk to the doctor who tended to you yesterday, just so we can be sure. Okay?"

"No, it's fine. I won't take the painkillers again. I'll feel better after a hot shower. My back and neck are a little stiff."

Luke stood up and held out a hand to her. Noa looked up at him and he saw a vulnerability in her which broke his heart. She placed her hand in his and Luke pulled her to her feet and into his arms. He stroked her back and waited for her to ease into the embrace.

"Noa, who hurt you?"

She shook her head against his chest.

"Sit down, I'll make you coffee. And after you've had something to eat, I'll run you a bath. Don't worry about King, he and I can play in the back-yard. If the weather permits, we might enjoy lunch out in your garden."

Noa wrapped her arms around his waist. "You don't have to stay with me the whole day. I'm fine. Matthew has rescheduled my sessions for the rest of the week and Kim is helping with my classes. Luckily the gym is quiet during winter."

"I'm staying with you. I just need to cancel something I had on for tonight and ask my dad to stop by my house to check on the renovations."

"Please don't cancel your date tonight. I'm fine. Can I make you a cup of coffee before you leave? It's the least I can do for you." Noa turned, but he reached out and laid a hand on her arm.

"I can't believe I have to say this, but I'm going to because it's you. I'm not seeing anyone else. I don't want too either. Today is Maddie's twenty-third birthday and we're having a family dinner at my parents' tonight. Please come with me?"

"I'm sorry, Luke. Guess I'm still a little shaken after what happened yesterday, not thinking clearly yet. Please don't cancel your plans with your family. I promise I'll be fine on my own. As much as I would like to meet your family, it's too soon, and I'm not in the best place at the moment. When I meet them, I want to make a good impression."

"They're going to adore you as much as Maddie and I do." Luke tilted Noa's head up and kissed her hard. Possessive. "I'll only leave you tonight, if Kim or Matthew come and stay with you. Tomorrow morning first thing, I'll be here to cook you breakfast. Go sit down, I'll call Matthew while I make coffee. Don't make me carry you to the couch."

Noa smiled at him and pulled his head down for her own possessive kiss.

Tuesday, 22 June, 8:00 a.m.

Jamie stared at the faces in front of her. "Where are you?" she asked. Only silenced answered.

In the past year three women had disappeared. The only commonality shared by the women, apart from their current where-abouts being unknown – their age. Early twenties.

The previous night Jamie had spent hours lying awake thinking of Noa and wishing she could be there for her friend. Luke would take better care of her than anyone else. As she'd stared at the darkened ceiling, she realised her brother might have found someone to love; the very thing Luke had spent years running away from. That he had insisted on taking Noa to hospital and stayed the night with her spoke volumes.

Jamie studied every nuance of the faces and notes on the board in front of her, until her concentration was broken by her phone ringing.

"Good morning, Luke."

"Good morning to you too. I can't talk long, Noa's taking

a bath. Any updates?"

"I hate going behind Officer Sheridan's back like this."

"I don't care, we're talking about Noa and you know as well as I do something is wrong." Luke kept his voice low.

Jamie hunched over in the chair and rubbed her neck with her free hand. "Sheridan went to Clarke's home, but he wasn't there. We don't have enough to get a search warrant. She said she would go there again today, and talk to Clarke's neighbours, if he doesn't answer the door."

"Please keep me updated. I hate the thought of leaving Noa alone tonight, but Kim and Matthew said they'll come and stay with her. They need to leave before five tomorrow morning to open the gym and Koffee. I'll try to be back here by seven, at the latest. Can you maybe arrange for someone to park down the street from her house for those two hours?"

"We don't have the manpower you had in the city, Luke. Before you say anything, I will do it myself. How is Noa?"

"Not good. She freaked when she woke up next to me this morning and she had a strange reaction to the painkillers the doctor prescribed for her. I phoned him before I called you and he said it shouldn't have had an effect on her."

"He spoke to you about his patient?"

Luke sighed. "I said I'm her husband."

"Listen, Luke, I know you and get that you're worried. We all are. But Noa won't be happy you went behind her back; she takes *personal privacy* to a whole new level."

"It's hard not being part of the investigation. Noa knew I *wanted* to talk to him. I have to go. I'll see you tonight and let me know if there are any developments today."

Luke ended the call and Jamie returned her attention to the board. Again, she wondered if this was a murder board. *A body does not a murder make.*

Jamie was desperate to ask Luke for his input. He had worked on various cases during his time in the police. Most days she envied Luke for getting out of River Valley and gaining notoriety as a homicide detective. Not to mention the drug syndicate he had spent two years infiltrating. If only she could get his opinion on *this* case.

If there were no new leads by the end of the week, Jamie decided she'd swallow her pride and ask him. The lives of the missing women were more important.

Tuesday, 22 June, 11:00 a.m.

Two hours weren't enough for what he had planned, but he prided himself in making the best of whatever life threw at him. He needed to improvise and hope he got the dosage right. He wasn't a psychiatrist, or a medical doctor, but a quick search on the internet would've eased his conscious, if he had one.

When other little boys were learning to swing a bat, he had wondered how it would feel to swing a bat at someone's head.

Emily had spoken to him on a level no one else before, or after, ever had. She was as much a predator as he was. If he believed in the concept of souls, then Emily was his mate.

"Your bodyguard just made this a lot easier for me. I'll thank him before I cut off his head."

He placed the last item in his backpack and walked over to his laptop. Emily sat next to the muscle monkey – her hands in his dark hair, her mouth on his.

"I will savour every second of our time together. After I am done with you, you will never allow the muscle monkey or any other man to touch you. Ever. This time you will say it. I'm counting the seconds until I taste your silky skin."

Chapter 16

Tuesday, 22 June, 7:00 p.m.

Noa returned her phone to the dining room table and realised Kim and Matthew were watching her with the same idiotic grin on their faces. She didn't want to be babysat, but appreciated not having to spend the night alone.

"What?" she asked, biting into a French fry.

"He cares about you. Why else has Luke been sending both of us messages since he left an hour ago?" Matthew said, placing his beer on the table. Kim placed a coaster under the bottle and kissed Matthew's cheek.

Noa sighed. "I feel guilty that he's thinking about me when it's his sister's birthday."

Kim reached across the table for Noa's hand. "Madison adores you. She was asking me questions about you when she came in for breakfast this morning with their father."

For as long as she could remember Noa had been jealous of the relationships other people had with their parents.

"Don't worry, I didn't tell her any scandals. Only because I don't know about yours from before you moved here, and we haven't made any together."

"How did the classes go today?" Noa pushed her plate of food away and eased back in her chair, rolling her neck from side to side.

"Are you okay? Do you need me to fetch you a painkiller?"

"No thank you, Kim. I'm just a bit sore, not bad enough that I need to take a pill. That reminds me, I need to drink my multivitamin." She hurried to the bathroom. In the mirror she gave herself a once over before turning her attention to the bottle of multivitamins next to the basin. A message alert sounded from the phone in her back pocket.

Luke: Having dessert and wished your mouth could be mine. You have the most delectable mouth.

Two sentences that made her entire body tremble. Noa placed her hands on either side of the basin. She smiled at herself in the mirror. "You look like crap. No matter how sore you get you're not taking a painkiller. You didn't need it last time; you won't need it now." She gave herself a stern nod and went back to the living room where Kim and Matthew were busy playing with King.

They settled in and watched a comedy series. Noa looked at her phone's screen more than that of the television. She didn't laugh when Kim and Matthew did.

Noa caught them both looking at her and felt her cheeks heat. "It's time for me to go to bed."

"Will you be sleeping or playing Luke with yourself?" Kim asked, wiggling her eyebrows.

Matthew dropped his head to his chest, unable to hide the visible shake of his chest.

"Kim, I swear if Luke wouldn't kill me for spending the night alone, I would send you packing. Goodnight." She walked to her bedroom with King trailing behind her.

"You didn't answer my question."

Noa turned and faced her friends. "Thank you for staying with me tonight. You have no idea how much it means to me. Please lock the door when you leave tomorrow morning."

"I will let King out before we go. Do you want me to wake you up so you can reset the alarm?"

"No, I get up around five every morning so it's fine. Thank you both." Noa walked over to them and kissed each of them on the cheek.

Before closing her eyes Noa read Luke's most recent message.

Luke: I don't think I will ever be able to sleep again without you in my arms. Too soon? Maybe, but life's short. Goodnight, Noa. I can't wait to have you all to myself tomorrow morning.

Wednesday, 23 June, 4:55 p.m.

In the darkness he waited until her friends' cars left the driveway. The muscle monkey's SUV still stood inside her garage; a big, phallic reminder that someone other than himself had entered Emily's world. He'd be damned before he allowed the gym junkie to enter her the way every man wanted to.

Emily was his, and this time, he'd break her. This time she wouldn't fight.

Without making a sound he opened the back door and checked the alarm's keypad. The alarm wasn't armed.

King ran up to him and he bent down to rub behind the dog's ear.

"Good boy. Today I have a special treat for you," he whispered, removing the sausage from his right pocket. King gobbled it up in a single bite. "Nighty night, King."

He tiptoed to her room and eased the door open. Emily looked beautiful, even though she glowed green through the night vision goggles. He lowered the duffel bag to the floor and removed the syringe from his left pocket.

He inched closer to where she was laying, serene, perfect.

This Emily he loved the most; vulnerable and at his mercy.

He placed his left hand over her mouth and stabbed the needle into her exposed shoulder. She woke instantly and thrashed against him, but he had anticipated this reaction. He knew her like no one else ever would.

Her hand searched frantically for the gun on the pillow next to her; a pitiful sight. For a mere second, he respected her fighting spirit.

This was the Emily he hated. The strong Emily who, after forty days, had still fought him.

Her thrashing calmed and her eyes lids fluttered. Once her muscles relaxed, he removed his hand from her mouth.

The rhythmic movement of her breasts hypnotised him. The same way it had the first night he'd seen her take a breath.

"Good morning, my love. We don't have much time."

He dragged the duvet off the bed.

Wednesday, 23 June, 5:05 a.m.

Jamie sat in her car staring at Noa's driveway. The coffee cup had long been empty, and Jamie needed to ease the pressure in her bladder. "Dammit, Luke. The things I do for you."

Her phone rang, and Jamie wondered if they, by some fluke of nurture, were telepathic.

"I can't reach Noa. Where are you?"

"Calm down, I'm outside her house. It's only just after five, she's probably still asleep." Jamie envied Noa for not having a brother she would do anything for after hearing what had haunted him for a decade.

"Can you please take a walk around her house? I have a gut feeling something is wrong. Matthew phoned when they left and told me he heard Noa go to the bathroom."

"Sexy. You and your infamous gut. Do you have any idea how cold it is outside?"

"Yes, dammit, Jamie. Just humour me. Please."

"Okay, okay. I'm heading for her door now."

A shot rang through the air.

"Gun shot. What's going on?"

"I'll phone you back." Jamie pocketed the phone and removed her service pistol as she ran up Noa's driveway. She stepped onto the front porch and rang the doorbell. "Noa, open up, it's me."

"Jamie! Back door!" Noa's voice was frantic.

Jamie ran around the side of the house. The back door and security gate were both open. Her heart pounded in her head, but her hands remained steady until she stepped closer and saw Noa. "What happened? Get inside, you're going to freeze."

Noa stumbled backwards. Jamie grabbed her in time before she fell over King. Jamie yanked a blanket from the couch and wrapped Noa in it. "Noa, what happened?"

"In my room. Shot. I shot him."

"Sit." Jamie helped Noa onto the couch and made her way to the main bedroom, her gun extended in front of her.

Jamie switched on the light. Total disarray stared back at her. Bile rose in her throat at the sight of a familiar item on Noa's dresser.

Out of Noa's sight, Jamie grabbed her phone.

Jamie: Please don't come here. Will explain later. Trust me. I'll take care of Noa.

She slipped the phone back into her pocket, ignoring the constant vibration of Luke's replies.

Jamie returned to Noa and took a seat next to her. "What happened?"

"Him. Found me." Noa's head swayed.

Jamie placed an arm around her friend. "Sweetie, I need to get an ambulance for you."

"Detective Davidson. In Marcel." Noa turned her head just in time as the remnants of the previous night's dinner made a less than dignified exit from her body.

Jamie fetched a set of clothes and a wash cloth, helping Noa to clean herself and get dressed.

"Answer your phone. It keeps buzzing."

Jamie smiled at Noa and said she needed to call this in. She stepped into the kitchen and answered her phone.

"I'm outside. I need to see her." Luke's voice was an echo of the fear in Jamie's stomach.

"No, you don't. Not like this. I'm taking care of Noa and will talk to you as soon as I can. Please trust me, Luke. This is my job." Jamie didn't say that Noa's house was now a crime scene.

***

Wednesday, 23 June, 11:25 a.m.

Noa's eyes remained shut throughout the examination. *You've done this before.* The thought brought her no comfort. Jamie stayed by her side and held her hand during the procedure.

A rape kit had been collected along with blood samples. After the nurse had left Noa couldn't look at her friend, opting to stare at the window, registering nothing on the other side of the glass.

Jamie's phone rang again and she excused herself from the room. Tears spilled down Noa's cheeks, but she made no effort to dry them.

Jamie returned and asked, "Noa, if you're up to it I need to ask you a few additional questions?"

"Did he rape me?"

"No honey, it doesn't look like you had any tears or swelling, but the lab is running tests on the items found in his duffel bag and an item found on your dresser." Jamie took Noa's hand in hers. "You were clothed when I found you, but you were so disorientated we had to make sure. I'm sorry to have put you through this."

"I asked. I've been through it before." Noa's stomach churned and pushed bile up her burning throat. Jamie held the kidney dish as Noa dry heaved into it.

Noa sucked on the ice cube Jamie gave her.

"When did this start?"

"Have you spoken to detective Davidson?" Noa stared at the window.

"Yes, he sent me the file. He gave me an overview of what happened. I'll read the file when we get out of here."

"I can't go back to that house. Where's King?" It wasn't lost on Noa that Jamie didn't refer to her *case* as if she was just another victim.

"Kim took him to the vet. They're running blood tests, as soon as the vet says he's okay to come home I'll make the arrangements for you."

"I can't go to my house, Jamie. I can't." Tears streaked Noa's face as she turned to face Jamie.

"You're not going to. I'm taking you to my parents. They have a guest house and twenty-four-hour security. You'll be safe there. Kim packed you a suitcase when she fetched King, which has already been delivered to my parents."

"Thank you." Noa reached for Jamie's arm, tears stinging her eyes.

"I need to ask you again. When did you first suspect he found you?"

"Friday night. I heard an air horn; he used to wake me up with one. On Saturday there was a rose on my windshield. He used to bring me a fresh bouquet every day. Then on Sunday a package was delivered for me at the gym, but with everything that's been going on, I haven't had time to open it. It's on my kitchen counter. Matthew brought the box last night. If you want to open it, go ahead. Oh, and on Sunday morning King brought me a rabbit's head."

"Yesterday you were attacked by spiders." It wasn't a question.

"Yes. Has the officer found Benjamin Clarke yet?"

"No, but she'll go to his house again today, and will speak to his neighbours." Jamie tried to warm Noa's hands between her own. "Has anything else happened in the last week? Anything, no matter how inconsequential you might think it is."

"I met someone on Friday night, Luke Taylor. This all started on Friday night, but Luke was with me when the air horn was blown. Is it possible that it's him?"

"I promise you, Luke Taylor isn't behind this."

"How can you be so sure?"

"Luke is—" Jamie's phone rang, and she excused herself from the room again.

It can't be Luke. Not him.

Chapter 17

Wednesday, 23 June, 5:00 p.m.

Luke found Jamie in the living room of their parents' home; the very home in which they'd grown up. Jamie was standing with her back to him, hands on the mantel of the fireplace, and her head down. "What happened?"

Jamie walked into his arms and a searing, pain-filled sound came out of her.

"My imagination is conjuring up the worst. Please tell me what happened."

Jamie asked Luke to sit with her. She took both of his hands in hers as they sat next to each other. She couldn't look him in the eye.

"Luke, it's bad." Jamie wiped her eyes. "But it's for Noa to tell you the details. If you're not serious about her, let Noa go. I don't know how she survived the first time, and now ..."

"What do you mean the first time?"

Jamie shook her head, then sighed and nodded. "He held her captive for forty days. *Forty* days, Luke. She was rescued by chance. But Noa needs to tell you the details, *if* she wants to. I beg you, back away from her if you're not serious." She lifted her eyes to meet his.

"If you, for one second, thought I wasn't serious about her, you wouldn't have brought her here." Luke held her gaze.

"You're right. I knew this morning when you called me." Jamie leaned her head on her brother's shoulder.

***

Wednesday, 23 June, 5:15 p.m.

Aaron saw Noa standing outside the door leading to the living room. She glanced at him and knew he noticed her unshed tears. Aaron reached out to her but pulled his arm back, letting it drop by his side.

"I'll go back to the room." Noa turned with heavy feet and walked towards the stairs.

"Noa?"

At the sound of Luke's voice, the tears broke free and fell to the hardwood floor.

"Noa, please look at me."

Behind her heavy footsteps moved closer. She waited to feel the warmth of Luke's hands on her shoulders, but Luke didn't touch her. Noa drew a deep breath and lifted her head, wiping her eyes before turning around.

She caught sight of Jamie standing behind Luke. "I'm sorry, Jamie, I didn't realise you're related. I'll go pack, if you can please take me somewhere else."

Luke stepped forward, holding a hand out to her. He didn't flinch when he saw her swollen left eye. Noa looked at his hand, then his face. She stepped backwards. Luke's arm slumped at his side, defeat on his face.

A storm erupted within her and she stepped forward, into his arms. The storm tore through her and Luke held her until calm returned. "I'm scared, Luke," Noa murmured against his chest.

"I know. But I promise to keep you safe and I'll do *everything* in my power to stop him."

Noa noticed the anger contained in his eyes.

Luke released his hold and cupped Noa's face. "What do you need from me? Whatever it is, you need to tell me. If you don't want me to touch you, I won't. If you do, I'll wrap you in my arms and hold you forever. Please don't push me away. I won't lose you because of him. You survived him before, and now you'll beat him, because you have me. Jamie. All of us."

Tears streamed down her face. Noa noticed Laura wiping her eyes with a tissue.

Madison rushed in behind her mother and came to an abrupt halt. "I told you they're in love, but no one ever listens to me. We should've made a bet on this. I could've made *a lot* of money."

Noa focused on her shoes in an attempt to hide her face from Madison.

"Madison Taylor. This is not the time." Laura chided her youngest.

Jamie gave Madison a stern look and took her by the arm, dragging Madison to the kitchen. Laughter bubbled up in Noa as Luke reached for her face, drying her tears with his fingertips.

"I spoke to the vet. He said I can pick King up tomorrow morning. He's fine."

"Thank you. I need to figure out where King and I'll stay until this is over. Your mother's guests are arriving tomorrow afternoon for the conference."

"You'll both come stay with me." Luke's fingers moved through Noa's hair and massaged the nape of her neck. "I have a spare bedroom and a fenced-in yard."

"I can't stay with you. This is my fight. I won't drag you or your family into this."

Luke took her hand and led her into the living room away from his parents. "Dammit Noa, let me help you. Let *us* help you. I realise you've never had anyone take care of you, but believe me when I tell you my family will go to hell and back for you, because it's who they are. They did the same for me thirty years ago."

Noa shook her head. "I can't. He will never stop. Not until I'm dead or somewhere he is sure no one will be able to rescue me this time. You and Jamie mean too much to me for me to drag you into this."

"I'm going to your house to fetch my SUV. I expect your bags to be ready when I get back. You're moving in with me.

Please don't fight me on this." Luke pressed his lips to Noa's right cheek. "Do you need anything from town?"

More tears welled in her eyes. "How can you care so much, that even when you're angry with me, you still think about what I might need?"

"It's not you I'm angry with. I'll be back in forty minutes."

Noa watched Luke leave, despair and fear settled over her. *I won't survive this again.*

Wednesday, 23 June, 5:15 p.m.

He slammed a fist into the couch, wincing at the memory of punching Emily's face. "I didn't want to hurt you. This is not what I had planned for our time together."

He slumped down behind the laptop and watched the previous day's recordings. It wasn't possible. She wasn't supposed to wake up. "Bitch, you played possum."

Hours' worth of recordings sped past his eyes until he found the reason his plan had failed.

"You, dear Emily, are responsible for everything I'll do to them. Their deaths are on your head. It won't be on your conscious because you, my love, don't have one."

He brought up the feed from a different house and rubbed his aching hand over his erection. "If I close my eyes, it will be you. Just like before."

Wednesday, 23 June, 6:05 p.m.

Jamie glanced at her brother sitting next to her with a stark expression on his face. She knew Luke well enough to know that he blamed himself for not being there to protect Noa. So did she.

"I'm sorry, Luke. I know better than to say this is my fault. We're not responsible for the actions of psychopaths or any other criminals, but I was right there while it happened. If you hadn't called when you did ..." Jamie's palms slammed against the steering wheel.

Luke stared out the car window at the passing trees. "Did he rape her?" His fingers dug into the flesh around his knees.

"No. He didn't have time, but he planned to. We found some items in his duffel bag. I need to talk to Noa about the significance of some items, but didn't want to put her through even more today. She was pretty drugged up when I got to her and doesn't remember much. From what I read in the report he often drugged her during her captivity."

"I should've been there with her. I should've gone to her last night after dinner."

Jamie glanced at Luke; he scratched his beard. "Give her time. Allow her to realise she has a choice to either be a victim or a survivor. Knowing everything she survived and had to go through to get to where she is, I have no doubt Noa will choose the latter. The fact she fought back is huge for her recovery. You just need to back off a bit and be less intense."

She lifted a hand from the steering wheel. "Before you say anything, I know you mean well. But Noa doesn't know you as well yet."

A shrill sound sliced through the ensuing silence. Jamie retrieved her phone from the front console and looked at the caller ID. "I don't have the energy for this man right now."

"Who is it?"

"Eric. I'm so tired, Luke."

"We need to talk about it. Let me take the call." He held out his hand towards her.

"Be quiet." She glared in warning at Luke before answering the call. "Eric the builder."

"Funny. Where is Noa? I can't reach her and I'm getting worried."

"Noa was attacked in her home this morning. She's okay. We moved her to a safe house and she'll stay there until we make an arrest." *Or I kill him.*

"I'm heading back to River Valley. Noa will come stay with me in Shadow Bay. The hotel has twenty-four-hour security. I hope you've arrested Luke Taylor, or at the very least taken him in for questioning."

"First of all, Eric, Noa isn't going anywhere with anyone. My boss and I are the only people privy to her location. It's for her own safety. You need to respect that it wasn't my call, but I agree with my Captain's decision. Second thing, why do you mention Luke Taylor?" Jamie dared to look at Luke before steering the car into a bend.

"They're seeing each other. And who happens to come to her rescue when a nest of spiders infested her Jeep? The hero ex-detective. Who clung to her like a haemorrhoid on Monday night, refusing to let me speak to her? Luke Taylor. You should arrest him. Don't you think it merits investigation, seeing as he returned to town and things started happening to Noa? He inserted himself into her life for a reason, Jamie."

"Thank you for your concern as an upstanding citizen and member of this community. I'll take your advice into consideration."

"Don't test me, Jamie. Noa's my best friend. I'll take this over your head."

"Please do and waste valuable time we could spend finding the real suspect. Noa's my best friend too, so don't you dare threaten me. Once she's safe she will contact you."

Jamie parked the car in Noa's driveway and stared at the crime scene tape covering the front door. Next to her, Luke stared at Noa's bedroom window, his fists clenched.

"I *will* take this over your head *if* you refuse to look at him as a viable suspect."

"Goodbye, Eric." Jamie ended the call.

Luke removed the spare set of keys from his jacket pocket and watched the garage door as it opened. "Has he always been so highly strung?"

"Oh, yes. That's Eric for you."

"Thank you for the ride. I'm going to talk to your Captain

and find out if there's a possibility of me assisting with the investigation, even if only as a consultant or whatever."

"Luke, I don't know where to start looking for a suspect. We know everyone in this town. The only viable suspect is Benjamin Clarke. He had access to Noa's vehicle on Monday. He excused himself long enough from their session to have placed the spiders inside her Jeep. Noa mentioned he acted stranger than usual. But we don't have enough to go on. Whoever put those spiders in her vehicle could've done it outside the gym, or even at her house."

"I need to be with her right now. Let me see if I can get more information from her. Will talk to you later."

"Noa's lucky to have you in her corner. My ten-days-older-brother."

Luke's smile was short lived. "I'm the lucky one. Now I just need to prove to her and myself that I'm worthy."

Jamie smacked a palm against the steering wheel, hitting the horn. "Don't you ever say anything like that again. You're a survivor too, Luke and you need to realise we all love you. We have *always* loved you. Yes, you and I fought growing up, it's what siblings do. Our bond will always be thicker than blood." Jamie reached for Luke's face and kissed his temple.

Chapter 18

Wednesday, 23 June, 6:15 p.m.

Noa sat cross-legged on the bed, staring at the laptop screen. The messages kept coming, but she couldn't bring herself to type a response. How could she help anyone when she couldn't help herself?

After Jamie had told her about the surveillance cameras the crime scene investigators had found inside her house, she'd covered the webcam on the laptop. Noa reached out next to her, but the space empty; King wasn't there. Her heart ached for him and how scared he must be after waking up in a strange place.

A knock on the bedroom door startled her.

"Noa? It's Laura. I brought you decaf coffee and something to eat. I'll leave it on the table outside the door. The sandwich will be fine later, but the French fries won't taste like much once it's cold."

Noa opened the door and found the Taylor matriarch holding a wooden tray. She stepped back, allowing Laura to enter the room. Noa watched as Laura placed the tray on the table at the window and waited for her to finish pouring coffee into both mugs. The delicious aroma filled the room.

"If you are up to some company, I'm desperate for a cup of coffee. New blend; delivered this morning." Laura picked up a mug and made herself comfortable on one of the wingback chairs.

Noa joined her, rolling the mug between her hands. Her

shoulders sagged as the warmth spread through her palms, and Noa leaned back in the chair. "I'm not much company. This isn't how I envisioned meeting Luke and Jamie's parents. Thank you for taking me in. I promise to be out of your way first thing tomorrow morning."

"Have you showered?" Laura studied her over the rim of the mug.

"Yes, thank you. Twice. I struggled the first time, kept thinking about the cameras the police found in my bathroom. In my shower." Noa's gaze travelled over the room. There was a kind of warmth in every small detail. She'd noticed the same attention to detail throughout the house. This was a place where people loved each other and Noa had never felt more out of place.

"You're welcome to stay as long as you want to. I overheard Luke telling you that he wants you to move in with him. But Maddie can go stay with him until she returns to Shadow Bay on Monday. You can stay in her room."

"Thank you, but it won't be necessary. Your family has already gone out of their way for me."

"Get used to it. You're one of us now." Laura returned her empty mug to the tray and placed her hands on her lap. "Not only are you one of our daughter's best friends, Maddie's hero, but my son cares about you. You might have noticed from your interactions with my children they are brutal in their honesty, which might offend most people, but it's how Aaron and I decided to raise them. No topic is off limits in this house."

Noa cleared her throat. "I call it your family affliction. It's refreshing and disconcerting at the same time."

"Do you want me to call your parents and tell them you're all right? Jamie mentioned she had to take your phone for your safety, something about tracking or some other lingo I'm too old to understand."

"No parents. No family. The only friends I have are aware of what happened."

"Aren't you tired of keeping people at a distance?" Laura

took a French fry and bit into it, without breaking eye contact with Noa. Noa did the same. "What were you doing before I came in? I see your laptop is on the bed. Luke mentioned you're an online health coach and a personal trainer. When did you decide you wanted to help people?"

Noa bit into another French fry and chewed without haste. "I've always enjoyed being active and after school I studied Biokinetics. When I moved here I started doing online health coaching and training to stay busy. Last year, after I moved into my house, I met Matthew. He lives three houses down the street from mine, and he offered me a job at his gym."

"Is that what you were doing now?" Laura reached for a quarter of the sandwich, handed it to Noa and took a piece for herself.

"No. I, uhm, run an online support group for young women who are victims of abuse, doesn't matter if it's bullying, domestic or sexual." Noa spoke as she poured them both more coffee.

Laura smiled and stared out the window. "You and Luke are so much alike."

"I can't move in with him."

"I know sweetie, and I respect your decision."

"When did you adopt him?" When Noa had seen all of the Taylors' in the same room, she realised Luke didn't resemble either of his parents or sisters. With his dark brown hair and matching eyes, he was the complete opposite of their more Scandinavian appearance. Except for Madison, but her similarity came from a bottle.

Laura's smile grew and, when she faced Noa, her eyes held unshed tears. "Luke was five years old when he came to live with us. We adopted him as soon as his father signed away his parental rights. Didn't take much convincing, the man had no leg to stand on being in prison for murder, and the attempted murder of his son."

Noa's eyes burned and she pursed her lips. With a quivering voice she whispered, "Luke's father tried to kill him?" Tears dripped onto her shirt, but Noa didn't dry her wet face. Her body was too numb; her heart too sore.

"Luke will be upset with me for talking to you about this, but I don't care. I can see how much you care about each other and I'd rather put my foot in it than allow a potential misunderstanding to get between you. He is stubborn, proud if you will, but we're even more proud of our son for who he was at five and the man he has become."

Noa listened as Laura told her how Luke became their son. She let the tears stream without reservation, her body remained still, her heart forever changed.

"Luke's mother was murdered in front of him?" Noa's hand lifted to her mouth.

Laura nodded, pressing a tissue to her eyes. "When I met Luke in the hospital, he was nothing more than a little shell. There was no spark left in him. I went home that night and told Aaron we're adopting him. Aaron agreed without me even telling him anything more. I was the social worker assigned to Luke." Noa picked up on Laura not referring to Luke's *case*; Jamie had done the same with her.

"I can't imagine what Luke has lived with all these years. You did an amazing job of raising him. I've never met a man like him. Not before, and certainly not since moving here."

"He always had it in him. But I've always believed nurture plays the biggest role in circumstances such as what Luke faced. Yes, nature plays a big role with certain individuals, but Luke has spent years fighting to be nothing like his biological father."

"He protects people because he failed to protect his mother. In his eyes, not mine."

Laura's eyes glistened. "You understand him. The thing is, Noa, as much as you need to be protected right now from whatever is going on, Luke needs to protect you because of who he is. But more than that, my son's falling in love with you. I know neither of you have said it, but I knew when he asked me for advice about your date on Sunday."

Noa covered her heating cheeks with her hands. "This is a strange conversation. I never spoke to my mother about my day, or a boy I was interested in."

"You'll see when you have your own children, more often than not you can sense things even before they tell you. Do you want children?"

"To be honest, I've never thought about it. And if I consider everything that has happened to me, I can't bring someone else into this world." Noa touched her swollen eye and ran her tongue over the cut in her lip. "I'll leave tomorrow morning first thing. Your guests can't see me like this, but thank you for offering me Maddie's room."

"Where will you go?"

"To Luke's. As you said, he needs me as much as I need him. Never thought I would ever say those words. But Luke can't get caught in the middle of whatever *he* is planning."

"Luke will do everything humanly possible to keep you safe. You'll make it easier for him if he knows where you are and that you're safe."

"Laura, I'm not ready to go to Luke's house just yet. Can he also stay here tonight?"

A knock on the door made them both freeze.

Wednesday, 23 June, 6:39 p.m.

With his back against the wall Luke sank to the floor. His body was exhausted from the tension of the day. Noa's and his mother's voice carried through from the other side of the door. Desperate to hold Noa and breathe in her scent, for him, fearing it might not be what she wants or needs. Over the years Luke had worked with many victims of assaults and home invasions, but Noa wasn't another victim.

He regretted the way he had spoken to her before leaving earlier. Jamie was right he had to back off and give Noa time.

Luke stood up and knocked on the door. For now, he

needed nothing more than to be in the same room as Noa.

His mother called out to him and he opened the door to find both women seated, facing him with red and puffy eyes. Noa's left eye showed the aftermath of what she had endured hours earlier.

"Hello, sweetie." Laura rose and kissed Noa's forehead before turning to Luke with the tray in her hands.

Luke stared at the empty plate.

"Are you hungry?" his mother asked. "Dinner is ready and waiting for you. I'll bring it to the adjoining room."

Luke frowned.

"You're staying here tonight. You'll be right next door, and tomorrow morning, after you fetch her dog, Noa's moving in with you. For the time being." His mother winked as she kissed his cheek and walked out of the room, closing the door behind her.

Noa eased up from the chair and closed the distance between them. She trailed her fingers along Luke's beard and touched his mouth with her fingertips. Luke pressed his lips to each of her fingers.

"I will not be his victim for another second. He has already stolen so much of my life; he can't have any more. I don't know what he did to me this morning or years ago. I only remember how I woke up and what I woke up to. On Sunday, when you kissed me, my body responded to you."

Noa's cheeks turned the most beautiful shade of red Luke had ever seen.

"He didn't break me. It's going to take time to come to terms with this, but I will. Please be patient with me and don't ever see me as *broken*."

Touching her chin with his fingertips, Luke eased Noa's head up until he could look into her eyes. "Noa, I will never see you as broken. You're a survivor. I have never respected anyone as much as I respect you. Take all the time you need. I'm not going anywhere."

"Is it weird that I really want to kiss you right now, but can't because of this?" Her tongue touched the tear in her lip.

Luke bent his head forward and brushed his mouth against the unhurt side of Noa's mouth. His heart clenched. He hugged Noa to him and waited for her to put her arms around him. The moment she did, gratefulness and rage collided inside him. *How can anyone hurt this amazing woman? My Noa.*

Chapter 19

Thursday, 24 June

Emily,

It's your fault she's dead. You need to go and look her parents in the eye and explain to them you could've prevented their daughter's death. Had you only said what you should've none of this would've happened. Thank you for reminding me how strong I am. You are my soul.

I'm sure the police believe you missed by accident, but we both know the truth. You don't have it in you to kill; it is the only way in which we are different. And it proves your love and devotion to me.

Don't be jealous, my love. She didn't taste like you. None of them do.

Admit what you are and come back to me.

You can't hide forever.

Chapter 20

Thursday, 24 June, 9:00 a.m.

Three women's faces stared down at her. Jamie pushed the brown file across the desk, and drank the last sip of cold decaf coffee. Her face scrunched up at the taste. *Instant coffee isn't for the fainthearted.*

This was a level of fatigue she hadn't expected even though the doctor had said it was normal. Neither she, nor Spencer, had said anything to their families. They wanted to wait, at least, until after the first ultrasound.

The brown folder held unimaginable horrors. It made her stomach churn.

Jamie needed to remain objective for Noa's sake. As a detective she couldn't allow her love for her friend to overrule logic. If she did, Jamie would tear apart the person, who had abducted and tortured Noa, limb from limb with nothing but her bare hands.

Jamie reached for her phone and dialled Detective Davidson's direct line.

"Davidson."

"Good morning, Detective. This is Detective Edwards from River Valley. You sent me Emily Gallagher's file yesterday. I have a few follow-up questions."

"Any way I can help." His chest wheezed like that of a thirty-a-day-smoker.

"I reviewed your notes of potential suspects, but didn't see Doctor Benjamin Clarke's name on the list. Apart from her ex-boyfriend, you didn't have any other suspects?"

"If Clarke's name isn't in the file, then his name didn't come up during the investigation. Why do you ask about him?"

"He's a person of interest in a situation we had here on Monday, involving wolf spiders."

Davidson sighed. "The same as what we found in the cabin."

"Yes. Do you know what happened to Emily's ex-boyfriend? I read he was the only person with a potential motive."

"I'll look into his whereabouts and what he's been up to over the past two-and-a-half-years. Will let you know what turns up, but back then his alibi checked out. I didn't think he was capable of the things that were done to Emily. He seemed too soft, cried through questioning and got sick when we showed him a few of the less disturbing photos. Either he is the best actor in the world or he really is innocent."

"Thank you, I appreciate your help. I would like to know whether he has moved on with his life."

Jamie stared at the faces of the three women. "Davidson, do you have any unsolved cases involving the disappearances of women in their early twenties? Don't have any more information other than they were last seen after a night out with their friends."

"It should be in the national database. You can access the information, but I'll also look on my end and ask around. Emily's was my last missing person's case; moved to homicide after she died. Is there a specific reason you ask?"

"Just a hunch. I might be looking for answers in the wrong place. Thank you for your time, I'll be in contact soon."

Jamie opened the file and stared at Emily Gallagher's photo. Her phone's insistent ringing brought her back from the darkness where her mind so often wandered.

"Edwards."

"We have a body; will text you the directions."

"I'm on my way." Jamie grabbed her jacket and rushed out of the office.

***

Thursday, 24 June, 10:00 a.m.

It was easy to understand why Luke had moved back and called this place home. The moist wind stirred Noa's hair, while she rocked on the porch swing and gazed at the mountain. On the other side of the river stood the constant visual reminder that some things were beyond a person's control. This moment, this feeling, Noa committed to memory.

Noa had moved to River Valley out of necessity, self-preservation, but being at Luke's home she realised this was a place she wanted to call her own. And Luke Taylor; a man she wanted to call hers.

The previous night she'd fallen asleep with Luke sitting next to her. When he'd tried to leave she reached for his hand. Luke had stayed, laying down beside her and Noa was the one who'd moved closer until she was nestled against him. Neither had said a single word. Long after, she had lain awake, listening to Luke's steady breathing. Every time her mind drifted towards ideas of running again, she became aware of Luke's warmth behind her and the safety of being in his arms.

Noa realised then she had only one option – fight. She'd fight for her own life, again, as she had done for forty long days and even longer nights. For a life with Luke, if he still wanted her after this ended. How it would end Noa didn't know. But she refused to allow the devil to steal one more day of her life.

Luke's SUV came into view, passing through the lane of oak trees. Her stomach did a slow roll, and she smiled with a content sigh. This man had an effect on her she had never experienced, even when she couldn't see his handsome face or his breathtaking smile. The SUV came to a stop. The instant the driver side door opened a grey streak came barrelling towards her. Noa jumped up as fast as her body allowed and bent down. King ran into her at full speed, sending Noa flat on the deck.

"I missed you my beautiful boy." She pressed her face to King's neck.

King lifted his head and scanned his temporary home. He ran off, darting in every possible direction. Noa laughed and caught Luke watching her.

"You're always beautiful, but when you laugh it does something to me here." He pointed at his core.

"Do I add to the eight-pack you have going on under that shirt?"

"Six-pack, working towards eight." Luke carried some items up to the house and placed them on the porch. He then helped Noa to her feet. "I know a very sexy personal trainer and I'm wondering about her fee." His eyes drew to slits. "You haven't seen me without a shirt?"

"I don't need to see you without a shirt. I can imagine what's going on under all those layers. How long before it's summer and you work shirtless in the garden?" Noa caught herself off-guard, imagining being here in the future. The mere act of wondering felt like a victory. *One day, one victory at a time.*

Luke opened his mouth, but turned his attention to the items at their feet.

"What were you going to say, Taylor?"

"You're a lady. I can't say it. What I will say is, seeing you here, the way the sunlight dances on your face and auburn hair, it makes me forget the reason you're here. It feels so … right. Having you here waiting for me."

Noa touched Luke's chest, feeling the strong beat of his heart under her palm. "I know. Since I woke up this morning, it's as if none of yesterday or anything before that happened. Until I see my face, or try to take a sip of coffee, water, eat, whatever."

Luke ran his fingers through her hair, trailing Noa's cheeks with his thumbs. "Soon this can be our life. No thoughts of stalkers or reasons other than wanting to be together."

Noa pressed her fingers to his mouth. "This needs to serve as a kiss until my lip heals."

In an attempt to avoid Luke's heated gaze, Noa turned her attention to the items at their feet. "What's all this?"

"I don't even have the most basic groceries, so I went shopping. Hope I got everything you like. I bought King food and his own bed. He's not sharing with us." Luke looked towards where King was sniffing under a willow tree. "I don't expect you to sleep next to me every night. Sorry, it came out wrong."

"I know." Noa wrapped her arms around Luke's waist and rested the unbruised side of her face against his chest. "Right now, I want to forget about the real reason I'm here and I just breathe. Luke, it feels as if I haven't breathed in years, maybe never."

"You haven't, you were too busy looking over your shoulder and surviving. I'm so glad you did."

"I still need to survive this round and ensure it's the last."

"Jamie called while I was on my way back. She needs to stop by later to talk to you, and she's bringing your gun. Perhaps you and I should go shooting later this afternoon. I need to see for myself that you can handle a gun."

Noa grabbed his shirt and clenched the fabric between her fists. "I missed because he drugged me."

"I know, I didn't mean you can't shoot. I'm so proud of you for how valiantly you fought him. I don't want to think about what would've happened if you didn't."

"I can. Is this how it's going to be now? One minute we're just two people, talking about you being shirtless, watching my dog, and the next a shadow moves over us and sucks the joy out of the air?"

"Not forever. I promise." Luke bent down, pressing his mouth to her hair. "My mom has decided to adopt you, but I told her it would make things a little icky between you and me. So she's settled on calling you her middle daughter."

"What kind of word is *icky* for a big man like you?"

"Maddie's been home too long. I told you my mom will love you."

"The feeling is mutual."

Noa had often hoped her own mother would give her up

for adoption. Watching Luke carry the bags into the house she wondered if her life would've been different had a woman like Laura raised her instead.

Chapter 21

Thursday, 24 June, 10:02 a.m.

The wind lifted the corners of the white sheet. Jamie waited for the woman underneath it to stand up; she never again would. The strength of the wind indicated a cold front was moving in. Rain would follow.

The forensic investigators searched the area. Like white ants they kept close to the ground, looking for any clue which might lead to the arrest of the monster who'd left a young woman brutalised and defenceless against nature and its creatures.

In the ten years Jamie had been part of the River Valley Police Department she'd never seen a more horrific sight. The medical examiner gave her time with the victim, to confirm this was one of the three women whose photos were pinned to Jamie's board.

DNA would be the only means of identifying the remains. Jamie wasn't the only person on the scene to step back and take a deep breath.

"Estimated time of death? Just ball park, I know you'll give me a more definitive answer once you've done the autopsy," she asked, pushing to her feet.

"Within the last six to twelve hours, but it's an estimate. Don't write it down and don't hold me to it," said Doctor Burger. Jamie had worked with him long enough to know one could carve it into stone.

Jamie moved around the scene, taking photos. She preferred to capture her own to remember how she saw and experienced the scene; not relying on someone else's lens and their eyes.

With one foot in front of the other she stepped around the body, careful not to disturb the foliage. Jamie had counted the steps from the road to where the body was laying.

Jamie turned towards the road, imagining the body rolling down the embankment until a tree stopped gravity. The victim's hand lay in the footpath used daily by trail runners. "You're either not familiar with this area or you wanted her to be found."

The vibrating phone in Jamie's pocket disturbed her train of thought. "Edwards."

"It's Davidson. I might have something for you on Benjamin Clarke. He hasn't paid child support in over two-and-a-half years. There's a warrant out for his arrest."

"I owe you a beer, Davidson. Thank you."

"Let me know if he's the bastard we're looking for."

"Will do."

Jamie contacted her captain and requested that he send Officer Sheridan to Clarke's address. Captain Johnson ordered Jamie to take over the investigation, and he assigned Officer Sheridan to work with her. It was time for the rookie to learn.

Thursday, 24 June, 11:11 a.m.

Officer Kori Sheridan waited outside Clarke's house as Jamie's car pulled up. The rookie averted Jamie's stare as her feet pounded on the pavement.

"We arrest him first and then I deal with you," Jamie said, knocking on the front door, her gun drawn.

Silence answered.

Jamie tried the door handle. It opened. Stepping into the quiet house she called out, identifying herself. No sound came from anywhere inside the house. Jamie walked into the foyer, Officer Sheridan behind her.

To her right a door stood ajar. Jamie eased it open.

They were too late.

Officer Sheridan gagged. "Do you ever get used to it?" she asked, covering her mouth with the back of her hand.

"No, and if you do, you have a problem." Jamie reached for her phone and noticed four missed calls from Eric. *He has to wait.*

She called it in and waited for the crime scene investigators and medical examiner.

So much for River Valley being a quiet little town where nothing ever happened.

Thursday, 24 June, 5:08 p.m.

The logs glowed bright orange in the fireplace. Noa welcomed the heat. Luke placed a mug of chamomile tea on the coffee table in front of her and sat down. He leaned back on the couch, closed his eyes and rested his hand next to Noa's thigh.

Noa threaded her fingers through his. "You make a good caveman. As long as you don't pull me around by my hair."

"Hey." Luke squeezed her hand. "I'm working hard to turn this place into a decent home."

"I love it. The quiet, the view." *Being with you.* "Though, I would change one thing, and it might be because I prefer open plan houses."

"I knew it. I saw you looking around the kitchen when we made lunch. Out with it. What am I doing next?"

Noa smiled. "Break out the wall between the kitchen and the dining room. It will open up the whole area and give you views of the river from the kitchen. Put an island in the middle for extra work space and, if you put cupboards underneath it, you won't lose any packing space."

"Okay." Luke's eyes remained closed.

"Okay?"

"Yes. I agree with you." He squeezed her hand. "This place needs a woman's touch."

"Why don't you ask your mother? I love their home. Never

thought this city girl would feel more at home in an old farm house than an apartment. But I prefer your home because it's be more modern and I've always liked a double-storey with a wraparound porch."

"The only woman who has a say is the woman who lives here." The wistfulness in Luke's voice made her heart ache. "Tell me about your life before."

Noa changed position to face him. Luke ran an index finger between her eyebrows until her frown disappeared.

"What if you don't like me once you know who I used to be?"

"I'm not asking because I care about your past, apart from the things which have a bearing on who you are now. You met my family and I know almost nothing about you." Luke reached for her face and she leaned into his palm. "You have this strength inside you. It leaves me breathless, Noa. But you also have a vulnerability that tugs at my heart and makes me want to eviscerate the person who ever made you doubt yourself, your own worth. It wasn't only *him*, was it?"

"No. My *mother* is to thank for that. At least she's dead, so there's a happy ending to those chapters of my life."

Noa thought back to all the days she had spent trying to win her mother's love or even a sliver of attention. No child should have to fight for that. She'd had an epiphany the previous night after her conversation with Laura. To her mother, Noa had been nothing more than an inconvenience.

A few weeks after Noa had been rescued her mother was murdered. The case remained open.

After her death Noa had spent countless hours trying to remember a single nice word uttered by, or a loving moment with, her mother. None ever came to mind.

Noa told Luke how her mother's rejection had led to her escaping into music. The day of her high school graduation was the last day she'd woken up in her mother's house.

Luke remained motionless, not needing to wipe a single tear from Noa's face.

"Did Detective Davidson ever consider your abductor might've been a disgruntled criminal your mother sent to prison, or someone related or affiliated to any case she presided over?"

Noa stared at the fire. "I don't know. After I was released from hospital, I became a recluse. I didn't speak to anyone, and didn't want to think about it. Then six months passed without an arrest, and I had started seeing Doctor Benjamin Clarke. He had proposed I move and start a new life."

"Why don't you take a painkiller? You keep rubbing your neck and your face must hurt too."

"I took one an hour ago." Not because she'd wanted to, but Noa's entire body ached, reminding her how lucky she was to be alive.

Luke lifted Noa's hand to his smiling mouth. "No comments tonight about how beautiful I am?"

"It's weird. I feel fine. I told you I was prescribed the same pills before and had no adverse reactions."

"The other night you took it with your multivitamin and your pill. Have you taken it tonight?"

"No, Kim only packed my pill. Why?"

"Most people I know take their multivitamin in the morning. Why do you take yours at night?"

"It helps me sleep."

It was Luke's turn to frown. "Do you always buy the same brand?"

"Yes. What are you getting at, Luke?"

"Capsules or tablets?"

"Capsules."

Luke jumped to his feet and rushed to the kitchen. "I need to speak to Jamie."

***

Thursday, 24 June, 6:08 p.m.

The police and crime scene investigators cleared out of Benjamin Clarke's house. He wished he could see Emily's face when she heard about his latest gift. When would she be informed? Who would tell her?

His fists clenched. "Where are you, Emily?"

He brought up the live feed to a room in a different house. "She isn't you, my love. None of them have lasted as long as you did. I swear if I could cut out the part of them that cries ... Emotional. Pathetic. Whores."

From inside the fireplace he retrieved an envelope and removed the contents, placing them on the table next to his laptop.

"You were so carefree and strong. Like me. Even back then." His index finger trailed over the face of the woman standing next to him in the photo.

They'd both changed so much over the years. The man staring back at him hadn't known true ecstasy. Deep within Emily it paced like a caged animal, waiting for him to unleash it. All he needed was more time with her.

Lifting her printed image to his mouth, his tongue touched the part of Emily he craved the most. "You're my drug, Emily Gallagher. Mine."

Chapter 22

Luke walked out onto the porch to meet his sister, pulling the zipper of the jacket up to the hollow of his throat. As Jamie exited the car Luke, again, noticed her exhaustion. He knew it all too well.

"When are we going to talk about whatever is going on? You're pale and you have bags underneath your eyes." He wrapped an arm around her.

"Don't you know how to make your sister feel pretty? Been one of those days."

"I'll fetch you a blanket. We can sit out here for a while and talk."

"No, I need to speak to Noa and then I want to go home and spend time with Spencer." Jamie smiled, rubbing her belly.

"Are you hungry?" Luke asked

"Famished. Do you have any decent food?"

"Mom brought dinner. Noa didn't want to eat. I don't know how Mom got her to eat last night."

They walked into the house and found Noa on the couch. Luke headed to the kitchen as Jamie placed two handguns on the coffee table in front of Noa.

As Luke waited for the leftover pasta to heat in the microwave, he watched Noa discharge the magazines, count the bullets and reload. She chambered a bullet in each weapon before returning it to the table. It was by far the sexiest thing he had ever seen. The ease with which Noa handled both guns, and the way she pulled the slide back, stirred a need in him. Luke turned towards the refrigerator thinking about his grandparents.

"Are you going to tell me what happened today?" Noa asked.

"I'm tired and haven't had time to eat since breakfast."

"Jamie, talk to me."

"It will be selfish of me to talk about my day with everything you have gone through – *are* going through."

"It will be selfish of you if you don't. We're friends. Your eyes are haunted and talking to me might help."

"I wish I could, but it's another case I'm working on. Noa, thank you for being you."

"Any time you need me, no matter what's going on in my life, you come talk to me. Or to Luke, or most definitely to Spencer. Do you tell him when bad things happen?"

"Nothing as bad as this has ever happened, not that I've seen. Definitely not in River Valley." Jamie stared at her hands. "It's unrelated to what happened to you."

"Okay. Why are you here apart from bringing over my guns?"

Luke handed Jamie the plate of food and took a seat on the floor. King climbed onto his lap. "Do you want me to leave so you can talk?"

Jamie's eyes met his. "It might be better for Noa if you did."

"No, please stay. Whatever it is, you're bound to find out one way or another."

Jamie finished her meal, and while Luke carried the plate to the sink, she whispered, "Noa, are you sure? I might ask questions you don't want to answer in front of him."

"I'm so tired of all the lies and half-truths, and I suspect Luke has his own investigation going on after your captain declined his offer to help."

Luke returned and waited for Noa to look at him. "Are you sure?"

She nodded.

Jamie took a sip of water and cleared her throat. "Noa, when did you first meet Benjamin Clarke?"

"He came to see me while I was still in hospital. He said he was doing a study on the prolonged psychological impact on victims of captivity."

"Who paid him?"

"He said his services were free because of the research he was conducting. Why?"

"Clarke received a monthly payment from a shell corporation. The first payment was made while you were in hospital; we found bank statements. It was the only deposits he received after moving here from Marcel."

Luke asked, "Have you found him?"

"Yes." Jamie said to the fire. "We're still investigating but it appears he's the person who attacked you yesterday morning. We found evidence."

"What kind of evidence?" Luke asked, repositioning King on his lap.

"Were you aware that he recorded your sessions?"

Bile rose in Noa's throat and she called King. He slumped down at her feet. She leaned forward and trailed a hand along his back. "No, I didn't. I would never agree to it. But it makes sense that he did. He never made any notes. Maybe he listened to the audio recordings afterwards for his research."

Jamie took Noa's other hand. "We found a video recording of your last session. He … He also recorded himself after you left. There's more footage we need to go through."

"What?" A muscle in Luke's jaw twitched.

"I knew I was right to end my sessions with him."

"When did you?" Jamie asked.

Noa glanced at Luke and returned her focus to stroking King. "On Monday. I had done everything he'd proposed in order to reclaim my life – rather – build a new life. Except, I refused to see a sex surrogate. He kept bringing it up, and I kept saying no." Noa pressed her hands to her face. "He even proposed to sit in on the session to help me through it. Like that would make the whole thing less disgusting. The idea of paying someone to have sex with me is bad enough."

"What made you decide to end it on Monday?"

"During our session on Friday Clarke talked to me about dating, and asked again if I'd consider a surrogate. On Monday, he asked about my weekend and I let it slip that I met someone."

Luke glanced at Noa, but she focused on King. "I refused to discuss the man I had met. He kept pushing and then excused himself. Five minutes later Clarke came back and asked if we could reschedule my session."

"And after you left his house there were spiders in your Jeep." Luke shook his head.

Noa rubbed her arms and shuddered. "Have you arrested him?"

"No." Jamie sighed. "Benjamin Clarke is dead."

Thursday, 24 June, 9:00 p.m.

Luke walked Jamie out to her car. "What haven't you told me yet?"

"It's up to Noa to tell you the whole story. I need to stay objective and, by telling you, I'd be your sister."

"What could be worse than learning her psychologist was a sexual deviant who broke into her house and tried to rape her?"

Jamie stopped walking and stared up at him. "It's one thing to want to keep Noa safe because it's who you are. She's my friend, but you're my brother, Luke. I don't want you to get hurt."

"Why would *I* get hurt?"

"You know how these investigations go. We're bound to find skeletons in her past, things you might not be able to come to terms with."

After Jamie drove off Luke stared at the house and wondered what Jamie had meant by her parting statement.

All Luke cared about was that inside his home sat the most resilient woman he had ever met. He didn't intend to let Noa go. Not when she cared about Jamie's well-being while going through hell. Again.

Thursday, 24 June, 10:30 p.m.

"The hairy wolf spider climbs up the whore's leg. She bucks, thrashes, squirms and begs. I remove the spider and spread her legs wider." He tapped a finger to his lips. "It needs work."

In front of him the pitiful shape laid strapped to the bed. Even with dyed hair she didn't have Emily's resilience. This little slut had begged for mercy within the very first hour. *Pathetic.*

The spider climbed on to his hand and he studied it. "I'm so sorry your brothers or sisters had to die. But it's the price we need to pay."

The woman squirmed; her eyes wild.

"Calm down, not *your* brothers or sisters." He shook his head and smirked. "Your generation is so self-involved. Selfie this. Selfie that. Like me. Follow me. Share me. Not everything is about you. But if you had come to that realisation on your own, you wouldn't be here."

She thrashed against the restraints as he touched between her legs. "You made my work easier and for that I thank you. I do prefer my women clean shaven."

He bent forward and whispered against the duct tape covering her mouth. "Say it."

Thursday, 24 June, 11:55 p.m.

Noa awoke to someone touching her face; the familiar scent filled her soul.

"Luke?" she murmured.

"Shh, it's me. Sorry I woke you." Luke removed his fingers from Noa's face.

"Hmm, don't stop." Her voice husky.

Luke reached for the lamp on the bedside table. Noa squinted in protest. "Dude, my eyes."

"Dude? Your pillow talk sucks."

"If you can blame Madison for *icky*, then I can blame *dude* on her too."

Luke laughed. The sound forced Noa to open her eyes and look at him. She loved the sound of his laughter, craved the feeling she got from the way his mouth, his whole face, changed.

Pushing herself onto her side to face him, Noa's fingers trailed along Luke's bare chest. The small circles she traced on his pecks made him shiver. The scant dark hair covering Luke's chest tickled her fingertips. *The perfect amount of man.*

Luke touched her mouth and she met his eyes. Their gazes held. Noa ran her fingers through the lushness of his dark hair. Noa fought the urge to tug even when Luke moaned in appreciation as her fingernails scraped against his scalp.

He rolled Noa onto her back and pressed his mouth to the hollow of her throat. Luke's tongue traced the path to her mouth, sending her body into an arch.

"We need to stop." His voice a rich, dark caress to every part of her.

No. Maybe. Please don't. "Okay."

Luke licked at her mouth and she wrapped her arms around his neck pulling him closer. "You're driving me crazy, Luke Taylor."

He feathered kisses along her jaw. "Good," he said against her skin.

Taking Luke's face between her hands Noa tilted his head up. The emotion playing in Luke's eyes made her breath catch. Her heart beat thudded in her ears. Never had she seen this emotion in anyone's eyes. Not when they were looking at her. Need. Not lust. "Good?"

"Now you know how I felt, watching you handle your guns earlier."

"Are you that easy?" The corners of Noa's mouth lifted.

"Maybe. I have *never* seen anything sexier."

"Guess we're going shooting tomorrow."

"Let's go now."

"You need sleep. You're not in your twenties anymore. Remember?"

"Oh, and you are?"

"On paper, I'm thirty."

"And the woman beneath me?" Luke whispered next to Noa's ear, making her arch again. Her chest pressed into his.

Noa wanted nothing more than to reach for him, to know how it would feel to be with a man she needed. A man who needed her. "Wager? If you shoot better than I do, I will tell you. Each time you hit the target of my choosing you can ask me any question you want."

"Deal. Only if we agree now to one day play strip shooter."

Noa laughed until her stomach muscles ached and her lip burned. "You have to make my lip better. It hurts. How is it ever going to heal if you keep making me laugh?"

"The only thing I have to do is take a cold shower."

Luke eased off her. Even in the faint light Noa drew a deep breath at the sight of his body's response to her. She had felt it pressed against her, but seeing it now she wanted to yank Luke's boxers down and explore every part of him.

With his back to her Luke faced the window. Noa walked up behind him and rubbed her face against his warm skin, wrapping her arms around his waist.

"I've wasted so much of my life. Noa Morgan, I want *you*. I don't care about your past or whatever I might learn about you, even the bits you'd prefer I don't hear. Promise me, no secrets between us. Ever."

"I promise." Noa pressed her lips to Luke's skin.

Chapter 23

Friday, 25 June, 6:30 a.m.

Jamie found Spencer at the dining room table and took in the sight of him. She often wondered how she could still be madly in love with him ten years after they first met.

When Spencer turned and caught her watching him, she knew.

"Good morning, Mommy. How is the most beautiful, radiant and sexiest woman in the world this morning?"

"You heard me, didn't you?"

"Hard to miss, my love. Reminds me of the nights we got drunk and had naughty sex all over town. I don't care. My child is growing inside you and there's nothing sexier than that. And of course, your boobs are getting bigger, which doesn't hurt." Jamie punched his shoulder. "Ow."

Spencer grabbed her wrist and pulled Jamie onto his lap. "I love you, Mrs Edwards."

"*Detective* Edwards to you."

"I only call you detective when you bring your cuffs into the bedroom." Spencer kissed her throat.

"Wish I had the energy to make you call me detective, but I need to get to work."

"Have you told Captain Johnson you're pregnant?"

"No, I'm not going to until we reach fourteen weeks."

"You can't keep working like this. It's not good for you or the baby." Spencer rubbed her stomach.

"I know, but I have two active cases. And I had to call in

favours to keep Noa's case. It should be closed soon. The only suspect we have is dead."

"How is she?"

"Surviving. Don't think I would've been as strong as Noa is. Not with what she had to survive."

"And Luke?"

Jamie smiled and pressed her lips to Spencer's forehead. "He's in love."

"You say it as if it is a bad thing. He deserves to have what we do. Jamie, you know he carried the guilt of Amber's death all these years and now that the truth has come out, you need to let go and allow him be happy."

"I want Luke to be happy. I'm just worried. There's this constant knot in my stomach."

Spencer traced his fingers across Jamie's belly. "You're hormonal and becoming more protective, which I read is to be expected."

Jamie hugged her husband tight. "You're right, Mr Edwards. Go conquer the wine world. I believe another award is bound to be in your near future. Please tell my mother last night's dinner was a winner. She can add it to the menu at Lamont restaurant."

Friday, 25 June, 6:45 a.m.

King ran across the lawn and dropped the ball at Luke's feet. Noa rolled the mug between her hands and leaned back against the front door.

Luke threw King's ball and ran up to her. Noa's stomach rolled and her eyes burned. It baffled her that a man like him wanted her.

"What's wrong?" Luke took Noa's face in his hands. He gently brushed his lips against the left side of her mouth.

"This cold wind stings my eyes."

Luke frowned, and Noa traced the line across his forehead

with her finger. "You and I are going shooting today." Mischief played in his dark eyes.

"I remember." Noa gave him a naughty smile. "But, I need a favour."

"Anything." Luke took the mug from her hands.

"Can you please take me and King to my house?"

"Why?"

"It's time to go. He's dead. I can carry on with my life now."

Taking Noa's hand, Luke led her to the porch swing and helped her to sit. "Do you see how difficult it still is for you to move around?"

"Nothing which won't heal in a few days."

"The investigation isn't over yet."

"He's dead, Luke. Unless Clarke was bitten by a zombie, I doubt he's coming back."

"Until Jamie officially closes the case, you can't leave."

"Technicalities."

"I don't want you to leave." Luke reached for her face and gently tugged her chin until Noa looked at him. "I'm going to ask again. What's wrong?"

"I need to leave so we can do this right. We're living together. Sleeping together."

"Sleeping isn't the problem. It's when you wake up while I'm admiring you."

Noa snuggled closer and took the mug from Luke.

"We can do *normal* as soon as Jamie closes the case. Don't run away because of what happened last night. You're done running. Unless it's into my arms, after King or when you jog, but that's it. Last night we took *a* step and who knows when we will take the next. I'll wait until you're ready." *Even if it kills me.*

"You're too much. I don't know how to do this."

"I don't either, but I'm liking how we're doing it now and how we will." Luke's laughter bellowing from the porch made King raise his head from where he roamed the garden.

"King judges you, and so do I." Noa slapped Luke's thigh.

"Tell me about your past relationships."

"Relationship. Singular. Not much to tell." Noa shrugged. "We met while I worked my last cruise and he was the kind of man my mother always said I should marry. From a good family, stable career, attractive, but not so much that I'd have to worry about him and his secretary. I had turned thirty a month before and the big three-o made me re-evaluate my life. He lived in Marcel, which made it easier for me when I settled there again. If I had to some up our relationship with one word, it would be – comfortable. We dated for six months, decided to move in together. On the day of the move I found him passed out in bed, two condom wrappers on the bedside table and another woman's pink lace *something* at the foot of the bed. That's the last time I saw him."

"Cruise ship?"

"I worked as a Biokineticist on several five-star cruise ships. Travelled the world for a few years. I loved travelling and meeting new people, made so many friends. It was exactly what I thought it would be. All throughout my years at university it was my dream. So, I never got involved with anyone because I didn't want to give up on my dream."

Luke stood and helped Noa to her feet. He called out to King and together they went inside the house. Once in the kitchen the discussion changed to Luke's past relationships while they made breakfast.

Noa stopped beating the eggs. "Wait … Amber told you she was pregnant and faked it for weeks?"

"Yes. I phoned her doctor to find out when her next appointment was scheduled, as she'd claimed to have gone to the first one without me because I got the time wrong. Turns out she wasn't even a patient. Her sister was. They had the same initials so Amber passed off the ultra-sound photo as hers. Ours."

"What did you do?"

Luke had planned to leave River Valley the day he ended the relationship. He had believed Amber. How could he not after knowing her for the better part of his life? Once her lie had been exposed Luke left for Marcel. Amber left him a voice note – she planned to commit suicide. The medical examiner had ruled Amber's death an accident as she was three times over the legal limit and the police found her car wrapped around a tree. Luke only heard the voice note hours later after the aeroplane had landed in Marcel.

"Why didn't you tell Jamie?"

"Amber was her best friend since pre-school. They were inseparable. I didn't want to tell Jamie that her friend was a pathological liar. I thought it would do Jamie more harm, and in the end, it did much worse. Now she knows. Jamie and I agreed not to tell you we're related until you and I were sure we are serious."

"Are you?" Noa whipped his squat-honed butt with the dishcloth.

"About taking you shooting today or never letting you and King leave this house?" Luke wrapped his arms around her and yanked the dishcloth from her grip.

"Not fair. I'm half your size."

"Technicalities." Luke held Noa's arms behind her back and lowered his mouth to hers. "You're mine." His tongue teased Noa's bottom lip. "I love the way you taste."

Luke's phone rang. He answered, but kept Noa against him with his other arm.

"I was about to contact you. Jamie, Noa wants to go home."

"She can't leave. Not until the case is closed. I'm heading to the morgue for the autopsy. I couldn't sleep last night. Luke, something doesn't add up. I didn't want to discuss the evidence we found at the scene as we're still working through it. I'll call you once I have the autopsy report."

"Why don't you tell Noa. Maybe she'll listen to you."

Luke held the phone to Noa's ear.

"Good morning, Jamie. How are you today? Did you get some sleep?"

"Noa, you're not leaving Luke's house. When this case is officially closed you can go home. There are a number of things I need to follow up on today. I'll talk to both of you later. And if you're thinking Luke won't want you now that you believe you're no longer in danger, you don't know him at all. We haven't spoken about you two dating, so let me be frank … You do *not* get to hurt my brother. Not after what Luke has been through."

"Okay, Jamie, calm down. I won't leave. Are you sure you don't want to talk about whatever is really going on?"

"Sorry, I'm just tired and I want you both to be happy. Get over yourself and be happy, dammit. Talk to you later. I'm off to see a man about a corpse."

Jamie ended the call and Noa turned her focus to Luke. "I can't remember her ever being so high-strung while working a case. Not even with those trucks getting hi-jacked a few months back."

"Don't take it personally. Jamie has another case which is also getting to her. And you are in the middle of something she can't figure out. You're her friend and it's a lot to process. The stakes are higher when someone close to you is in danger."

Friday, 25 June, 7:55 a.m.

Two bodies waited on the other side of the door. One a victim. The other a suspect. Jamie rolled her shoulders. The immensity of the riddle weighed on her.

The smell of disinfectants assaulted her senses as she pushed through the doors and stepped into the cold room. Jamie made a mental note to ask her gynaecologist about the baby's safety with her being exposed so often – too often – to the lingering fumes.

Doctor Burger walked in behind her, cleaning his reading glasses on the hem of his shirt. "Good morning, Detective. Which one do you want to start with?"

"Let's start with our female victim. We need to rush the DNA identification. The tattoo on her thigh isn't enough for me to contact her parents. Did you locate all of her teeth?"

"No. Five are still imbedded in the jaw. Two I extracted from her throat. Found one in her oesophagus. Are you ready?"

In all the years Jamie and Doctor Burger had worked together not once did he ask if she was ready. She understood the reason he asked this time. "No. Couldn't get her image out of my head last night. But there are two other missing women whose faces stare at me every single day. If the same person took them, then I need to find him. Before they end up here like her."

"Okay, let's start at the top." He removed the sheet and Jamie clenched her eyes shut. She drew a deep breath before forcing her eyes open.

Doctor Burger waited for Jamie to regain her composure. "Time of death is between 2 a.m. and 6 a.m. From the scalp fragments I deduce her hair has recently been dyed. It still shows stains. It's with the lab for analyses."

He didn't discuss the injuries to the victim's face apart from mentioning an object such as a cricket bat was used. Official cause of death – blunt force trauma.

"Her armpits, legs and genital area were recently shaven. As she was reported missing two weeks ago, I assume she didn't do it herself or perhaps not of her own free will."

"You think he has kept her this long?" Jamie asked, focusing on his face.

"Yes. There are abrasive marks on her wrists, ankles, legs and chest. Here." Doctor Burger pointed to the discoloured lines across the victim's breasts and upper thighs. The bruise across the victim's thigh was lighter than the one across her chest.

"She also has multiple spider bites on her legs. Some have started to heal. I've sent samples of the surrounding skin tissue to the lab. They can tell us the precise species."

Jamie inspected the victim's hands and feet and noted the distinct colour applied to her nails. "This was done not too long ago. There's polish on her cuticles."

"Yes, again, sent chips to the lab. My wife likes to wear a similar bright pink in summer."

Jamie dreaded her next question. She had only seen it before in books. "At the scene I noticed something protruding from her ..."

"Yes." Doctor Burger retrieved an evidence bag from the back of the refrigerator. "I kept this out of my staff's view and wanted you to see it first." He held the bag out to Jamie. She took it and studied the contents. "Most women blush, giggle or grimace at the sight of one of these."

"Not the first time I've seen one in the last few days." Jamie continued examining the object inside the evidence bag. The irony wasn't lost on her. Jamie handed the bag back to Doctor Burger and washed her hands at the sink despite having worn latex gloves.

"When did he do *it*?" Jamie asked, using a paper towel to dry her hands.

"Prior to death. The victim would've bled for quite some time. It must have been excruciating because of the thousands of nerve endings."

Jamie squeezed her thighs together. "What did he use?"
"I found teeth marks on her mons pubis." Doctor Burger shook his head. "The bastard bit her."

Chapter 24

Friday, 25 June

My most beloved Emily,

I cheated on you again last night. If you were where you belong, I wouldn't have to resort to this. I hate myself for it. No, that's a lie.

Sometimes I wonder if you would like to watch. If you too would experience the pleasure I do. Before you get jealous, it is not, and never will be, the ecstasy I experienced with you.

None of them compare to you. They are weak and beg and scream and try to touch me. As if their submission will change the outcome. You, my love, are unique.

Do you remember the games we played? It feels like a lifetime ago. Perhaps it is. I'm going to let you in on a secret – sometimes I let you win. There was nothing more infuriating than knowing another man was touching you and I was forced to touch another woman.

You know how much I hate losing, even to you. Even when I won, I lost, because it wasn't you. Those who looked like you made it a little more bearable.

You called them 'my type'.
I call you an acquired taste.

Chapter 25

The second body remained covered. Jamie waited for Doctor Burger to pull back the sheet. No one who'd died from natural causes ever ended up in this morgue. If only after each case Jamie could erase the faces of the dead; the ones who would forever linger in her mind. *Who and what haunts Luke?*

"Are you ready for this one?"

"Yes," she said, rubbing her belly.

"Cause of death is obvious. Ballistics pulled the bullet from the wall and matched it to the .38 Special he had in his hand."

"What's this on his wrists?"

"I sent a swab to the lab, but if I had to guess – glue from an adhesive tape. This is where it gets interesting. His time of death is close to that of our Jane Doe." He pointed towards the woman on the table behind him. "But his stomach is empty and his body shows signs of dehydration."

"A patient of Doctor Clarke said he mentioned not feeling well on Monday. Could it be due to him being sick?" Why Jamie didn't want to say Noa's name, she didn't know.

"Possible, but not at this level. Most people would take an anti-nausea pill, but there was nothing in his stomach and the toxicology report came back with traces of Etomine. At the recorded levels Benjamin Clarke would've been sedated at the time of Jane Doe's death." Doctor Burger moved towards the neck of the body. "If you look here … there's a puncture mark." He handed Jamie a magnifying glass.

A piece of the puzzle fell into place for Jamie after she looked at the tiny hole left in the skin on Clarke's neck. "Someone set Clarke up. Etomine also showed up in the toxicology report of a victim who was attacked in her home on Wednesday morning." Jamie headed towards the door. "Thank you, Burger. I owe you."

"The only reason I can give you these answers today is because of the private laboratory processing the evidence in your stalker case. Whoever is paying for it, it's costing them a fortune."

Jamie left the morgue and braced herself for the cold wind outside. As she climbed into the car Jamie reached for her phone and turned the heater on full-blast.

"Captain, we need to send the object found inside Jane Doe to the private lab and compare it to what we found in the homes of Noa Morgan and Benjamin Clarke. I don't think Clarke is our stalker. He was restrained long enough to become dehydrated before he died. There are traces of what looks like glue residue on his wrists and ankles. Doctor Burger also found fibres in his mouth and throat. His toxicology report came back positive for Etomine. Clarke wouldn't have been conscious during the time of Jane Doe's murder."

"I'll put someone on it. But Jamie this means—"

"Noa Morgan is still in danger. And her stalker is a sadistic killer." Jamie dragged her hand down her face. "Captain, we need to have all the evidence from the case in Marcel sent to us ASAP. I'll talk to Detective Davidson, but I'd appreciate it if you could also put a call in to his superior to speed up the process."

Friday, 25 June, 12:03 p.m.

The chorus got the best of her; she sang along. Noa danced around the kitchen while preparing lunch. She hated being the reason Luke had to delay refurbishing his home. The wall separating the kitchen and dining room mocked her. Noa wished she could pick up a sledgehammer and pound it until only dust and rubble remained. To her the wall was a visual reminder of the emotional wall inside, and around, her. Walls *he* had built over forty days and cemented with fear. Noa longed to break free and live without dread as a constant companion.

She sang louder.

The rhythmic typing on the keyboard stilled, and she turned to find Luke watching her with a grin on his gorgeous face. Noa held his gaze and appreciated his features. From Luke's dark eyes and hair to the beard she loved feeling against her skin.

"Don't stop on my account. If I had some cash on me I'd stick it in your pants." Luke pushed away from the desk.

"It's my victory dance. Told you I can shoot." Noa stared at the floor. "When I'm not drugged."

With three big strides Luke closed the distance between them and pulled her against his chest. He bent down and whispered against her hair, "This is how I'm going to dance after we play strip shooter."

"Excuse me, Mr Taylor." Noa's hands moved along his arms, feeling every curve of muscle and wrapped her arms around his neck. "You're going be buck naked, while I will be fully clothed. I took out all the targets long before you even released the safety."

"Can you blame me? The way you handle a gun does things to me. I forgot why we were there." Luke pressed his mouth to the spot below Noa's ear.

"Sit. Eat."

"My, my, aren't you bossy, Annie Oakley." Luke returned to sit at the desk, which was, for the time being, positioned next to the front door. "Who taught you to shoot?"

"The detective who worked my abduction case. Every time he came to visit me, I stared at his gun. After Clarke cleared it, Detective Davidson took me to the shooting range every week and helped me to apply for a permit."

As Luke stared at the laptop's screen Noa noticed his frown; another thing she adored about him.

"What's wrong?" Noa placed the plate next to his arm.

"You said the person who held you captive was at the cabin every day."

"Yes, when I woke up, when I fell asleep. Some days he left me alone for a couple of hours, and other times I heard him outside the door moving around. Why?"

"Benjamin Clarke was on a fourteen-day tour of Europe during the time you were held captive."

Noa shut her eyes, trying to suppress the memories of the sounds, the smells of him. She placed a hand on Luke's shoulder. His presence kept her grounded. "How do you know that?"

"Social media. It either makes you or breaks you. Clarke hasn't been active in the past two years and I contacted the people he tagged in his photos. I sent direct messages to the ones whose security settings are off. They all confirmed Clarke was on the trip with them and sang his praises."

"It isn't over." Noa sank to the floor. *It never will be.*

Luke pulled her up into his arms. He tried to still her rocking body by pressing his lips to her temple and drawing her tight against him. "It might be. How much did you tell him about your time in the cabin? Did you tell him any specifics?"

"No. I didn't want to talk about it; having it in my head is bad enough. I told no one about the spiders, or the other things."

Noa stared at the wall. She pushed out of Luke's arms and marched to the pantry where he stored his tools. Armed with a sledgehammer, she started beating at the wall. Rage, tears and dust mixed together until Noa sank to the floor, spent.

"I will not let him hurt you again. I protect what's mine." Luke sat down behind her and pulled her closer. Noa turned and buried her face in his shirt.

Two and a half years worth of rage and fear burst through her.

"I'm getting you dirty," Noa said, wiping her eyes with the back of her hands.

"I don't care."

"Can't he just walk in front of a bus or get stabbed to death during a mugging?"

"Good, you realise he's human."

"He isn't, Luke. He's the devil. A demonic clown with only one goal – to destroy me. Why does he hate me so much?"

"It's not you that he hates, Noa. It's what you represent to him."

Chapter 26

Friday, 25 June

I'm tired of playing this game. Where are you, Emily? It's not as if I can spot your face in the crowd. And I don't remember you ever wearing a striped red and white shirt, or any stripes either.

Who's taking care of you, my love? Do they care for you like I did? I cooked for you every day; you needed for nothing. How do you not realise this is love? I blame your bitch mother for destroying you. She deserved far worse than she got.

If you won't come to me, then I'll smoke you out.

Predators thin out the herd from the back, starting with the weakest.

This, my love, is *your* fault.

Chapter 27

It's never that easy. Luke thought back to Noa's plea for her tormentor's death. Luke had carried her to the master bathroom and turned on the shower. While Noa showered he'd changed and cleaned himself up. He waited on the bedroom floor for her, listening to Noa's anguished cries. The curse words made him smile. Her distress stabbed through him.

Laura took Noa to the stables while he cleaned the carnage left in the dining room. Noa returned with a smile. Laura had taken her for an outride. Noa spoke of getting her own horse upon her return so Luke asked which one she liked best; she could take her pick of the horses on the estate. This offer didn't include his thoroughbred nor Madison's Arabian.

The light in Noa's eyes had flickered briefly as she told him about rubbing the horse's soft muzzle.

Luke took a seat next to her on the porch swing, glancing at Noa's smile as he held a glass of Merlot towards her.

"Who knew I could still ride a horse?"

"It's like riding a bike. And I thought it might take your mind off things."

Noa turned, tucking her legs under her bum. "You asked your mother to do this?"

"Yes."

"Thank you, and you didn't have to clean. I would've."

"It gave me something to do. When I get angry it's best if my hands stay busy."

"Is that why you're so ripped?" Noa's fingers trailed the veins on Luke's forearm, sending a shiver through him.

These small moments of intimacy made him crave her to the point of a physical ache.

"I avoided relationships because I didn't want to turn out to be anything like my biological father. If people didn't get close to me, I couldn't hurt them. It was a decision I made as a teenager when I first started noticing girls."

Noa gently pushed her fingers through his hair and in her eyes, Luke saw understanding. "You know about how I became a Taylor?" *And still, you want me.*

"Yes, Laura told me. Not to break your confidence, but to make me understand you need me as much as I need you." Noa trailed her fingers along his jaw, savouring the tickle of his beard. "What made you decide life is short? You've said it more than once."

Luke took Noa's hand and kissed her wrist. He heard the quick intake of her breath as he inhaled her subtle perfume. Noa's scent was right up there with the sight of her handling a gun.

"The last two years I was part of Marcel's Homicide Division. I spent every single day with Jeff, my partner, and I didn't see the warning signs. On Sunday, it will be three months since he died."

Noa pressed Luke's hand to her chest and held it there, waiting for Luke to continue.

"He went home after our last shift, took his service pistol, killed his wife and their three children. Then turned the gun on himself."

Noa blinked, sending tears dripping onto Luke's arm. "You can't blame yourself for what he did."

"He was my partner. I should've realised he had PTSD. We saw things you can't forget. I worked out my frustration and demons in the gym. Jeff held on to his."

Noa bent forward and placed the wine glass at her feet. She tried to wrap Luke's hand in both of hers.

"When he murdered his family and killed himself, it forced me look at who I thought I was. All my life I waited to turn into my father, but Jeff came from the best, most stable family, like the Taylors, and still he was capable of killing his own children in cold blood."

"You're a Taylor. Maybe not by blood, but something more, something deeper and far stronger. And never forget, you are your mother's son. She protected you with her life. You have *nothing* of that man inside of you. Every cell in you consists of her courage and strength. You're kind, compassionate and, I'll say it again, you, Luke Taylor, are the most beautiful man in the world."

Luke moved closer, brushing his lips against hers. He searched Noa's eyes. "Where were you when the nightmares kept me awake? When I used women to fill my nights to dull the images and voices in my head? The nights I stayed in the gym until I could barely drive myself home?"

"You're done carrying the world's burdens on your own. It ends right here. Right now. If, in the future, you decide to take any of it on yourself, then I'll be right next to you."

With her mouth Noa showed him how beautiful he was. She kissed Luke's eyes, nose, cheeks, forehead and then returned her mouth to his.

Luke eased her on top of him, desperate to get closer, to have more of her. He gripped Noa's thighs, making her moan into his mouth. The sound coming from her throat made him fight to keep control and give her the time he had promised.

Luke forced himself away from her hungry mouth despite every part of him aching to be one with her.

Staring at the green flecks in Noa's eyes, the content smile on her face, Luke knew there was no way he could live without her.

The front gate's intercom sounded.

***

Friday, 25 June, 5:02 p.m.

Jamie slumped onto the couch, dropping three files by her side. Noa sat down and took Jamie's hand in hers while Luke made Jamie something to eat. Noa compared the dark circles under her friend's eyes to the bruise on her own and wondered how Jamie remained on her feet.

"What's going on?" she asked, opening a bottle of water and giving it to Jamie.

Jamie finished half of the bottle before Luke handed her a sandwich and lowered himself onto the coffee table. "James, talk to us. What's going on?"

Jamie's hair moved from side to side. "Work. Not enough sleep."

Noa glanced at Luke and noticed he also picked up on the lie. "Okay, let's talk so you can head home and get some sleep. Talk to Spencer if you won't discuss it with us."

While Jamie cleared her plate, they discussed Laura and Noa's horse ride.

Jamie patted Luke's knee. "I don't think you should be here for this."

"Jamie, you're scaring me. What happened? If you came here to tell us Benjamin Clarke isn't my attacker, stalker, abductor, captor, whatever, we already know," Noa said.

"How?" Jamie asked her brother. "I forgot you're conducting your own investigation. Not that you have a lot of time on your hands with you two getting close."

At the sound of King barking Luke walked to the front door. King ran in and went from woman to woman for an ear scratch. He settled at Noa's feet.

"You and I will chat later about where you were the whole day," Noa said and returned her attention to Jamie, not without noticing Luke's smile at her comment to King.

"Luke did an online search. Clarke was on a fourteen-day European tour during the time of my captivity." Noa tried to distance her current reality from the memories, but to no avail.

"We need to discuss those forty days and everything that happened before your abduction. Noa, I've read the file. Talking about this will be hard for you. Perhaps it's best if Luke leaves."

"No, I want him to stay. All of it will come out when this goes to trial. It's better for Luke to hear it now."

"No secrets?" Luke asked, cupping her face. "You need to be sure. Nothing in that file will ever change how I feel about you, or how I see you." He pressed his mouth to Noa's and remembered his sister's presence just as he was on the verge of deepening the kiss.

"This isn't just some passing fling? You two are serious?"

"Yes." They both said without taking their eyes off each other.

"Okay." Jamie's smile faded as fast as it appeared. "We have proof Clarke was sedated, tied up and gagged during the time an unidentified woman was murdered. The reason I mention our Jane Doe is because there are striking similarities between what happened to her and to you, Noa. Not only now, but two-and-a-half years ago. I realised it when I reread your file, and went through the evidence photos of the items found inside the cabin and your house. Let's call it *items*, because until you tell me more, I don't know what else to call them."

Jamie sighed and shook her head. "Noa, you didn't tell Detective Davidson about everything that was done to you during your captivity, did you?"

Noa massaged her temples, craving a cigarette for the first time in years. Not since the day the demon clown had given her a cigarette which made her violently ill. Whatever he had used to lace it with, it had put Noa off cigarettes for the rest of her life.

"Noa?" Luke placed his hands on her knees.

"No, I didn't. When he questioned me about certain *items,* I said I couldn't remember. I was humiliated, having been found naked, tied to a bed by that poor man and his son. The shock on their faces. I didn't want to go through it again in court. My mother told me so many stories about victim blaming and how defence attorneys would tear into victims. So, I kept certain things to myself. My past isn't very vanilla."

"Noa, I need to be Detective Edwards now and not your friend. Please keep in mind that I'm asking because I need to find the person responsible before he kills another woman."

Noa gasped and brought a hand to her mouth. She looked at Luke and laid her palms on his cheeks. "I'm sorry. I have to tell now." Tears streamed down her face.

Luke smiled and pressed his lips to Noa's forehead.

"Okay, Detective Edwards, I'm ready. I won't stay quiet and allow him to kill again." Noa wiped her eyes and straightened her spine. She stood and walked to the fireplace.

Jamie cleared her throat. "What is the significance of the dildo?"

Noa hugged herself and stared at the fire. "He made it for me. A gift, he said. I threw it as far away from me as I could and he hit me. Sometimes I woke up with it ..." She shook her head.

"I realise this is difficult, but I need to know."

Noa gagged, closing her eyes and swallowed hard. "Inside me," she said so softly they might have missed it were they not focused on her every word. "He drugged me and raped me with it. I'd wake up and it would still be in there."

Noa ran to the bathroom and leaned over the basin. At the sight of her reflection, she remembered how he had worn the demon clown mask and watched her take a shower. No amount of soap had ever made her feel clean. When she had refused to shower, he dragged her to the bathroom and washed her himself. This only happened once. She had fought him until he removed a syringe from his back pocket and injected the contents into her neck. The next morning, she'd woken up as sunlight trickled into the room. He had shaved her.

Noa turned around with her arms still wrapped around her waist. She didn't meet Luke's eyes. "Did he shave her? Legs, armpits, private areas?"

"Yes," Jamie said. "I saw the photos; the ones taken after you had arrived at the hospital. Jane Doe's body has similar marks across her breasts and thighs. Why did he tie her down?"

"Can I see it?" Noa asked. "The photos of myself and Jane Doe?"

"You don't want to. Trust me."

"Dammit Jamie, I need to see them. Maybe I'll remember something or pick-up on something which might tell us who he is."

Luke pushed his hands through his hair. "Did he only rape you with the dildo?"

"As far as I know. He often drugged me, and when I woke up he'd done something to me. Why?"

"Our suspect might be a woman," Luke said. "You mentioned never seeing your captor's face so how can you be sure it's a man?"

"I can't."

Friday, 25 June, 6:30 p.m.

Dinosaurs would roam earth again before she said what he wanted to hear.

A single tear ran down her temple, into her hair. He hated her chestnut brown hair and had changed it. She wasn't sure what colour it was now; she hadn't been allowed to move around since. Except when he escorted her to the bathroom where he watched. He always watched.

Who are you, Emily? I hate you.

He said it was Emily's fault that she, Sarah, had found herself here. *Sarah.* She clung to her own identity, desperate to remember her name no matter how many times he screamed, begged or moaned, '*Emily*'.

Why don't you just kill her?

Sarah stared at the exposed concrete ceiling, wondering if someone realised she had disappeared.

Her eyes followed him as he walked towards the shelves. Next to them beckoned the only reminder of another world. Days and nights fused in the darkness of this room. No windows. No light. No hope.

Only hell and him. The devil.

Who knew evil had such a beautiful face? He returned with a syringe and another tear trickled into her hair.

"It's time for a taste," he said as his eyes trailed over every curve of her body.

Sarah tried to forget she was naked; clothing didn't matter in hell.

The devil took what he wanted.

Darkness enveloped her. This time, Sarah hoped she wouldn't wake up.

Chapter 28

After receiving a phone call Jamie left Luke's in a hurry. She thought about Noa en route to the crime scene. How Noa had managed to overcome so much and cared more about those around her baffled Jamie. She understood why Noa and Luke grabbed onto each other and knew they'd continue to hold on once this was over.

Jamie still carried the guilt of not being more accepting of Luke when they were children. Going from being an only child to having a brother of the same age had taken a toll on her. However, she'd made up for it whenever one of the other kids had bullied Luke. Jamie had seen the hurt others caused him and, even as a child, she would make anyone who wronged him pay with blood. Luke was her brother in every possible way.

With Noa around she no longer felt the need to protect Luke. After seeing them together earlier it became clear – they were in love. Jamie would fight to protect them both. If only she knew who *he* was. *Or she.*

As Jamie stepped out of the car, she braced herself for what waited on the other side of the crime scene tape. Doctor Burger leaned over the shape and called for more light. Strobe lights brightened this area of the forest. It illuminated the darkest moments of a person who didn't deserve to have their life ended.

She squatted next to Burger and, had someone not told

her it was a human being in front of her, Jamie might have mistaken the form for foliage.

"Before you ask me for a time of death, this one will take longer. The animals got to her," Burger said.

"The face?" Jamie asked, averting her gaze from the shape on the forest floor.

"Appears to be blunt force trauma. I won't lift the sheet, but there's an object that's been left inside her. Poor woman doesn't need gawkers staring at her humiliation."

"He makes it and rapes them with it."

"You spoke to her?"

"I had to." Jamie pushed down her emotions and focused on the victim.

"I'll finish up here and give you a call when I'm ready to start the autopsy tomorrow. Go home and rest. This isn't good for you or the baby."

"How did you know?"

"I might work with the dead, but I can see new life growing inside of you. Go home, Jamie."

"I have to stop him."

"And you will, but not if you're physically and mentally exhausted."

Jamie left, not before taking her own notes and photos of the scene as usual.

As she laid her head on her pillow, Jamie lost the fight. No detective is immune to the horrors they see every day. This hit close to home for Jamie as one of her best friends had suffered unthinkable torment. Spencer held her until her breathing calmed.

Saturday, 26 June, 00:36 a.m.

Luke stepped away from Emily Gallagher's file and placed more logs on the fire. He stared into the flames, gripping the mantel.

The woman in his bed couldn't have survived everything he'd read in the file. More details emerged from the information in Jane Doe's autopsy report. *The bodies of the dead speak; the living hold their tongues.* Luke understood why Noa chose to not speak about what she had endured.

Emily Gallagher's face haunted him. He remembered her face from the ensuing media reports after her rescue. How had he not realised it was her, his Noa?

Two-and-a-half-years was a long time and Noa had changed the colour of her hair and the style. The faces of the homicide victims Luke had sought justice for must've overshadowed the face of a survivor. That's what Luke told himself to stop dwelling on how he'd not been able to see Emily Gallagher when looking at Noa Morgan.

Luke stared at the wall separating the kitchen and dining room. The extent of Noa's rage, fear and pain was evident by the missing chunks of plaster and brick.

Never before had Luke felt so torn. He wanted to walk up the stairs and make love to her; the intelligent, strong, brave and beautiful woman he craved. But Luke remained rooted in front of the fire.

How would Noa ever allow a man to touch her again?

How did he dare think of showing her what she meant to him when she was in the midst of hell? Noa deserved better.

War raged inside him. Luke stormed to the pantry with clenched fists.

Saturday, 26 June, 00:45 a.m.

Noa sat bolt upright at the clap of thunder, which was followed by King's incessant barking. She reached for Luke, but his side of the bed was empty. Cold.

She fumbled for the bedside lamp while trying to calm King.

Noa grabbed her Glock and made her way down the stairs,

her heart thundered to the beat of the sound coming from somewhere in the house. Noa tried hard to keep her hands steady.

Dust and sweat mixed on Luke's shirtless torso; a faint white layer of plaster covered his hair.

"Luke!" Noa shouted above the deafening sound of the hammer smashing against the wall.

He didn't respond. Again, she called out to him.

Luke kept raising the sledgehammer and slamming it into the wall. Noa stepped through the living room, noticing the files on the table. Emily Gallagher stared back at her.

She placed the Glock on the dining room table and walked over to Luke. Noa hugged him, pressing her face against his back.

"Let me go."

"No. Luke, look at me." Noa moved around him, placing her palms against his chest.

"I won't hurt you."

Noa grabbed his face and stood on tiptoes. It wasn't close enough. Luke stepped back. Noa jumped, wrapping her arms around his neck, her legs around Luke's waist.

He dropped the hammer and gripped her thighs, resting his head against hers.

"Baby, look at me. Please."

Luke rubbed his forehead against hers.

"No secrets. We promised."

"I can't do this."

Noa wrapped her legs tighter around him and placed her hands on either side of his face. Luke backed her up against the wall.

"I want you so much that every part of me aches." She knew Luke meant it; the pressure of him against her made Noa's stomach clench. "I read what he did to you and it's selfish of me to want you. It's wrong. Noa, I've wanted you since we met and every day you make me ache for you. You're compassionate, strong, beautiful, and you're everything to me."

"It's not wrong." Noa pressed her mouth against his and licked against his lips until Luke took control of the kiss; dominant and leaving no doubt in her mind.

Noa dug her fingers into his back as Luke thrust against her.

With a growl he released his grip on her thighs. Noa held on. Luke's eyes met hers and she saw the same need she had before, but it held so much more.

"I'm in love with you," Luke whispered. "I've never felt what I do with you. You're what I've been running from my whole life, but you're exactly what I've wanted to run towards."

Noa couldn't control her breathing or the fire burning within her. "I want to take another step."

He lifted his eyes to hers and Noa reached between them, finding him more than she imagined. As she stroked his length, Luke shuddered and pressed her into the wall.

"Please, Noa. I can't." He rubbed his forehead against hers. The throbbing cock in her hand told her differently.

"I need this. Another victory." Noa lifted her head and against his mouth she whispered, "Luke, I need you."

His eyes darkened, and he ate at her mouth, keeping his tight grip on her thighs. The sheer act of giving Luke pleasure gave Noa more than she ever thought possible. Before it had always been about her, but with Luke she wanted to give him everything. Every day of her life. Every part of herself.

Noa kept her eyes on his face as the last shudder rippled through him. The intensity resonated through his hands into her thighs. The sight? Mesmerising.

Luke braced himself against the wall, his legs shaking. Noa slid down to the floor, pressing her face to his chest and listened to the thunder in his heart.

"Thank you," she said. He smiled, and she knew the sight of victory. *I'm not broken.*

"You're thanking me?"

"Yes. You don't understand how big a step this is for me. I've never experienced anything like this." Noa wanted to run her hands up Luke's beautiful chest and into his hair. "You will never hurt me, Luke Taylor. I might not be ready for everything … yet. You gave me more now than I ever thought possible. My past was wasted because this is …"

"I know. It's big." Luke's smile was wicked.

"Yes, that too." Noa's cheeks heated even though she knew what he meant. "I think we found a better way to relieve stress because at the rate we're going we won't have any walls left."

Luke's laughter filled her soul. Noa pressed her mouth to his chest. This wasn't a small step, but a giant leap.

Saturday, 26 June, 6:35 a.m.

Jamie reached for the irritating thing interrupting her sleep. "Edwards," she mumbled.

Jamie removed Spencer's arm from around her waist and got to her feet. "I'll be there as soon as I can," she said and ended the call.

Spencer reached for her across the bed and placed his hand bellow her naval. "What's wrong?"

"I need to get Noa. Please take your gun with you today and stay at Lamont until I get home."

Spencer pressed his lips to her neck. "I would much rather stay in bed the whole day with you. You and the baby need rest and you're not supposed to be working this weekend."

"I know, but I'm in the middle of a multiple murder investigation and he – or she – just upped the stakes. This is going to destroy her. Please promise me. Gun. Stay at Lamont."

"You're scaring me." Spencer hugged her.

"Good, because I *am* scared."

Chapter 29

They strolled into the house hand in hand. King ran in ahead. Noa smiled, watching him sniff every object and surface. It wasn't lost on her that both of them had settled into life with the Taylors' far more easily than they had to living on their own. Luke hadn't missed her comment about them tearing down *their* walls. He welcomed it, and had teased her as they fell asleep with their bodies intertwined.

Aaron sat at the dining room table reading on his iPad. From the kitchen, Laura called to Madison and the young woman shouted from somewhere in the house.

Noa's heart clenched. Luke became the man he was today because of the love of this family. She would be forever grateful to them for giving him a good life. For the rest of his life, she'd ensure Luke knew how deserving he was. And how loved.

"Ah, you came to see a man about a horse?" Aaron placed the iPad next to his plate and crossed his arms over his chest.

"Good morning, Aaron. How are you today on this misty morning? Can't remember last winter being this cold."

"Weather, Noa? Your response is to talk about the weather when I'm offering you your pick of the horses." He gestured to the chair to his right and Noa sat. "You know Luke and Maddie's horses are off limits. Which one will it be then?"

Luke laid a hand on her shoulders and gave a light squeeze. "Tell him which one you want."

Noa's head tilted back. "You people are insane. Who *gives* a horse to someone?"

147

Aaron cleared his throat. "Do you hear this, son? *You people.*" He reached for Noa's arm. "We are *your* people now. Your *family.* Giving Jamie's friend, and Luke's *special* friend, a horse is a small welcome to the family gift."

Luke laughed when Aaron's eyebrows moved up and down.

Noa touched her face, arms and legs. She poked at the fading bruise on her cheek bone. "I'm not dreaming? You talk of being family when I barely know you, and you me. My own mother never even referred to me as her daughter or us as a family."

"Do you see the light in my son's eyes? You're his light. I knew within the first week of meeting Laura we would get married. Don't give me any crap about it being too soon or whatever. Suck it up middle daughter." Aaron pushed to his feet and pulled Noa into an embrace. "You're my daughter now. I think Maddie has been home too long. I've never used the words *whatever* or *suck it up* like that in my life."

Noa wrapped her arms around him and tried to stifle the sobs, but as Aaron caringly rubbed her back, she embraced being called *my daughter* and being part of this family. Her own father had never called her his daughter. He never had the chance as they'd only met once.

When prompted again about her choice of horse, Noa chose a young thoroughbred mare Laura had saved a few weeks before. The Taylors saved whoever needed saving. Noa was grateful to be one of their rescues.

Laura and Madison joined them, carrying in serving trays filled with scrambled eggs, bacon, croissants and a variety of cheeses. Noa's stomach grumbled as the aroma filled the room.

"She gets a horse, but I can't get a new guitar. Not fair. Even with another sister I'm still the youngest. And you know the youngest has to get spoiled rotten. It's a fact of life." Madison rested her chin on her fists and pouted.

"I believe sisters help each other. What if I offer to help you write some original songs for your band? I've been inspired to write lately." Noa patted Luke's leg under the table and watched as a cheeky grin transformed his face.

"You write songs?" Madison jumped out of her chair and nearly strangled Noa by wrapping her arms around her neck.

Noa coughed, tapping Madison's arm. "Yes, a couple of my songs have been bought by record producers. You may recognise the artists who perform them. But non-disclosure agreements stipulate I can't divulge any more details."

"I love you more than Jamie. I swear." Madison kissed Noa's bruised cheek.

Noa ignored the pain as the front door opened and King made his way to greet the late arrivals. Jamie entered the dining room, unable to hide the fear in her eyes. Behind her, Spencer didn't seem to be his usual happy self.

"Mom, Dad, I'm sorry to do this on Maddie's farewell breakfast, but Noa and I need to leave."

Noa pushed her chair back. Luke did the same.

Jamie's focus shifted to her brother. "You can't come with. If you do, Noa's safe house might be compromised. We can't risk it." Jamie rolled her shoulders and shut her eyes. Spencer wrapped his arms around her.

"What happened?" Noa asked, walking towards them.

"Kim was in an accident last night. Hit and run. I'll tell you more on the way to the hospital."

"Noa is not leaving." Luke placed his hands on Noa's shoulders and pulled her back against him.

"Dammit, Luke, I don't have the energy to fight you. Get off your alpha-male, testosterone-fuelled horse and let me do my job."

"I'll follow you and provide back-up if needed."

Jamie sank into the chair Spencer pulled out for her. She looked at the faces of her family before returning her attention to Noa and Luke. "It wasn't an accident. We can't discuss the details here or now. Noa and I need to leave. Can you all please stay on the estate today?"

"I have a gig tonight in Shadow Bay so I need to leave," Madison said, biting into a croissant.

"Okay, but you call me as soon as you get there and don't take the back road through town. Get on the highway and keep going. Is one of your friends driving back with you?"

Madison rolled her eyes. "I'm not a child, James. I won't take candy from a stranger or stop for hitchhikers. Emma is driving back with me. I promise you there won't be space for a butterfly, never mind another person."

"I don't like this," Luke mumbled.

Jamie got to her feet. "You don't have a say *civilian* Taylor."

Luke turned Noa to face him. "I don't want you to go. But I know you will because your friend is hurt. Do you have your gun with you?"

Noa stepped back and took his hands, placing one below her breasts and the other at her lower back. "Who's your girl?" She winked.

Luke lowered his head and whispered, "If we were alone right now, I'd push you against a wall and do to you what you did to me this morning." His hands remained in place.

Noa's cheeks heated. In his voice she heard a promise she wanted him to keep.

"I'm not allowed to have a guy stay over even once, but these two are practically making babies in front of us. Do you want me to clear the table for you and usher everyone out before they have breakfast *and* a show?" Madison leaned back in the chair, crossing her arms over her chest with a sly grin.

Saturday, 26 June, 9:30 a.m.

If there was one thing Emily could never resist it was a friend in need. Wasn't it a shame little Emily had grown up unloved and when love had stood right in front of her, the damage done to her had blinded her? He pulled the collar of the coat closer to his skin and stared at the hospital's main entrance.

There he sat, in the cold, waiting for her.

His mate.

The other half of him which he didn't know existed until she'd stood in front of him.

"Play this right and she'll be back where she belongs." His heart stilled as she exited the car.

"Not as beautiful as you were with your natural black hair, but you still have the same effect on me." He massaged his erection. "Hello, my love."

Reaching for the door handle he reminded himself now wasn't the time to grab her like before. No, this time, Emily would come to him.

He braced for the cold outside by remembering her sweet, wet heat.

Eeny, meeny, miny, moe, who will be my next ho?
Maybe Jamie. Maybe Maddie.
Eeny, meeny, miny, oh.

Saturday, 26 June, 9:45 a.m.

Kim turned her head towards the door as Noa and Jamie entered the hospital room. Noa grabbed Jamie's hand but kept her face from showing the horror which screamed inside her. A sickening sweet smell hung in the air. Noa's stomach tightened.

"I know it's bad. The doctor said after a few skin grafts I should look good as new. To think of all they money I wasted on anti-wrinkle creams." Kim tried to smile, grimacing instead.

"Once the swelling goes down and the bruises fade it will look much better." Noa inched closer to the bed, not paying attention to the casts on Kim's legs or her right arm.

"The flowers in the corner came for you. Both of you."

Noa and Jamie turned as one and stared at the bouquets of white roses next to the washbasin. Noa pushed down hard on the need to scream; later she'd further her and Luke's progress on the wall.

"He sent me a bouquet too. Matthew read the card. You're

free to take it, Jamie. The flowers too." A tear slipped from the corner of Kim's eye.

Jamie removed a latex glove from her coat pocket and read the note aloud. "If only Noa didn't kill Emily. You're collateral damage. No hard feelings."

"Who is Emily?" Kim asked.

Before Jamie could protest Noa said, "I'm Emily."

Chapter 30

"This is all because some psycho is obsessed with you?" Kim asked, pain and fatigue heavy in her words.

Noa helped her take a sip of water. "Yes. I'm sorry. I should never have moved here."

Kim ignored Noa. "What are you doing to stop him?" she asked Jamie.

Jamie stood with her back to them and removed the envelope addressed to Noa from the bouquet. She opened the card, but didn't read it out loud. Noa walked up behind her and read it over Jamie's shoulder.

You will always be mine.
Soon my love, you will beg me.
You will say it. YOU WILL.

xoxo

"Open yours." Noa's voice came out low and shaky.

Jamie did and placed a hand to her stomach.

You can't protect them all.
Not even the one you carry.
Give me my Emily. She's mine.

Noa touched Jamie's stomach and whispered, "I won't tell and he will *not* touch you."

They turned to see Kim had fallen asleep. Jamie kissed Kim's forehead and made her way towards the door.

Noa leaned over Kim and whispered, "I'm so sorry. I won't let him hurt anyone else."

Matthew and Eric waited for them in the corridor, both

153

with vacant expressions on their faces. Eric hugged Noa.

"Jamie, you better find the person responsible, and the rest of you need to get in line. I get first dibs on breaking every bone in his body." Matthew slammed his fist into his palm.

"I'll get to him first and after one minute he'll wish for broken bones." Eric patted Matthew on the back.

"How is she?" Matthew asked.

"Sleeping. I think rest is what Kim needs most now. I'm so sorry, Matt." Noa hugged him.

"Jamie, please tell me you've heard something?" Matthew asked.

"It wasn't an accident. CCTV footage shows the driver speeding up. The car was discovered outside of town, burnt up, but the VIN number was traced back to a vehicle stolen in Malmesville. Noa, it's time for us to leave."

Eric grabbed Noa's hand. "Wait a minute, Jamie. You can't take my friend from me. Noa and I haven't spoken in a week. What's going on?"

"It's all my fault. And I need you to be extra careful until this is over."

"Sweetie, you're scaring me. What's going on? Where are you staying? I can't even call you, and all Jamie will ever tell me is you're safe."

Noa glanced at Jamie; Jamie shrugged. "You said you're tired of the lies. The truth might help them to be more vigilant."

Noa asked her friends to follow her to the restaurant in the lobby. Once seated, she told them and watched as both men's mouths dropped to the floor.

"Why didn't you tell us?" Matthew reached for Noa's hand.

"I started a new life and wanted to forget about it. I don't know how he found me, so please be extra careful until this is over."

"Where are you staying?"

Noa looked at Eric. "I'm staying in a safe house in a neighbouring town. He abducted me off the street last time … We're not taking any chances."

Matthew cleared his throat. "Does Luke know about this?"

"No. We only started spending time together when this happened. I don't want to drag him into it. I sent him a message telling him I'm out of town visiting friends and will see him when I get back. Jamie, if you think Luke might be in any danger, you should contact him."

Matthew squinted. "Why isn't he helping with this investigation? He has a ninety-eight percent arrest rate. The conviction rate from his arrests is just as high. Check his records."

Jamie held up a hand, silencing him. "Luke's a civilian now. Noa and I need to leave. I promise to get justice for Kim."

As they walked towards the car Noa asked Jamie why she didn't want their friends to know she was staying with Luke.

"You never know who might have been eavesdropping."

Bile rose in Noa's throat at the idea of *him* being within earshot.

Saturday, 26 June, 12:00 p.m.

Jamie switched off the ignition. She and Noa stared at the Taylor family home. The twenty-minute drive back from the hospital had been filled with silence.

Noa reached for Jamie's hand and rubbed it for warmth. "Why haven't you told anyone you're pregnant?"

"It's only seven-weeks; way too early and I've been busy the past week." Jamie changed position to face Noa. "Any idea who could be behind this?"

"I've spent the past few days trying to think of anyone who could hate me this much. And to be honest, I can't. I might not be everyone's favourite person, but I can't believe someone can hate me this much. Were you able to locate Justin?"

"No, not yet. He disappeared the day before his wedding and no one has heard from him since. Tell me again about Emily and the years before the abduction."

"She had a normal student life. Never got involved with anyone because of the plan to work on cruise ships and travel the world. Did that for five years. Met Justin. Moved back to Marcel. Settled into relationship-life. Then he cheated, she left him and contacted the cruise company to ask for another contract. A week before she was supposed to fly to Amsterdam he abducted her."

"Why do you speak of her as if she is a different person?"

"Because she is. I haven't been Emily since I was rescued from the cabin. I didn't come out as the same person he had dragged in."

"No other boyfriends or scorned lovers?"

"No boyfriends. As far as lovers go, the list might be a bit long. I'm not proud to admit it, but I don't remember all of their names."

"Any issues with female friends?"

"None that I recall. We were a big group of friends, but I never had the kind of friendships with them that I have with you and Kim."

"Noa, if it wasn't for you being attacked, I might never have known the truth about your past." Jamie rested a hand on Noa's shoulder. "I understand why you didn't tell any of us."

"I'm going to go pack. Take me back to my house. I won't let him hurt any of the people I love."

Jamie turned to face the vehicle coming to a stop next to them. Both women kept their gazes fixed on the man getting out. Luke strode up to the passenger side door of Jamie's car and yanked it open. He squatted and reached for Noa's face.

"Are you okay?" Luke wiped at the wetness under her eyes with his thumbs.

"No. He's coming after the people I love. I need to go pack. If he wants to come for me, so be it. I won't be the reason anyone else gets hurt or lose someone they love." *Or someone I love.*

"But you expect me to be fine with it?" Luke pushed to his feet and stormed towards the house.

"I thought you understood him." Jamie sighed, leaning her head back against the headrest. "Running away isn't going to help. We just need to regroup and review the evidence again."

"I won't risk you or your baby getting hurt, Jamie. And I can't lose Luke."

"If you don't want to lose him, then you need to fight back. Luke's in love with you and if you have feelings for him, you would want him by your side through this. I get where you're coming from, but this is no longer just about you." Jamie reached for Noa's hand and waited for her friend to face her. "Are you in love?"

"Yes. For the first time in my life. Luke makes me feel safe, alive, wanted and needed."

"Have you told him?"

"No. And you're right. Running away isn't the answer. But how do I keep everyone safe when I don't even know who we're looking for?"

"Go talk to Luke and apologise. Do what you need to do. I'll be back later and then we can talk this through. I need to update my captain and head to the morgue."

The colour drained from Noa's face. "Did he kill someone?"

"Yes. Two victims we are aware of so far. Another woman who fits the victim profile is missing. Noa, I need you to find the strength you had in you for those forty days and fight back." Jamie took Noa's face in her hands. Determination radiated from her eyes. Desperation filled her voice. "Fight. Back."

Chapter 31

Saturday, 26 June

My love,

I can't tell you how wonderful it was seeing you today. You have always been a world-class performer. Faking concern for Kim reminded me of how you faked orgasms. The best way to describe your performance today – marvellous.

Imagine my surprise when I noticed a certain Luke Taylor in the hospital's parking lot. He watched you, much as a shark watches a seal before going in for the kill. Naughty boy. Your mine. He won't get to play with you.

I don't believe there's nothing going on between the two of you. Did you lie to your friends? Are you perhaps sleeping under his roof? In his arms? If you are, my love, I'll make you regret cheating on me.
You're mine. Forever.

The hero detective will suffer a fate far worse than poor Kim.
No one looks at my woman the way he did.
Oh, what big eyes you have, Luke Taylor.

Chapter 32

Luke stood in front of the window in the living room with his back to the door.

"My entire life I have taken care of myself. I've never needed anyone until I moved here and became friends with Jamie and Kim and, by extension, Spencer and Matthew. Eric took me in when I first came here and I depended on him so much the first year when we lived together. Now the people I care about are being targeted by someone from my past. A person who has hated me for years. I can't think of a single person I've wronged to the point of hating me." Noa stepped closer.

"I have no words to describe how you make me feel, Luke. You're both my calm and my storm. I never dreamed this passion, joy and peace existed. It's overwhelming and comforting ... I don't know how to keep you safe." Noa laid her hands on his back and rested her head between his shoulder blades. "Please look at me." *I'm in love with you.*

Luke didn't face her. "I will find the person behind this. And kill him for what he did to you."

"*We* will find the person responsible. Together."

"What do you want, Noa?"

"To break down more walls. To take more steps and sit with you every day on our porch looking at the sunset and at King chasing the Egyptian Geese." The corners of Noa's mouth lifted. "I want a life with you Luke – not Lucas – Taylor."

"Then stop talking about going to your house. It's just that – a house. Whenever you talk about my place you talk about *our*

159

and *we*. It's your home now, Noa. *Our home.* And yes, I realise it has only been a week, but we've lived a lifetime in the past few days. We know more about each other than some people do by the time they get married. I never want to hear you say the word *leave* again."

Noa wrapped her arms around him and Luke caressed her arms.

He continued, "I'm going to ask you something for three reasons. First, I can keep you safe here. I'm having security cameras installed all over the property right this minute. Second, how pissed off will he be when he finds out you have moved, and he can't get to you? Angry people make mistakes. But more than anything, when this is over, and it will be soon, I want to keep waking up to your beautiful soul. I want to hear you sing in the kitchen every morning and fall asleep with you in my arms every night. King has approved of me and you can't deny he loves the freedom of roaming the farm."

Luke turned and ran his fingers through Noa's hair. His thumbs traced her jaw. "Noa Morgan, will you move in with me?"

Saturday, 26 June, 2:19 p.m.

Darkness spat her back out at his mercy. *Mercy?* He had none.

Sarah no longer cried.

She still hated Emily, but not as much as she hated *him*.

Without making a sound he moved around the room. "I'm sorry my dear, but our time together has come to an end," he said and returned to stand beside her.

She made a muffled sound; the duct tape kept her lips unmoving.

"Your death will not be in vain. Your blood will remind her of my love for her, and she will come home to me." His fingers trailed the length of her skin. "You are a rare beauty. I would've enjoyed spending more time with you. But alas, I need to shift my focus elsewhere and I'm not the monster you envision me to be. I won't leave you here to rot. No, your body will give back to the earth until someone finds you. Just as you have given me bliss, so you will bring joy to the animals and insects."

He lifted his arm, bringing a cricket bat into view.

This time darkness kept her.

Saturday, 26 June, 3:00 p.m.

Jamie stood in the doorway of her home and watched as crime scene investigators inspected every object and corner. She placed her hands under her navel and whispered, "Mommy will keep you and Daddy safe, my love."

An investigator removed a book from the shelf and placed it inside an evidence bag. He nodded at Jamie when their eyes met. A fire ignited in the pit of her stomach.

"How did it get there?" Captain Johnson asked from behind her, startling Jamie.

"I don't know. Spencer and I discussed installing an alarm system when we first moved in, but it was one of those things we kept putting off. For almost ten years." Jamie shook her head. "He got around Noa's alarm system so it wouldn't have made a difference."

"How is she?"

"Not good. She wanted to leave the safe house and return to her house. I talked her out of it." In a low voice Jamie added, "I'll go see her as soon as I'm able to pack some of our things. Spencer and I will stay with my parents until this is over."

"I want you to instruct Officer Sheridan to do more of the legwork. You need to make time to rest, not only so you can keep a sharp mind, but also for the baby."

"How did you know?"

"You really didn't hear me walk up behind you?"

Jamie exhaled out loud. "I went to the morgue earlier. Both

our victims were identified. Linda Christie and Brie Doyle; our missing woman. Sarah Poe is still missing. I'm worried we'll find her like we did the others. On the way over here, I made a few calls. No one has reported any women, fitting our victims' descriptions, missing at stations in the area. Either more women will disappear, or he will come for Noa."

"I've heard nothing from Detective Davidson regarding the ex, Justin's, whereabouts. Do you think he might be behind this?"

"To be honest, from what I read about him and the nature of his and Emily's relationship, I can't see him doing this. He moved on, got engaged, and he has a stable work history. He disappeared the day before his wedding. Maybe he just got cold feet. The date of his disappearance doesn't coincide with what has happened here. He's been missing for a month."

"I also don't make him for it, but you should speak to Noa again. Does she prefer being called Noa now that her secret is out?"

"I haven't even asked her yet. My focus is on finding this sonofabitch. What name Noa chooses to go by is up to her."

Captain Johnson stepped away to take a call and Jamie watched as more of their belongings were placed inside evidence bags. The mirror from the master bedroom being among the items being carried out of her home.

A cold chill ran down Jamie's spine. She bit back the curse words and stormed up the stairs to pack. This had to end.

Chapter 33

Saturday, 26 June, 5:30 p.m.

Kori Sheridan sat in her car in Detective Edwards's driveway. *How can she afford to live like this on her salary? Oh yes, the handsome, perfect, award-winning vintner.*

As she stared at the manicured lawn and red brick house her phone rang. "Hello handsome. I miss you."

"Not as much as I miss you. What's my favourite police officer up to? Saving the world as usual?" her caller asked.

"No such luck for me today. Just running errands for the detective to whose case I've been assigned."

Kori wondered how she had ever gotten so lucky that a man like him would be interested in her. With his handsome face, melodious voice and expert love making skills, she found herself head over heels in love after only a few nights.

"Do I need to have a word with her superior? You can't waste your investigative skills on silly errands."

"Flattery will get you everywhere. What time can I see you tonight?"

"I'm sorry, Gorgeous, I'm meeting with a client tonight. He is only in the city for one more night. I promise to make it up to you, and I know *just* how to ..." He explained in vivid detail what he had planned the next time they saw each other.

"Stop before I get the victim's possession's wet."

"Such a filthy mouth you have, Kori. I might need to spank you for such dirty talk. Is that the errand you were referring to?"

"Yes, it appears our *victim* will be staying in a safe house. With the amount of stuff I had to pack, I don't think she intends to ever return to her home. I wish this case was over. Then I can spend every night with you."

"I know, Gorgeous. Soon it will be all over for you. I promise. Listen, I need to run. I'll talk to you soon and, in the meantime, I'll think of ways to reward you for that slick, dirty mouth of yours."

He ended the call and Kori watched Jamie storm towards the car. *Here we go. Couldn't this bitch end up in the forest?*

Saturday, 26 June, 6:05 p.m.

From the corner of her eye Noa watched Luke typing on his laptop. He had moved the table closer to the couch, which allowed them to sit next each other and tend to their day jobs. King lifted his head and rolled onto his back in front of the fire. From where Noa sat, he reminded her of a grey bat.

Luke caught her looking at him. He removed Noa's hand from her laptop and lifted it to his face. "I'm putting up a punching bag in the garage for you and buying you better gloves. There are still marks on your knuckles."

"I think you're more worried I'm going to take out another wall."

"Do you blame me after the way you ran earlier? Your legs are almost half the length of mine and I struggled to keep up with you." He ran his hand down the side of her thigh. "Not that I didn't appreciate the view."

"You body builder types all lack stamina. All weights and no cardio."

"And no Pilates. Don't forget that waste of time." Noa noticed the quirk in his mouth.

"Not even if I offered you another lesson free of—"

"No."

"Free of clothes." She turned and stared at him.

Luke drew the laptop closer to his stomach. "When is this class scheduled?"

"Oh, but Mr Taylor you just declined my offer. Carry on checking your emails."

"How am I supposed to focus when all I can think about is you naked, doing a bridge pose?"

Her left eyebrow raised. "Perhaps if you focused on your work and stopped undressing me with your eyes, you'd find something to distract you. Discussion over."

"You're a cruel woman, Noa Morgan." Luke reached for her face. "No naked bridge pose for me, so no naked bridge pose for you." Luke's smile reached his eyes, making Noa's stomach flip.

"Focus on your work. We've both lost countless hours and you need to make the world a safer place." Noa's attention returned to the teenagers in the chat room and, after letting out a soft curse, Luke focused on the unread emails in his inbox.

Undisturbed, they continued working and Noa exhaled aloud a few times as the pain of the children in the chatroom mirrored her own youth.

Deep in thought and drafting replies in her mind, Noa at first didn't register the sound coming from Luke's laptop. When it finally registered, she stared at Luke's screen in shock.

"You're watching porn? Seriously? With me right next to you on the day we decide to live together."

"No. Someone emailed me a link."

Noa tried to get a better view of the image on the screen. "No. No. No." She placed her laptop on the coffee table and jumped to her feet. "Turn it off!"

Luke paused the video and reached for her hand. Noa yanked it away. "I swear I wasn't watching porn. I received an email with a message saying I should reconsider *my involvement*, and *should I require further proof it will be sent in due course*. I thought it pertained to one of the schools." Luke placed his laptop next to hers and touched the back of Noa's leg. "What's wrong?"

"Who sent it to you?"

Luke searched for the sender's details – therealem@email.com.

"I need to watch it. Without you."

"No."

Noa spun around. "Yes. Now."

"No. We're in this together and it was sent to me."

"Don't you see it? *He* sent it to you. He knows about us. That video was made without my consent."

"Wait, it's you? How can you be so sure?"

"I remember the outfit."

Luke stared at the screen and recognised a twenty-something Emily Gallagher. Even on her back, there was no mistaking her eyes. Emily stared back at him, as if frozen in time.

Noa sank to the couch, dropping her head in her hands. "He taped me having sex. Who does that? Oh, I know, the same person who put cameras all over my house and watched me for who knows how long. Who has hated me for so many years?"

Luke tried to pull Noa closer and into his arms. "Perhaps we're looking at this all wrong. Maybe it's not about hate, but love."

"Love? I might be new to this emotion, but how can destroying someone's life be considered love? If that's love, I don't want it."

"What I meant is – *obsession*. He *thinks* he loves you and sent this to me to put me off pursuing a relationship with you. Nothing in this video will change how I feel about you. Do you remember anything about this *incident* which might identify him? Who is the guy you're with?"

Noa shook her head and stared at King. "I can't remember his name. It was at a dress-up party during my third year at university. I went as an Amazonian warrior, hence the outfit."

"At least your sword is bigger than that of the guy you're with." Luke laughed.

"This is *not* funny."

"I'm sorry, but it's kind of funny. Not someone filming you having sex, but the fact he thought it would get me to back off. The only way he could know I feature in your life is if he saw me in the hospital's parking lot."

"Or on Friday night. Or Saturday outside the gym. Or Sunday. Even on Monday he could've seen us together. He was there. He has always been there. Everywhere. Hiding in the shadows."

"Maybe he or she isn't hiding in the shadows. He or she might be standing in plain sight."

"Thanks, that makes me feel a hell of a lot safer."

"Watch this with me so we can figure out the significance of this specific video. I'll look at it as a detective and not your boyfriend."

Noa shook her head. *My boyfriend?* How could she allow Luke to watch another man have sex with her? Her memory of that night was foggy. Except she remembered waking up around midday with a killer headache, still wearing the outfit.

Before she could ask Luke again to let her watch it alone, he pressed the play button. As much as Noa wanted to look away, she couldn't.

Before the video ended, Noa ran to the bathroom.

Chapter 34

Jamie leaned her head against the steering wheel. *I can't do this again.* A knock on the window made her jerk upright. She turned and stared at the dark figure standing outside the car.

The figure opened her door. The cold wind whipped Jamie's hair into her face. She reached for the elastic band around her wrist, tying it in a bun at the nape of her neck.

"I've never had a week like this. How you holding up?"

"Not good. I'm tired, Burger. Tired of innocent women dying. Tired of not being able to take down the man who hurt two of my friends and has threatened my family."

"Then let's get to it. And you're going home as soon as you've seen the victim. Instruct your sidekick to take photos of the scene. It's about time she learns. Johnson's going to need another detective when you go on maternity leave."

"I'm telling you as my friend, but I don't think I'll be coming back. I don't want to leave this baby at home while I witness what monsters do to other people's babies."

He placed an arm around Jamie's shoulder and hugged her to him. "I get that. Some days I lock myself in my office and cry before I go home and face my family."

"You cry?"

"Don't sound so shocked. I told you when you first came into the morgue – the day it no longer gets to you, is the day you know it's time to get out. Why did your brother leave the police force?"

"We haven't had time to talk about it yet, but knowing Luke, he realised he'd had enough. I'll go see him when we finish up here. Luke might not be officially on the case, but I can still ask for his input. He's a legend in Marcel."

"You're a legend here. Jamie, every detective feels this despondent on their first serial case. I've seen it countless times over the years. This is my eighth serial case and I question my capability every single day. The pressure is so immense I review everything three times, no matter how inconsequential."

They walked in silence to where a photographer was hunched over the remains of the third victim. There was no mistaking this was the work of the same killer. Jamie breathed through clenched teeth and asked the photographer to hurry up; the other people on the scene didn't need to witness the poor woman's humiliation.

"Is this your other missing woman?" Doctor Burger asked.

"We will need DNA to confirm, but the heart-shaped birthmark on her bicep is as much confirmation as I need right now. This is Sarah Poe."

A rustle of leaves made Jamie spin around and reach for her gun.

"My apologies for being late, Detective. I had to drop a gift at my friend's house on my way here. It's her birthday."

"Please save your apologies for the woman lying on the ground. The one who had her head bashed in. I'm sure she doesn't mind you taking care of something which could've waited until morning. First you screwed up on the Benjamin Clarke investigation. And now you're running personal errands instead of getting your ass to a crime scene. Go home, Sheridan. I'm going to request you be removed from the case." Jamie reached for her phone.

"Please, Jamie, don't call Captain Johnson. I'll try harder, do better, I promise."

Jamie bent down and watched the blowflies land in the gleam of her flashlight. "*She* deserves better."

***

Saturday, 26 June, 7:15 p.m.

Luke poured two whiskeys while he waited for Noa to return to the living room. He walked to his laptop and reread the words which signified the end of the video. *Is this who you want? There is no pleasing a psychopath.*

Whoever had sent it didn't know the first thing about Noa. *My Noa.* Since the night they had met, Noa's compassion and warmth drew him in. Her beauty the bow on the most mesmerizing package of a woman he had ever met.

Luke replayed the video. This time with the sound muted. The camera didn't move as one would expect from footage filmed by someone holding the camera. Luke wondered if it had been placed there to record anyone, or specifically, Emily Gallagher.

Noa returned to the living room and drained the whiskey without saying a word or meeting Luke's eyes.

"Can you remember anything about this room?" Luke asked.

"Such as the ceiling?"

He ignored Noa's sarcasm, understanding it all too well. "A bookshelf, or dresser, something where the camera could've been hidden? Who hosted the party?"

"I was pretty wasted that night. If I hadn't been, do you think I would've acted the way I did? But then again, back then I was known for not being easy to please." Noa sighed.

"You were pretty clear about his inability to satisfy. Even without saying a word, you reaching for a cigarette gave away your lack of enthusiasm."

"I'm sorry." Noa drew her legs to her chest.

"For what? Do I have a little performance anxiety now? Maybe. But you were right, Noa. The guy didn't know what he was doing. I really enjoyed the bit where you showed him how to do it." Luke bumped his shoulder against her.

"You're not making this any easier."

"I'm teasing you. I hate the piece of shit who recorded the

video and thought sending it to me it would change how I feel about you. It doesn't. It only makes me more determined to hunt him down and make him pay for what he's been doing to you for years. Or her, if we're looking for a woman."

"How are you not disgusted with me after seeing the way I behaved?" Noa stared at him.

"There are only a handful of people in this world who wouldn't mind if every second of their days, or mostly nights, at university was distributed for the world to see. Most of us had nights like this. I had them, as did most of my friends. Even Jamie did before she met Spencer. I don't want to say it, but I know Maddie hasn't taken a few names over the years. Forget about what we saw and focus on the fact he or she chose this specific video to send to me. Unless it's the only video they have, which I doubt because of *further proof*."

Luke pulled Noa into his arms and pressed his lips to her hair. "The girl in the video is Emily. The woman in my arms is Noa. During my varsity days I would've been all over Emily, but now, I want to live life with Noa. Don't ever think I don't know the difference." He drew her onto his lap, burying his face in her neck. "I'll do whatever it takes to keep you safe."

Chapter 35

Luke showed Jamie the live feed from the motion detection cameras he had installed along the perimeter of his farm. And, with their approval, he even went as far as installing hidden cameras on the properties of the neighbours. Luke had to get their permission to open the shooting range in order to complete the task.

Noa stood in the kitchen and took it all in. The sight of Luke hugging Jamie. The ever-present threat and the fact Luke's house was now her home. Where Emily had been a planner, Noa realised she now enjoyed living in the spur-of-the-moment. *Old dog, new tricks.*

Jamie leaned into Luke's embrace; the sound of her frustration stabbed into Noa's heart. Luke met her eyes, and she noticed tortured understanding in his stare.

Noa made a cup of decaffeinated coffee and carried it to Jamie. "You found another woman, didn't you?" she asked, making herself comfortable on the table.

Jamie nodded, holding on tighter to Luke. She lifted her head and stared at her brother. "How did you do it? How did you spend two years undercover to move onto homicide and here you are, strong and loving as ever?"

"I don't know what to tell you. Except the only way to get through it, is to keep seeing the victims. Hear their silent voices. And fight for justice. The day you arrest the person responsible, it makes it all worthwhile. You'll never forget the victims, but knowing the person responsible is rotting in prison for the rest of his or her natural life, makes it easier to move on to the next case."

"I don't want him to sit in prison and remember the horrible things he did to these women or to Noa. He needs to be burned alive."

Noa reached for Jamie's hands. "What can I do to help?"

"Tell me who he is."

"I don't know. Luke and I have spent countless hours talking about my past and I spent the last few hours trying to remember the men I've had sex with."

Luke leaned forward, glancing at both women. "Why am I the only one who keeps considering the possibility that our suspect might be a woman?"

The crackling sound of the fire engulfing the logs filled the silence. Jamie glanced at Noa and shrugged. Noa shook her head, her stomach churned.

"Our suspect is definitely male. He left *something* in his duffle bag in Noa's house. The DNA the lab extracted from the *something* led us to an ex-convict who is now a prostitute in Shadow Bay. Said man gave officers a detailed description of our suspect. We might need a rocket though as he described an alien. He was higher than a kite when he was approached for a *sample* by a two-headed, blue and yellow creature with large eyes." Jamie eased back on the couch.

Luke pushed his fingers through his hair. "What did you find in the duffle bag?"

Noa focused on Jamie's face, answering Luke. "A used condom. He often left them for me on the dresser, or on the pillow next to my head." She clenched her eyes shut, willing the memories to stop from surfacing. But Noa was unable to forget the horror of not knowing what he had done to her. She often wondered if knowing was better.

"Did you compare the DNA from the condoms in the cabin to the prostitute?" Luke asked Jamie.

"They found no condoms at the cabin. Before you ask, the

prostitute was in rehab during the time Noa had been held captive. We checked his alibi."

Luke reached for his laptop. Noa stood and walked to where King was laying. The instant her bum met the hardwood floor King snuggled onto her lap. Noa leaned her head back against the wall and closed her eyes.

Jamie didn't utter a word while she watched the video.

"Yours is much more flattering than mine. Angle is key." Jamie grinned and pursed her lips.

"You Taylors are a weird bunch of people."

"Hey, watch your tongue, we are *your* people now," Luke said.

Noa wanted to joke about leaving, but knew she had reached her daily quota for pushing Luke.

"Any idea who the guy is?" Jamie reached for the mug of coffee. She glanced at Noa who gave a slow blink before Jamie took a sip.

"What was that?" Luke asked.

"What? Can you show me photos of the victim whose body you found today?"

Jamie sighed, handing her phone to Luke. Noa waited for Luke to give it to her, but he didn't.

"Something has been bothering me for a few days now and today I finally figured it out." Luke handed Jamie's phone back to her and growled when Jamie handed it to Noa. "She doesn't need to see it."

"I don't have the energy to fight with either of you. Noa has seen the files of the other two women, and this one's body is in better shape. Doctor Burger estimated she was killed a few hours before her body was dumped on the footpath and she was found soon after. He's getting bold."

"Good. He thinks he has the upper hand. Soon, he'll make his next mistake."

"Next?" Jamie asked as she stared at Luke's laptop.

"Why did he go through the trouble of setting up Clarke, only to come out of the woodwork shortly afterwards? How did he even know you no longer considered Clarke as the main suspect?"

Jamie sighed. "He has a god complex. Maybe he didn't want Clarke to get the recognition he believes he deserves. I don't know."

"For years he stalked Emily, but abducted her when she was about to leave the country, again. He kept her, fed her, bathed her, but didn't kill her. Then he followed her here. He's patient, meticulous and has spent years perfecting his M.O." Luke stood and paced the length of the living room. "Have you received the results from the analysis of Noa's multivitamin?"

"Yes. He replaced the contents of the capsules with Dormicum. There is no way of knowing how long he has been doing this, but each pill in the bottle tested positive."

Luke stopped pacing and leaned against the opposite wall. "Okay, so he has been doing who knows what to her for who knows how long. Again, he didn't play his hand. Now he has started killing, but there's not much of a cooling-off period between kills. He holds more than one woman captive at the same time."

Jamie nodded. "We need to look for similar unsolved cases in the area. I asked Detective Davidson to review open cases in Marcel, but I haven't heard back from him."

Noa cleared her throat. "You need to review my mother's murder."

"Your mother's, why?"

"She was bludgeoned to death. Of course, I didn't see any photos of the scene, but I can't help to wonder if he's responsible." Noa shrugged. "She was murdered shortly after my rescue, while I was still in hospital. Perhaps the investigating officer didn't connect the two. Her being bludgeoned fits with your victims. Wouldn't a gang-banger have shot her or stabbed her in order to send a message? To bludgeon a person to death … seems personal to me."

"He destroys their faces, their identities," Luke said.

Jamie rested her hands on her stomach. "Because they don't

look like Emily even after he dyes their hair."

"All three were abducted after a night out with friends. I was abducted after I played a gig for a friend. I stepped outside the club for a cigarette and …" Noa slammed her hands on the wooden floor. "Bam. Goodbye Emily. Did any of the victims smoke?" she asked Jamie.

"Not as far as I know. They might've been social smokers."

"Social smokers always smoke with a friend. I averaged a packet or two a day back then. He hated it. I asked him for a cigarette once, after he had asked me what he could do for me. The bastard laced it with something because it made me sick."

"I'll have someone dig even deeper into our victims' lives."

Noa rose. "How are you getting test results back so fast? Doesn't it take a couple of days for DNA and toxicology?"

"The evidence is being processed by a private facility."

"Who is paying for it?" Noa asked.

"The private laboratory is analysing the evidence free of charge. We figured the suspect wouldn't be paying for us to track him down faster, so I haven't given it much thought as Captain Johnson is handling the arrangements. I suspected it might be my parents or Luke. All communication has been going through their lawyer, and from the first contact, they were explicit in covering the costs in regard to evidence related to your case. We contacted the lawyer once we linked the murders, and he reiterated that they'd process whatever we send them. Even if we're unsure it relates to your case."

"It's not me, and not Mom and Dad. I agree with you. He isn't behind this." Luke looked at Noa. "Who?"

"There's one person I know who has the resources." Noa closed her eyes and shook her head in disbelief. "My father."

Saturday, 26 June, 10:00 p.m.

Madison walked off the stage, adrenaline pulsing through her veins. Nothing came close to the rush of performing in front of such a large crowd. The people went wild for her band's new song. Noa had sent her the sheet music earlier in the day and the band had only rehearsed it once. It was so close to Slay's original music, it might have been written by their founding member. Maddie wondered why Noa no longer performed.

"You were fantastic tonight. I think this was your best performance yet."

Madison glanced up at the man whose hand was splayed against her lower back. The intensity in his eyes made her heart skip a beat. She smiled up at him, admiring his handsome face.

"Thank you." She tucked a strand of hair behind her ear.

He removed the hair from behind Madison's ear. "It looks better this way. More rock star, less student."

Madison's eyebrow raised. "How do you know I'm a student?"

"Lucky guess. This club is close to campus, and I've seen you perform before. That new song you played tonight … your voice is perfection. Did you write it?"

"No, my brother's girlfriend wrote it. I wish she was here tonight."

"I'm glad she isn't because I'm going to buy you a drink and I want to know everything about you. Come, join me."

Madison drifted on his every word, his voice intoxicating. "Okay."

Placing a hand at the small of her back he steered her towards an empty table at the back of the club. Madison rubbed her arms as she lowered herself into the chair the stranger pulled out for her.

"Are you cold?"

"No," she lied, grateful the man couldn't see the goosebumps on her arms.

"Let me guess, whiskey on the rocks?"

"How did you know?" She smiled.

He moved his chair closer to hers. "A sexy, bad-ass, rocker like you won't drink a fruity girly drink. It goes against the leather pants you're wearing."

He reached for his pants pocket, withdrew his phone, checked the screen and switched it off. "No more disturbances. I need to know everything about the most beautiful woman in wine country. What's your name?"

"Madison Taylor. Nice to meet you." She stuck her hand out towards the stranger and as he took her hand in his, electricity pulsed through her.

His thumb brushed against her skin; the left corner of his mouth quirked up. "Pleasure to meet you, Maddie. Please call me Rick."

Chapter 36

Luke's fists slammed on the coffee table. "He told you to kill yourself? What kind of person tells his own child to commit suicide?"

"If you allowed me to finish – it was his idea for me to become Noa Morgan."

Jamie settled back on the couch and removed her phone from her pocket. "Let me see if I have the facts straight. He helped you to fake your own death? And he helped you to obtain all the documentation needed to become Noa?"

"Yes. Like I said, he came to visit me in hospital and said if I wanted to start a new life, he'd help me."

Luke rubbed his forehead. "Well, it was the least he could do after abandoning you while your mother was pregnant."

"Things weren't quite as simple, but yes. I didn't take him up on the offer, not at first. After months of the police not being able to identify any viable suspects or make an arrest, I contacted him. It's ironic, I am who I am today because of Richard Davenport. How many children can talk about their fathers with affection?" Noa smirked.

"Hold on, your sessions with Clarke were paid for by a shell corporation." Jamie paged through the file. "I remember seeing the name Richard Davenport and here it is. He's listed as the director of said corporation."

"That can't be right. Clarke saw me free of charge for his research." Noa placed her hands on her hips.

179

Luke couldn't help but remember a younger Noa in an Amazonian outfit. Her stance mirrored that of a certain fictional princess. He stared at his woman in wonder.

Noa caught him gawking. "What?"

"Nothing, you just reminded me of someone. Do you still have the outfit you wore in the video?"

"Luke. I need you to think with your other head right now." Jamie's fist struck his leg.

Noa shook her head, walking over to Luke. She ran her fingers through his hair. "I'm going to have my hands full with you."

"You already do. Remember?" Luke's teeth sunk into his bottom lip.

"Enough, both of you. Let's finish up here so I can leave and get some sleep. You can do whatever it is you do *after* I've left. Enough with the verbal foreplay."

Jamie touched her stomach and noticed Luke watching.

"What did his note to you say?" Luke asked. "Noa told me about hers but refused to tell me about yours."

Noa shrugged. "Your call, Detective."

Jamie's gaze fell to her hands cradling her stomach. "You can't protect them all. Not even the one you carry. Give me my Emily. She's mine."

"You're pregnant?" Luke's face lit up.

"Yes. We haven't told anyone yet, as it's still very early."

Luke lowered his head to Jamie's stomach. "Hey baby, this is your Uncle Luke. I'm going to keep you and your mommy safe. You just hang around or do whatever it is you're doing and keep growing." He laid a hand on Jamie's stomach and kissed her cheek. "I won't let him hurt any of you. Your behaviour this past week makes perfect sense now. Your constant exhaustion, and the fact that you cried this morning. James doesn't cry in front of people. I should've known."

Luke looked at Noa and caught her wiping her eyes. "Thank you for keeping my sister's secret even from me. So much for us not having secrets." He smiled.

"This is her news to share and doesn't affect you and me."

"I'm teasing you. Again. But you're wrong. This affects all of us. We're going to have a baby in the family. Jamie, we need to find him and end this. For now, go home and sleep. Send me everything you have from today's crime scene. I don't care what Johnson said, I'm helping you. No one threatens my sister, or the life of my unborn niece or nephew."

Luke wrapped Jamie in his coat as he walked her out. This was one of the best days of his life. Noa had moved in and another family member was growing inside Jamie.

As Luke held Jamie's door open, she turned to him. "Does Noa know you replied to the email?"

"No."

"So much for the two of you not having secrets. Tell her Luke. Noa deserves to know that you've put yourself front and centre in his crosshairs."

Sunday, 27 June, 5:31 a.m.

After Jamie had left the previous night, Noa and Luke spoke about the facts surrounding her conception. Noa didn't believe her father was involved; Luke disagreed. They had gone to bed and slept. Not at all what Noa had envisioned or planned for their first night living together.

Noa made her way downstairs in search of Luke and found him on the couch. He watched her intently as she entered the room. "Luke, I'm sorry. I shouldn't have gotten upset with you last night. You made some valid points."

Luke held his hand out and pulled Noa into his arms as she took it. "I just want this to be over for you, Jamie and all of us. I might've looked at the information more as an investigating detective than I should've. How can I make it up to you?"

Noa rubbed her face against Luke's chest, his scent and warmth enveloping her. "Don't let me wake up alone again, not after the dream I had."

Luke ran his hand over her thigh, and she melted into him. "What dream?" His voice was husky.

"I can't tell you."

"No secrets, remember?"

"Tell me yours first. You're keeping something from me. Out with it, Taylor."

Luke eased away from her, went to the kitchen and returned with two mugs.

"If you make me coffee every morning, I'll love you forever." Noa pursed her lips.

Luke cupped her face and brought her mouth to his. Against her mouth he whispered, "I'm going to do so much more for, and to you, than make you coffee every morning. Show me what you dreamt." He kissed Noa, easing her down onto the couch.

Luke's fingers skimmed up Noa's stomach and found her breast. He looked down at her and smiled. "See, even your boobs are the perfect fit for my hands. I wonder about my mouth." He ran his tongue over her nipple and Noa arched against him. She dug her hands into his hair and brought his mouth back to hers.

"What's wrong?" he asked.

"I'm scared." Noa closed her eyes. "I want you so much but I don't know how to do this. Just being under you is confusing."

Luke eased up, pulled her shirt down and moved away from her. "Okay, talk to me." He reached for mug on the coffee table.

Noa pushed herself up and covered her face with her hands. "What if I can't do it? I don't know what he did to me. Maybe I have subconscious triggers. Luke, what if he broke me and I won't be enough for you? What if you regret asking me to move in because we can't have sex? I don't want you to regret us." She failed to control the shaking of her shoulders.

Luke pulled Noa closer, pressing his face to her hair while handing her the mug. "I will never regret us. I'm so in love with you. Now I understand why people write songs and poems about it. You will never be broken in my eyes. When I look at you, I see nothing but strength and resilience. I'm sorry for pushing you. It's the last thing I want to do. But dammit, Noa, look at everything you are. How can I not want you? Especially when that tank top leaves so little to my imagination. I can and will wait for you to be ready. So what if there are triggers we don't know about? We will get through it together."

"I'm sorry." Noa pressed her lips to the stubble on his neck. "You deserve better."

"Maybe there is another way for us to do this, but we just haven't thought about it. And don't you ever say I deserve better. You're all I need. Okay, so to get my blood back up north I'll tell you my secret."

Noa sipped the still hot coffee.

"I sent a reply to the email address he used to send the link to the video."

Noa choked on the coffee. Luke patted her back and continued, "I called him out and thanked him for destroying Emily, because if he hadn't, I would never have found *my* Noa. I thanked him for the video. Now I know women, like good wine, get better with age. And more flexible."

"You poked the monster, Luke. He won't take kindly to you calling me yours."

"Well, it's a good thing he isn't the first monster I've encountered or slayed."

Noa handed the mug to Luke. "Speaking of Slay, I wonder when Maddie will realise I founded the band?"

Chapter 37

Sunday, 27 June

Emily,
There is something to be said for the stamina and agility of twenty-something-year-old women. Not to mention their insecurities and constant need to please. And the effort they put in to coming across as more experienced than they are.

She is so much like you.

Of all the women I have had since you, she could truly pass as your doppelganger. From the way she flirts, to the way she undresses, and the incredible things she does with her mouth. Best part? I don't even need to change her hair colour.

For the first time, I'm not bereft with guilt – ah, just a little joke. In the past I felt I wronged you when I had been with another woman, but looking at her lying next to me, I want her.

This one I want to keep for myself. I want to teach her the things I tried to teach you. Thus far she has been far more accommodating to my requests. I didn't even need to ask her to say it. She is more Emily than you have been in years.

She bares herself to me and in her eyes, I see the same adoration – hero worship if you will – yours held when we first met.

Emily, her taste gives me pleasure I haven't known since our first night. After years of searching for this, for her, I did far better than I did with you.

Thank you for forcing me to find her.
I'm going to enjoy having both of you.
Both of you are mine.
Forever.

Chapter 38

Sunday, 27 June, 8:15 a.m.

Madison's back arched off the mattress. Her fingers dug into his scalp. This was how she had awakened and damn if she didn't feel more awake than she ever had before in her life. No other man had satisfied her as he did. Therein laid her answer; Madison had never been with a *man* before Rick. He hadn't told her his age, but the fine lines on his handsome face set him apart from the inexperienced young men she'd wasted her time with.

She reached for Rick and rolled him onto his back. Madison eased herself over his body, taking him inside her in a fluid motion she knew he liked.

"Good morning," she said as Rick ran his hands down her back, and dropped her mouth to his. "Lay still, I want you to feel what you just made me."

Rick yanked her hair back and bit her exposed throat. "Let's see what you've got inside you. Other than me."

Sunday, 27 June, 12:05 p.m.

Officer Sheridan paced across her living room. "Where the hell are you?" she asked the phone laying on the coffee table. At the sound of her ringtone, Kori jumped and snatched it up. "Where are you? I've been trying to get hold of you since last night. I'm worried about you."

"Now, now, my pet, you knew I was tending to business. I don't answer my phone when I'm with you, so why wouldn't I show the same courtesy to my client?"

She sighed and fought to stop the tremble in her hand. Rick wasn't her ex; he wouldn't cheat.

"Oh pet, why are you so pouty this morning? Tell me so I can make it all better."

"I was removed from the case last night. That bitch Edwards had me removed. This was going to be my chance to prove myself."

"Don't let this be a defining moment for you. Life is full of them, and I know what you're capable of."

"There's only one thing that will make me feel better now and it involves you being naked. When can I see you?"

"Stop touching yourself, only I'm allowed to do that."

"You're not here to ... wait. You can see me?" Kori rushed to the window overlooking her front garden.

"I don't need to see you to know your sounds, my pet. You're an open book to me. Go look outside on your porch."

On her welcome mat she found an unmarked brown box.

"Open it. I like your hair down."

Kori yanked her head up and scanned the street, adrenaline coursing through her. "Where are you?"

"Go back inside. Open the box and put it on. When you're done, come back to the window with the other item in the box. I will tell you what to do next."

She grabbed the box and rushed back into the house. Kori ripped it open and found a few interesting things inside. "You even got the right size. I love it."

"Stop talking. Change into it, and remember to bring the other gift back to the window. Hurry, I want you in front of the window. Now."

She obeyed and then rushed to the window wearing one of her gifts. "Can you see me?"

He laughed. "Yes, my pet. Now, put it in your mouth."

"I want you in my mouth." Kori licked the tip of the item.

he'd given her. This man and his games would be the end of her. Who knew she had a kinky side? Kori wouldn't make the same mistake with Rick that she had with her ex.

"Stop talking. Do as I say or I'm not coming in."

The last thing Kori Sheridan ever did – stick a pink dildo in her mouth.

Sunday, 27 June, 1:45 p.m.

Remnants of the front window lay scattered across the oriental rug. A crimson pool surrounded the victim's head. She wore nothing but lingerie. The thing of Jamie's nightmares protruded from the deceased's mouth.

"I guess you never truly know someone," Doctor Burger said, squatting down next to the body.

Jamie's head moved up and down. "No, I guess you don't. I wonder how he got to her."

One of the crime scene investigators called Jamie over and showed her the call history on Officer Sheridan's phone. "He was on the phone with her when he killed her. Sonofabitch. We need to put a trace on the number. Now."

A junior officer called it in while Jamie walked out to the porch, scanning up and down the residential street.

Next to her, Doctor Burger cleared his throat. "You're going to ask, so I may as well tell you. It was a high-powered rifle. They're busy extracting the bullet from the wall. I'll send the dildo to the independent lab, but from the looks of it, it's your guy. Scary how familiar I am with the length and girth of another man's penis."

Jamie winced.

"What was it?"

"Girth." Jamie and Doctor Burger shared a knowing look. This wasn't the time to laugh. "He sat in his car and shot her without even looking Kori in the eye. Why?"

The same junior officer came up behind Jamie and patted

her shoulder. "Sorry Detective, but I scanned Officer Sheridan's call history for the same number as the last one. The first time she received a call from this number was on Monday."

"Sheridan was the first officer on the scene after our victim's car accident. He was there. I wonder if she fed him information. It would explain a lot."

"Kori was in a vulnerable place after her husband left. She would've been easy prey for him."

"I don't care if Sheridan found out she was dying. There's no excuse for sharing confidential information on an ongoing case with someone outside of law enforcement. May she rest in peace," Jamie said, bowing her head. She wondered if sharing information with Luke could put him in even more danger.

Burger nudged Jamie's arm. Across the street, an elderly neighbour waved at them. Jamie walked over to the old woman, sighing internally. It wouldn't be the first time Jamie got called from a crime scene by a nosey neighbour who had no value to add to the investigation. Next to the front gate Jamie noticed a blanket, a small shovel and gloves.

"Good afternoon, I'm Detective Edwards. Did you place the emergency call?"

"Yes. I saw him kill her."

"Mrs?"

"Eastwood. Flora Eastwood."

"Can you please talk me through what you saw, Mrs Eastwood? We can talk inside if you prefer."

"It's such a lovely day today, but I don't want to see Kori's body in one of those black bags. She was such a lovely young lady and having a police officer living across the road made me feel safer."

Jamie frowned.

"I watch a lot of television, mostly crime series. Don't think I'll be able to stomach it again."

Jamie followed Flora inside her house and declined her offer of a glass of water.

As Flora recounted what she had witnessed before the

shooting, Jamie made notes in her notepad. "Have you seen this car before?"

"Yes, I noticed it for the first time on Monday night. And it was still parked in her driveway when I left for my doctor's appointment on Tuesday morning, which must've been around eight."

"Thank you, Mrs Eastwood. If you remember anything else here is my contact details." Jamie handed her a card as she stood up to leave.

Once Jamie reached her car, she called Luke.

Sunday, 27 June, 5:30 p.m.

Noa placed more logs on the fire and went back to the kitchen to check on dinner. A few hours earlier, Luke had received a call and left, after ensuring Noa had her gun on her.

For the first time since Tuesday morning, she'd found herself alone. It gave Noa the freedom to scream, cry, and pound away more of the wall separating the kitchen and the dining room. King ran outside the instant the sound of metal against plaster and brick began to echo through the house. Covered in sweat and dust Noa sank to the floor. Since waking up she hadn't stopped thinking about Luke and how deeply she was falling in love with him. Making love with Luke would be the ultimate victory over the clown demon. Yet, so much more.

The front door opened, followed by the sound of King's nails on the hardwood floor. Noa poured two glasses of wine.

Luke found her in the kitchen and wrapped his arms around her. He brushed Noa's hair from her neck and pressed his lips to the exposed skin. Warmth spread to every part of her. How could Luke make her feel so much joy with the slightest touch?

"I need to go shower and then we need to talk," Luke said.

Noa nodded, stroking Luke's clothed arms around her waist. *Too many layers of clothes.*

Luke kissed Noa's temple, and she smiled at the tickle of his beard against her face.

"Luke, I'm—"

"I need to go shower and it smells like the food is burning. I promise we'll talk as soon as I'm done."

He left her standing alone in front of the stove. Noa listened to Luke walking up the stairs and down the upstairs hall.

I'm done talking. Done wondering. I love you and I need to tell you. No, it's time I show you.

Noa switched off the stove and marched up the stairs, leaving clothes in her wake.

Sunday, 27 June, 5:45 p.m.

This girl he could love as much as he loved Emily. An afternoon of allowing him to do the most amazing things to her had left him yearning for more. More of her. More of Emily. *Fine wine*, Luke had called her.

Madison finished her meal, and he wondered how it would be to have Emily again. No man who'd tasted Emily would take the time to reply to an email. Luke Taylor was a liar. Poetic justice, he had thought while savouring Madison's taste.

Killing the shrill Kori had left him hungry for Madison. He called her as he'd driven away from Kori's house and asked Madison to join him at his hotel room. The moment she'd stepped through the door he did all the things he had thought about during his drive back to Shadow Bay.

He wondered what Madison would say if she knew he was going to kill her brother.

There was only one way to kill Luke Taylor and killing Kori reminded him of how capable he was. Bat or rifle, it didn't matter. Any weapon was nothing more than a means to an end.

Chapter 39

Water cascaded down his chiselled back. Noa had only seen perfectly symmetrical bodies in photos of pro-athletes in textbooks. *How many demons did you fight?* Luke's body was perfect; from the scars to the freckles dotted across his back and shoulders. The sight of him hunched over, hands splayed against the tiles, made Noa's heart thunder.

She took one step forward, into the shower.

Noa pressed her body against his and reached around him, finding him aroused. Taking a deep breath Noa closed her eyes against the spray of the water, and to the memories of horror.

Fear no longer had a hold on her. Not with Luke. In nine days, they had lived a lifetime.

"I'm done thinking, done living in fear and giving him power over us. I'm done talking." She released her hold on him, pushing her hands up his stomach, up to his pecks and shoulders. Noa eased him upright and trailed his arms with her fingertips, pressing her mouth to his wet back.

"We need to talk," Luke said in a low voice, making Noa ache for him.

"Weren't you listening? I'm *done* talking. Please, look at me." Noa licked the water running down his back.

Luke leaned forward, bracing himself against the wall, his legs shaking. Noa traced his length with her fingers, pressing her mouth to his back over and over.

"I can't look at you. I want to be inside you too much."

191

Luke shuddered when Noa gripped him with both hands.

Her hands stopped moving, but Noa didn't release her hold. "You've been inside me since we met. In my head, my heart, my past, my present and you have given me a future. Now, I *need* you inside me. I want to show you what you've done for me. Please." The last word was said on a whisper.

"I don't know how to do this without the risk of hurting you. I don't think I can take it slow."

"I don't care what you do. Luke, I need you, to show you." Digging her nails into his side, Noa pressed her body against his.

"Give me a minute. This has to be perfect for you." Without glancing in her direction, Luke stepped out of the shower. "Dry off."

Sunday, 27 June, 6:05 p.m.

Luke lay on his back, his arms extended towards the headboard. Desperate to control her breathing and the violent beating of her heart, Noa bit her lip. *I want him, for me, for us.*

"Why the cuffs?" she asked, closing the bathroom door behind her.

"I don't trust myself to take it slow. And I don't know what you're comfortable with me doing. This way, you're in full control of whatever happens."

Noa's breath caught in her throat as she realised what Luke was doing; always putting her needs above his own. "I'm in love with you Luke – not Lucas – Taylor. I love you with every part of me, and I will love you more every day we are together. Even in death, I'll still love you."

Grabbing the poles of the headboard, Luke pulled himself into a seated position. "You waited until I'm unable to touch you to tell me you love me?"

"It's not like I planned it." Noa stepped closer to the bed.

"I want to kiss you." His smile matched hers. Luke kept his

eyes on Noa as she reached for the key on the bedside table.

Noa bit the inside of her cheek. Now wasn't the time to ask when or why Luke had handcuffs. She climbed onto the bed, swung her leg over his body, straddling him. Without breaking eye contact, Noa tossed her towel on the floor.

Luke kept looking at her face as she bent forward, brushing her mouth against his. With her chest pressed against him she unlocked the handcuffs. "Let me show you."

Luke whispered against her lips, "What do you want?"

"You."

Luke took possession of her mouth, hard, unrelenting and rolled Noa onto her back.

She stared up at him. Both of them breathing erratically, but her heart wasn't racing from fear. In his eyes Noa saw reverence as Luke took his time gazing at every part of her. She squeezed her thighs, desperate for his touch.

"You have no idea how beautiful you are, *my* Noa." With his mouth on hers, Luke's hands explored. Her breasts, stomach, down to the part of her he had not yet touched. She arched her back as he slid a finger inside her. Noa plucked the towel from around his waist, tossing it aside, not caring where it fell. She reached for him.

"No, wait, if you touch me again it will be over. This is about you. Tell me what I'm allowed to do." Luke grazed Noa's bottom lip with his teeth.

Noa took a deep breath and exhaled with a smile. "What do you want to do?"

His eyes flashed. "Noa, I want to know how you taste."

Yes. Please. "Mr Taylor, anything you do to me will be done to you." Noa brushed her lips against his grinning mouth.

The last thing Noa saw was his captivating smile as Luke buried his face between her legs. With every lick of his tongue, kiss, nip of his teeth to her most sensitive part, she became lighter. Freer. As the orgasm crashed through her, Noa grabbed at the sheets and pulled them with her as her back lifted from the bed.

Luke kissed his way up her body and tasting herself on his tongue made her ache for him to do it again. Noa reached between them, wrapping her fingers around him.

"Wait, I need to get a condom." Luke tried to pull away; Noa wrapped her legs around his waist.

"No. I can't stand the sight of it. *Please*. Besides I'm on the pill; we're good."

Their bodies became one. Their mouths were hungry against each other's, their gazes locked. As he filled, her Noa's soul became full. Digging her fingers into Luke's shoulders, she met him thrust for thrust. She swivelled her hips to get more of him, to be closer to him. His release followed. The shudder of his body rippled through her.

Luke rolled off her, still holding her to his chest, their bodies joined. For a long time they simply held each other.

Luke kissed her forehead, skimming his hands down her back. "And I thought the other morning was big. This is … I don't have words."

"No words needed. I feel it too."

Chapter 40

Sunday, 27 June, 6:28 p.m.

Jamie dropped her phone on the bed just as her father tapped rhythmically on the bedroom door.

"What's wrong, honey?" Aaron eased the door open and leaned against the doorframe.

Jamie placed both hands on her stomach. "How could he know about his own child and make no attempt to contact her or be a part of her life? He claims he had loved her mother, but the strangest thing is, neither of her parents ever married or had more children. Emily simply existed, and neither of them cared about her existence. If that makes any sense."

"Not everyone who has a child deserves a child. One of the saddest facts about this world. Who were you talking to?"

"Emily's father. He acknowledged making his laboratory in Shadow Bay available to process all the evidence. Pro bono."

Aaron crossed his arms over his chest. "How did he even know Noa's in trouble?"

"That's the kicker – he received a call from Benjamin Clarke hours before Noa's last appointment with him. Clarke voiced his suspicion that the abductor tracked Noa down and claimed he was concerned about her safety. Of course, her father was in a symposium and let the call go to voicemail. By the time he returned the call, Clarke's phone was switched off."

"Did Clarke perhaps give him any specifics which might help you?"

"No. Just said he had his suspicions. After Richard Davenport – that's Noa's father – couldn't reach Clarke, he contacted a private investigator to look into Noa's wellbeing. The PI learned about what had happened to Noa from none other than Kori Sheridan. I swear if she wasn't dead, I'd strangle her. Heaven knows what she told the killer, Emily's stalker, her abductor. I'm not sure what to call him. He's all over the place." Jamie pushed her fingers through her hair and sighed.

Aaron gave her a knowing smile. "Why don't you come down for dinner? I need a break from your mother and Spencer's wine talk. After dinner you get straight into bed. You and the baby need the rest."

Jamie didn't blink.

"Don't be so surprised. Your mom and I put two and two together on Saturday night when you cried."

"Does everyone really see me as some robot?"

"No, not at all. You've never cried easily, even less so in front of others. And we've noticed you often touch your stomach. Your mom did the same when she was pregnant with you." Aaron closed the distance between them and wrapped his arms around his daughter. "We are both happier than you can even imagine. Our family is getting bigger by the day, and we're thrilled."

Jamie couldn't make sense of a parent choosing not be in their child's life. "Was it difficult for you to accept Luke as your son?"

Aaron rested his chin on Jamie's head. "No. I never saw Luke as anything other than my son. He needed us and we were happy to bring him into our home. I know it was rough on you, but look at the relationship the two of you have built over the years."

Jamie was grateful her father didn't say anything about the years she and Luke had rarely spoken. "Well, I'm waiting for your son to phone me. I need to talk to Noa, and Luke's been home for hours."

She showed Aaron the live feed of the motion detection cameras on the properties, and the exact time Luke had driven up to his house.

"I don't think he installed it so that you can spy on him," Aaron said with a smirk.

"Well, Dad, then he shouldn't have given me access. I'm in the middle of the biggest investigation of my career. And my friend – his girlfriend – happens to be the key to all of this."

Aaron shrugged. "Maybe the two of them got side tracked. Do you remember how it was in the beginning for you and Spencer? I considered using a crowbar to separate the two of you."

"There's no time for anyone to get side tracked. A police officer was killed in broad daylight. So far, we've found the bodies of three victims. He's escalating. I'm worried about what he will do next."

"You will catch him, Jamie. I know what my daughter is capable of."

"Was it hard for you when you retired?"

"Yes and no. I loved being a detective, making a difference, but when it's time to get out, you know."

Jamie nodded and rubbed her belly.

"Honey, if you decide to resign, we will all support you. There are other ways to make a difference in the world. So, hunt this sonofabitch down so that you can decide what you want for the future of your family and yourself."

Sunday, 27 June, 6:54 p.m.

Careful not to disturb the warm body sprawled over him, Luke reached for his phone. "James?" he whispered.

"Why are you whispering?"

"Noa's asleep." He rested his cheek against Noa's damp hair.

"Then leave the room. We need to talk."

"I can't." He grinned.

"Dammit, Luke, you haven't spoken to her, have you? And why can't you move?" Jamie cursed. "You two had sex."

"It's more pleasurable when two people are involved."

"Wake Noa up and get dressed. I'll be there in five." Jamie ended the call.

Luke held onto Noa. He wasn't ready to pull her, or himself, back into reality. Not when reality held a killer hell-bent on taking her from him. Noa's soft skin was warm under his fingertips. She shivered as Luke traced the length of her spine.

"Do it again," Noa murmured against his chest.

"This?" Luke brushed the back of his fingers down her back.

"No, what you did to send me into bliss."

He hugged her closer and remembered the second time they had made love. Luke had never seen anything more beautiful than Noa reaching climax. He wanted her on top of him again. *Dammit.* "Detective cock-blocker is on her way."

Noa burst out laughing and rolled onto her back.

Luke took a moment to simply admire her, from the sound of her laugh to the perfect body he would never again allow her to hide under clothes when they were home. "I told you earlier we need to talk."

"Say that again and you'll carry the consequences of what I'll do to you, as soon as I can walk." Noa reached for his face and rubbed her palm over his beard. "You're so pretty, Taylor."

Luke pressed his mouth to hers. *Dammit.* "Detective Edwards is on her way, and she doesn't need to see either of us like this. You know what we should've done? Made our own video and sent it to him."

Noa sighed, pressing her palms against Luke's chest. As she swung her legs to the floor, Noa looked back at him. "That's some way to spoil the moment, dude."

"Dude?"

"I miss Maddie. I'm worried about her being on her own in Shadow Bay. The last victim was abducted there. Wish she could stay at home until this is over."

"She won't, but I know Jamie gave her a proper talking to. Maddie is young, but she knows how to take care of herself.

Who do you think got Jamie into kickboxing?"

They both got dressed and raced downstairs after the third time Jamie rang the doorbell.

King rushed past Luke's legs as Luke opened the front door. He disappeared into the darkness.

Sunday, 27 June, 6:59 p.m.

Jamie took a seat at the dining room table. "Can you wipe those ridiculous, post-coital smiles from your faces?"

Still smiling, Luke and Noa glanced at each other. Luke pushed Noa's hair from her face. "I'm sorry, but we really should talk now." Luke pulled out a chair for her and took the seat next to it, threading his fingers through Noa's under the table.

"I spoke to your father," Jamie said.

"Why? He has nothing to do with this." Noa rubbed her free hand against her thigh.

"I needed to know why he's making his resources available, considering you've only met him once. He wants to see you."

"He's been a non-entity my entire life. Why change it now?" Noa kept rubbing her thigh.

"Because he's worried about you. Clarke phoned him after each of your sessions to update him on your progress. He paid for your sessions."

"I don't want to see him. Maybe I'll send him a fruit basket to thank him for his lab processing evidence after the clown demon has been convicted."

"Why do you keep referring to him as 'clown demon'?" Luke asked.

Noa tied her hair in a high ponytail. "Clown demon. Demon clown. Same shit. Same horrific colour."

Luke and Jamie gazed at her with quizzical stares.

"He always wore an evil clown mask while he had me in that cabin. I've already told you this."

"I know and trying to find out where he bought it is pointless." Jamie leaned forward, resting her elbows on the table.

Noa's brow furrowed. "Why are you asking about the mask?"

"He wore it to Koffee, and also while delivering a parcel to Officer Sheridan's house."

Noa stood and walked to the window.

"Get away from the window." Luke jumped to his feet and yanked the curtains closed. Noa stared at him in shock. "A lot has happened over the past few days. We believe Officer Sheridan was involved with him. Earlier today he killed her, shooting her through the front window of her house."

"He killed a police officer?" Noa stepped back, placing a hand to her forehead. "In broad daylight? While she was inside her home?"

Jamie nodded. "We found evidence indicating they were in some kind of relationship. At the time of her death, Officer Sheridan was wearing designer lingerie and a pink dildo was found at the scene." Noa turned to Jamie. "Before you ask, yes, I reviewed your mother's case. I'm sorry. It appears he might've murdered her. She was wearing the same pink lingerie we found on Kori Sheridan. Your mother's wounds are also consistent with what Doctor Burger found on our other three victims."

Noa sank to the floor, pulling her knees to her chest. Pained screams echoed through the house. She had never loved her mother, but to hear *he* was responsible tore Noa's soul apart.

Luke pulled Noa up and into his arms. "I'm sorry," he said.

After a few minutes Noa pushed away from Luke and took her seat at the table. "Tell me."

Jamie informed her of the footage they'd found on Officer Sheridan's dashcam. The video showed a hooded man stepping onto Kori's porch and as he walked back past her car half of a demon clown mask came into view. Why Officer Sheridan hadn't turned off her dashcam, was anyone's guess. Her ex-husband had made multiple threats towards her. The possibility existed she did it to capture him vandalising her house as Kori had suspected him of doing so before.

"Do you know anyone who drives a black BMW sedan?" Jamie asked.

"No, but isn't it a common car around here? It's the reason I chose a red Jeep – blend in even when standing out."

"Yes. Our eyewitness gave a basic description but couldn't see the licence plate from where she was hiding."

"Do you know anyone who hunts?" Luke asked.

"Just about everyone in Marcel. Especially during winter, when it's hunting season. Why did Officer Sheridan allow him into her life?"

Jamie shrugged. "We don't know yet, only that he first contacted her on Monday. We suspect he was at the scene of your accident. And we have reason to believe Kori told him sensitive information about the investigations. Not only yours, but also about our other three victims."

Noa pressed her palms to her eyes. "Linda Christie. Brie Doyle. Sarah Poe. Kori Sheridan. My mother. And of course, Benjamin Clarke. Not to mention the attempted murder of Kim. How is she?"

"We're keeping her in the hospital because of the twenty-four-seven security."

"Kim must be going out of her mind." Noa managed to give a faint smile.

"The staff are losing their minds. Our friend, on the other hand, is quite happy having people at her beck and call."

"Can't blame her when she has to serve people every day. Will Kim be okay after this, physically?"

Luke placed his hands on Noa's shoulders. "Matthew said the doctor is optimistic, but she'll require physical therapy."

"I'll work with her when she's ready. Fun fact – I'm a qualified Biokineticist." Turning her attention to Jamie, Noa asked, "May I contact the parents of the three women he murdered? I need to tell them how sorry I am that their daughters were sucked into his twisted game and have paid for it with their lives."

Luke exhaled hard. "Did you kill them?"

"No, but I have a part in all this. I'm not responsible for *what* he did; he chose to commit murder. But I still want to offer my condolences. It's the least I can do, and it will never be enough." *Not even Emily's death was enough to end it.*

Luke pressed his lips to the top of Noa's head. "You keep on amazing me."

Noa laid her hands over his, still protective and comforting on her shoulders. "Okay, you said he was at Koffee. Who did he hurt?"

Jamie glanced at Luke, shrugged and dropped her shaking head to her chest. Taking the chair next to Noa, Luke sat and turned to face her. "He left a note for you."

"Did someone see his face?"

"No, he wore the mask. Scared the caffeine out of the staff and customers. He strolled in and handed an envelope to the waiter closest to the door. Told him to ensure you get it. The waiter told Matthew, who then contacted me."

Noa rubbed her thighs. "Give it to me."

From inside one of Noa's boxes – still standing unpacked in the foyer – Luke retrieved a red envelope. Jamie handed Noa a pair of latex gloves. Reluctantly, Luke gave her the A4 envelope.

Noa studied the outside of it. "It's open."

"I—".

Jamie interrupted. "I asked Luke to look at it for me. Screw protocol."

Opening the envelope Noa peeked inside. On top of white rose petals, the red card was a stark contrast. Bile rose in Noa's throat. She forced herself to remove the card.

youremineemily@email.com
Password: 40days_mine

Noa returned the card with less care than she had taking it out. "Have either of you accessed this email account?"

Jamie shook her head. "We spoke about it but decided it's best if you see it first. As you know him and might pick up on something the rest of us might miss."

"I don't know him! Do you think, for even a second, I'd allow him to continue killing if I knew who he is?" Noa stormed out of the room.

Chapter 41

Sunday, 27 June

Emily,

By now you should have received my note and read some of the emails I drafted for you. For every excruciating day we have been apart, I wrote you an email. Don't you think there is something romantic about lovers taking the time to write a letter for each other? In our modern age, emails are the equivalent.

Oh, my love, how I wish I could gaze upon your beautiful face when you read of my undying love and devotion to you. Don't worry about what I said about her, I have enough love for both of you. In time, I know, you will both realise how much I love you. I will never favour one of you over the other, but she is special, Emily.

As I type this symbol of love, she is lying next to me. Her skin is youthful and smooth; sweet and delectable, just like she is. But you will see how wild she is once I push inside her, just as I know you will be. The biggest mistake of my life has been to deprive myself of the ecstasy I know I will feel once I'm inside you. Not that I haven't been in your mind, and your soul, since the day we met.

Please understand everything I have done, I did it all for you.

Would he kill for you?
Would he follow you to the ends of the earth? No, my love, only I will do whatever it takes to ensure we are together forever.

Soon you will be in my bed, as flushed as she is.

But first, I must remove the last obstacle in our way.

Chapter 42

Noa sat on the couch with her legs crossed, laptop balancing on her thighs. A muscle twitched in her jaw. Noa stared at the screen. A mixture of swear words erupted from her mouth.

Jamie and Luke turned to each other, staring wide-eyed. Neither of them had ever heard such a combination even from their police colleagues or criminals.

"Let's play. I *will* end you. Think you can scare me into submission? I'm going to use your dick to choke you and laugh as you gasp. Like you laughed when you put those fucking spiders on me."

Noa slammed the screen shut. "I have no idea who he is!" She placed the laptop on the coffee table next to a water bottle, making its contents vibrate. A strangled laugh escaped Noa's throat. "It looks like that scene in that dinosaur movie."

"You have quite a rich vocabulary for a woman."

Noa stared daggers at Luke. He lifted his hand into the air but didn't try to hide his smile. "Don't you start with me, Taylor. I've read the first few emails he drafted. He could be *anyone* from my past. Is this karmic justice for me being a little promiscuous in my youth?"

Jamie leaned her hip against the couch. "You know better than to victim blame. He could've fixated on you simply by seeing you walk down the street. You know this."

"But he isn't some random stranger. I've been intimate with him, as he recalls in great detail." Noa reached for the water bottle and sent it crashing into the opposite wall. It rolled out of sight. "I can't even respond." Pulling on her ponytail, clarity came. "I can! The email address he used to send Luke the video."

"No, you're not going to poke the demon clown." Luke stepped closer to the couch.

"Like hell I won't. You did." Luke's mouth opened; Noa cut him off. "But I'm some defenceless woman who can't protect myself against him. I'm not the ex-cop, larger than life, silver-bullets-and-wooden-stakes-can't-kill-me, hero you are."

Jamie walked up to Noa and grabbed her shoulders. "Good, you're angry. Direct your anger at him and not at the man who cares about you. The very man who will give his life to protect you. Cut the shit and focus."

"I'm sorry, Luke." Noa closed the distance between them and stood on tiptoes, pressing her lips to his jaw.

Jamie checked her phone. Throughout the time they'd spent talking, both Jamie and Luke's phones kept pinging alert tones.

"King setting off the cameras again?" Luke asked, removing the phone from the back pocket of his jeans.

Noa watched the colour drain from Jamie's face. Luke ran to the front door.

"Luke. Wait." Jamie called after her brother.

Sunday, 27 June, 9:15 p.m.

He crawled underneath the fence and positioned the rifle over his shoulder as he rose to his feet. *Who would've guessed I'd play soldier. Ah, love is war. Luke Taylor the enemy. King? Collateral damage, if he tries anything.*

Through the scope he watched King roam around the garden surrounding the house. A two-year-old puppy at heart, capable of ripping anyone's throat out. He wasn't taking any chances, not with King and not with the Neanderthal.

Animals, like humans, can be unpredictable.

The house came into view. He pressed the butt of the rifle into his shoulder and trained his sight on the figure as it moved closer to where he hid. A glimpse of a wagging tail made him lower the weapon.

"Good boy, King. Soon we will be together. You didn't think I'd leave you behind?" He reached out with one hand and scratched behind King's ear.

"King?" The muscle monkey called into the dark.

"Go on, distract him long enough for me to get a good shot. Tell her I love her."

Grinning, he tapped his palm against King's side. Through the scope he watched the first living thing Noa had ever loved run towards the house.

"King?"

On one knee, with his shoulder pressed against the oak tree, he raised the barrel. The muscle monkey rubbed King's back.

He focused on steadying his breathing as the object in the crosshairs came to his full length.

One day you'll thank me, Emily. He squeezed the trigger.

Sunday, 27 June, 9:18 p.m.

A shot cracked through the suffocating silence inside the house. Noa's heart pounded violently in her chest. "Luke?" She rushed towards the door.

Jamie grabbed her arm, but she yanked free. Noa's feet pounded over the porch. She pulled the gun from the holster at her side, aiming into the darkness. Noa stumbled down the stairs, running towards the form lying next to Jamie's car.

"Noa, get back inside!" Jamie ordered from behind her.

Noa hunkered down and belly crawled to where Luke was laying. With each movement forward, dirt mixed with the tears streaming down her face. King rushed to her side and nudged her with his head.

"Inside," Noa whispered and waited for him to obey.

Noa crawled the remaining distance. When she reached Luke Noa grabbed his face. "Please don't die. I love you. Please, Luke, I need you."

She pressed her mouth to his; a warm breath touched her skin.

"Kevlar," Luke managed to say with a groan.

"I'm getting you inside." Noa crouched low, balancing on the balls of her feet, gripped the Kevlar vest and pulled Luck towards the house.

"I'm coming to help." Jamie stepped onto the porch.

A shot bellowed through the darkness. Noa threw her body over Luke's.

Another shot followed.

"Jamie, stay where you are. I'll get him inside."

A less distressing sound filled the air. "Now isn't the time to take a call," Noa said next to Luke's ear.

Ignoring her, Luke removed his phone and answered. "Did you get him?"

"He got away, but Greg managed to put a bullet in him and one in his car. Tell Jamie to get her people out here." Noa recognized Matthew's voice. "Are *you* okay?"

"Yes, will be as soon as Noa allows me to stand up and get this vest off, to ensure the bullet didn't go through." Luke's breathing was shallow and filled with pain.

In a frenzie Noa clawed at Luke's leather jacket.

Luke reached for both her hands. "I'm okay." He smiled. "Who said you're not a hero?"

Noa gave a shaky laugh, yanked her hands from his and tried to unzip the jacket with trembling hands. *He's alive.*

Jamie rushed down the stairs and helped Noa to get Luke inside the house. He didn't need their help, but they insisted, flanking him on both sides.

Luke winced, easing out of his jacket. "My turn to have a nasty bruise."

"Paramedics and police are ten minutes out. I'll get you ice for your chest." Jamie jogged to the kitchen.

Noa helped him remove the vest; the mangled bullet held her attention. Luke placed his palm against her cheek. "I'm okay. I was prepared for this."

Wiping moisture from her face, Noa lifted her eyes to his. "I wasn't. I watched you put on the vest. Heard you talk to Matthew before walking out the door. Heard the shot. Saw you go down and stay down. I couldn't breathe."

"You're my hero, Noa Morgan." Luke pulled her close and smiled.

Chapter 43

Sunday, 27 June, 9:47 p.m.

Pain radiated from his side. He pressed his palm to the spot, trying his best to keep the car on the road with his other hand. "Shit."

On the back seat lay an unmoving form. "I'm sorry, my love. I should've left you where you would've been safe. If that sonofabitch shot you, I would've bashed his skull in."

He winced as he drove over a pothole and stared down at the warm fluid seeping through his fingers. "Shit."

Up ahead, a dirt road turned off the main road heading north towards the foot of the mountain. He eased his foot off the accelerator.

"We'll be home soon. I need to make a call; this wound won't heal by itself."

He drove towards the house and parked inside the garage. Switching on the interior light, he removed his phone and snapped a photo of the woman lying on the back seat. Only one person would come.

Dragging the woman into the house, he whispered, "I'm sorry I killed your brother. In time you'll realise it was the price you had to pay for us to be together. Now we only need Emily and then our family will be complete."

He eased her down on the couch, covered her with a blanket and pressed his lips to her forehead. Until his guest arrived he'd make do with the first aid kit hidden in the kitchen.

The woman stirred; her eyes remained closed.

"You, *we*, will be happy here. Welcome home, my love. My beautiful and delicious, Maddie."

Monday, 28 June, 00:18 a.m.

Who are you? Noa wondered what it said about her that she had attracted the attention of a psychopath, one who thought her to be as much a monster as he was.

The second last unsent email he'd written forced Noa to breathe through her nose, willing the nausea away. Her nails dug into the leather of the lazy-boy chair. "Shit," Noa whispered into the darkness.

A sound came from the bed. The duvet rustled. Luke switched on the bedside lamp.

"What's wrong?" Luke rubbed his eyes, squinting at the bright light.

Noa welcomed the yellow glow after spending almost two hours facing the glare of the laptop screen.

Luke eased himself up against the pillows, the bruise on his chest darker than before. If he hadn't worn the Kevlar vest …

If the shooter had used a higher calibre bullet …

If only Noa had never met the devil.

"Why aren't you asleep?" Luke reached for the bottle of water next to him.

Noa waited for him to return the bottle to the bedside table. "He has met someone else."

"Good, now he can leave you alone. But not good for her. We'll find him. Hopefully, he's in the system and the police can track him down using his DNA."

Noa shook her head, pushing her hair behind her ears. "He wants both of us. I think he has her, as in he's holding her somewhere like he held me."

"We don't have much time before he kills her."

"He won't kill her; he thinks he's in love with her. I've been reading the draft emails and in the last two he wrote about her and how special she is. He even states he *loves* her, but he isn't capable of it."

Luke patted the empty side of the bed. Noa stood, leaving the laptop on the lazy-boy. She settled her head on Luke's chest, tracing the bruise with her fingertips. "I don't know what I would've done if he killed you."

Luke pressed his lips to Noa's head. "He didn't kill me. Greg shot him and we got blood. Not a bad night, considering the alternative."

"But you're still dead. On paper at least."

"Death has worked out well for you. You get me, our home, a future." Luke hugged Noa as tight as his aching muscles allowed.

"I'll only be able to think about the future once he's behind bars or dead. I prefer the latter."

"It's a matter of time before we find him. Did you learn anything new from the drafts?"

"Nothing. Except he believes I'm his soulmate. And apparently, I'm also a psychopath. I get the idea that he and I didn't have sex, but *something* happened. Not even that gives me a better idea as to his identity. I spent most of my varsity nights properly drunk. Luke, I hate that you need to hear *every* detail about my past."

"I've told you before, I don't care. None of us are the people we were back then and if we were, it would be sad, and an utter waste of our lives. Consider everything you've survived and how brave you were rushing out to save me. You, Noa Morgan, are unlike any other human I've ever met."

"Your bravery rubbed off on me I guess." The dark hairs on Luke's chest tickled her palm.

"As soon as I can breathe properly, I want to find what else I can rub off on you."

"It was selfish of me to ask you not use a condom. I'm sorry."

"After what you went through, I'm amazed you don't get sick just hearing the word. We're both clean. I was tested after

I left the police, and you were tested on Tuesday morning. Besides, we're in a committed relationship and in this for the long run."

With her face resting on the hollow Luke's shoulder, Noa absorbed his warmth and words. "We need to stop him before he hurts whoever he has fixated on. I'm terrified about what he'll do to her."

Luke ran his fingers along Noa's cheek, down to her chin and tilted her head up. "I love your heart. Get some rest. Tomorrow we'll be a day closer to finding him." He kissed the tip of her nose.

He loves me. Noa's heart clenched. "I can't sleep. Not until I reread the drafts. I'm missing something."

"Sleep now. Think tomorrow." Luke eased back down and pulled Noa with him, holding her to his chest. "Do you hear my heartbeat? As long as there is life in me, I will hunt him down and make him pay. For all of it."

Once Luke's breathing calmed and his hold on her eased, Noa manoeuvred herself off the bed and tip-toed to the lazy-boy. Starting from the first draft, she reread every drafted email.

Monday, 28 June, 5:52 a.m.

Madison snuggled into Rick's arms and inhaled his scent; he smelled different. She forced her eyes open. Either Madison was getting old, or all their physical activities had left her exhausted. She yawned and ran her fingers down Rick's body, feeling nothing but material at his side.

Reaching for the lamp on the bedside table, Madison's hand touched thin air. The room was much darker than the previous morning.

Rick stirred and reached for her. "Come back, I'm cold without you."

"Where's the light?"

"It's too early to get up and I want to wake you up like I did yesterday morning. In order for me to start your day in the best possible way, you need to sleep now."

A muffled sound made Madison reach for Rick's arm and draw the covers up to her chest. "What was that?"

"Don't worry about it. Sleep Madison. Please."

"Dammit, Rick, it sounded like a person. Where's the bloody light?"

He grunted and switched on the light positioned above their heads.

A horrified scream deafened her. It took Madison a few seconds to realise it was coming from her mouth.

"Hush, my love. It will all be over soon."

Madison hugged her knees to her chest. "What have you done? Who is he?"

He laid a hand on her back and Madison flinched. "I'm still the same man you spent the weekend with. I did this because I love you. It's the only way to make her come to us."

"Rick, what are you talking about?" Madison stared at the man laying hog-tied in the corner of the room. A piece of silver tape covered his mouth. A faint red line trailed down the side of the man's head.

"Seeing as we're going to spend the rest of our lives together, it's time I tell you the truth. My name isn't Rick."

Madison scampered off the bed. "Who are you?"

The devil smiled.

Chapter 44

The heat from the mug transferred to Noa's hands. It didn't register, her brain too focused on the throbbing pain in her skull.

"Are you done hitting your head against the wall?" Luke rested his legs on the coffee table and crossed his ankles.

"The whole night I read through the drafts and I'm still no closer to figuring out who he is."

"I hate to say I told you so, but sleep, even for a few hours, would've made a difference."

Noa rolled her forehead against the wall and faced him. "Not in the mood, Taylor."

"Are you in the mood for something else?" Luke winked.

Noa smiled and walked over to him. She laid a hand over the bruise on his chest. "You're wounded."

"My chest is wounded. However, other parts of me are in perfect working order. I'll show you." Luke took the mug from her hand, setting it on the table. Pulling Noa onto his lap, Luke kissed her neck.

"I can still feel you inside me."

Luke yanked his head back and stared at Noa with his mouth open.

"What, didn't think I could say anything naughty? Get used to it. When I'm tired, I don't have a filter."

"You're never sleeping again."

Noa ran her fingers through Luke's dark hair, yanking hard

215

enough to make him groan. "That should keep you for a few hours. I need to go upstairs and read the drafts. Again. Until this is over, I can't take a moment for us to be a normal couple who don't have a psychopath hunting them. Perhaps he has delusional disorder. It doesn't matter what's wrong with him."

"Well, technically I'm dead, so I can take all the time I want." Luke's fingers skimmed across Noa's stomach. She swatted at his hands and pushed away from him.

"Not as long as he has her. I'm sure of it." Noa found her phone on the kitchen counter. Jamie answered on the first ring. "Jamie, have any women been reported missing in the past forty-eight hours?"

"I can make a call, but all personnel in the district gets a notification as soon as it is filed."

Noa knew this had become protocol after a recent spate of child abductions. The police had tracked the paedophile down, but not all the children had made it home. She had spent countless hours talking online to the siblings of some of the victims.

"I read through the drafts. No, I still don't know who he is, but I'm convinced he has abducted another woman. He wrote about her in the last two drafts, about how much he loves her, and that she reminds him of me when I was her age. Jamie, I'm terrified of what he'll do to her if she doesn't play to his fantasy."

"His fantasy?" Jamie yawned in Noa's ear.

"Yes, he believes the three of us will live happily ever after together. He wants both of us."

"I'll make a call and find out if I missed a notification. Will call you back as soon as I hear something."

Noa sighed. "Thank you. Have you spoken to Madison? Has she been informed that Luke isn't dead even though the papers will run an article this morning?"

"No, I was about to contact her when you called me. Will do that now. Thanks, Noa, talk to you later."

Noa stared at nothing in particular. "I can't let him hurt

someone else because of me. Today is the day. I have to figure out who he is."

Luke asked Noa to join him. They discussed all the information they had. The things neither they nor the police had answers for.

No matter how many times she searched her memory of the men she'd had sex with, Noa couldn't name him. No one stood out. None had tried to maintain contact after the night they'd spent together.

"My mother dated someone while I worked on the cruise ships. She boasted about how young he made her feel. Do you think it was him?"

"It's probable. His interactions with Kori Sheridan were sexual. The evidence points to it."

Noa gritted her teeth. "Did the police find anything in her house that might help us identify him?"

"Fingerprints were hers. The bed sheets contained her biological fluids. No used condoms or wrappers in the trash. A single hair was retrieved from one of the pillows. We hope it will match the blood found where Greg shot him. It's possible the hair belongs to Sheridan's ex-husband as he liked to screw with her and sleep in her bed while she was on shift."

"How were you able to pull off last night?"

Luke told Noa about the two retired detectives he had worked with while he was undercover. They owed him a favour for saving their lives. Matthew and his brother had been posted on the other corners of Luke's farm. Matthew might not have been the best shot, but his brother had served in the military. Until the police made an arrest, they would continue to keep watch. The security at his parents' farm had also been increased with plain clothed guards in order not to alarm visitors. At least it was winter when business tended to be slower.

Noa reached for her ringing phone and pressed the speaker icon. "Jamie?"

"I can't get hold of Maddie. Her phone's switched off and

her roommate hasn't seen her since Saturday afternoon."

Noa stood up so fast that she swayed. "He has Maddie, doesn't he?"

"We don't know that. Her roommate said she met a guy on Friday night, spent the night and went to his hotel room again on Saturday afternoon and Madison hasn't been home since."

"How can I help?" Noa asked.

"Reread the drafts. We have to figure out who he is. Go through the case files I left you. I'm heading to Shadow Bay to retrace Maddie's steps. The moment I hear something you'll be my first call. Noa, I haven't told my parents."

"I understand, I'll tell Luke." Noa ended the call and watched Luke storm into the kitchen. He returned with the sledgehammer and started on the wall.

Tears streamed down Noa's face as she ran to the bathroom. After her stomach cleared itself, Noa prayed Madison would play his game and keep herself alive. *I'm sorry, Maddie.*

Monday, 28 June, 8:00 a.m.

Madison dunked the cloth into the water and wiped the blood from his face. "Who are you?" She knelt in front of the stranger who laid tied up in the corner of the dank room.

"Richard Davenport. What's your name?"

"Madison Taylor. Why are you here?"

"He sent me a photo last night and said if I ever wanted to see my daughter alive again, I had to come alone, which I did." Richard winced as Madison pressed the cloth to his forehead.

"Why did you think I was your daughter?" Madison sat back on her legs and studied him.

Richard stared at the floor. "You look so much like Emily did at your age. I haven't been in her life and knowing what he's been doing, seeing it … I couldn't let him hurt her or anyone else."

Madison frowned. "I don't know anyone called Emily."

"You might know her as Noa Morgan." Richard lowered his voice. "As long as you play his game, you'll live. You need to buy time until Detective Edwards finds you."

"Jamie Edwards?"

He nodded, and Madison helped him to sit upright. Before the devil had left the room, he'd tied Davenport's hands in front of him. His hands remained tied to his ankles. The devil had fastened a shackle to Madison's right ankle, the other end bolted to the floor. The sound of metal against concrete grated on her nerves, but Madison reminded herself it was the sound of life as she moved around the windowless room.

"Did you bandage him?" she asked.

"Yes, he held a gun to your head."

"Thank you for saving my life." Madison gave a weary smile; Richard did the same. "Is he the man responsible for the attack on Noa and the murders of the three women whose bodies were found in the forest?"

"Yes. But it's four women. He killed a police officer over the weekend."

Madison stared at her hands. "We weren't together the whole weekend. How did he get me here?"

"I suspect he drugged you with Dormicum. You were unconscious for a few hours. It's what he used on Emily, sorry Noa. It has no lasting effects so you'll be okay."

"I had unprotected sex with him." Madison turned her head in time for the vomit to not land on Richard's feet. With the back of her hand, Madison wiped her mouth and cleaned the floor with the blood-stained cloth.

"As soon as we get out of here, I'll test you at my lab. No one has to know."

"Thank you. Noa never mentioned she has a father. I was under the impression both her parents are dead."

"To her, I am. Can't fault her for not acknowledging me. I did it to her for years and I've regretted it every day. When Emily was a baby, I tried to be a part of her life, but her mother refused."

"Who is he, other than the devil? How can I be so stupid?"

"As much as I want to say we tend to see people as inherently good because of who *we* are, he's a master manipulator. I believed he's my daughter's best friend and allowed him to move to River Valley with her." Richard grunted. "I thought he'd protect her and help her heal emotionally. He convinced all of us he's gay. Don't blame yourself. Just do whatever you have to and stay alive. No matter what he does to me."

Madison nodded as the steel door opened and the devil stepped back into hell.

Chapter 45

The drafts mocked Noa. The idea of him being this close for so many years sent her running to the bathroom more than once.

After the last time, she walked out of the bathroom and into Luke's arms. "Have you heard from Jamie?" Noa held onto Luke's shoulders for strength and to steady the storm swirling inside her.

"No. People at the club Madison played at on Friday night saw her talking to a man. The best description Jamie could get was 'smoking hot fox'."

"Dead end on my side. I'm missing something and it's eating at me."

"Noa." Luke ran his hands down her arms. "Who, besides Davenport and Clarke, knew of your staged suicide and your new life as Noa Morgan?"

Noa dropped to her knees. "He's gay. He can't be responsible for all of this."

"Who? Eric?"

Noa nodded. "He changed his name to Eric Foster when we moved here to protect me and give me further anonymity. That's what he said."

"Is he Foster Ericson?" Luke eased himself onto the floor next to Noa.

"Yes. Why?"

"I had an idea earlier to look at your past online presence.

221

Foster Ericson had liked or commented, on every single photo Emily Gallagher had posted. Your security settings were not set at all. I could access everything, all your photos, posts, friends."

"He's gay and won't touch a woman again."

"Again?" Luke asked.

"Yes. He wasn't always gay. Well, he was, but when he came out to me, he said he hid it because of his parents. He lived a double life."

"Did the two of you ever …"

Noa nodded and told Luke about the night Foster had dared her to seduce him. It had been their game – whenever they went out, they would see who could go home with the hottest guy or girl. Some nights they both struck out and laughed about it. Nothing more than a silly game. The night before Emily had left for her first cruise, Foster dared her to seduce him. She agreed purely because it had been Foster's most ridiculous idea to date. They both drank more than a reasonable young adult should and had ended up in bed.

"Did you?" Luke's eyebrows lifted.

Noa stared at their joined hands resting on the floor. "No. Okay, you need to be a detective right now and not my boyfriend."

"I promise." Luke kissed the side of Noa's head.

"Foster was busy going down on me and the next moment he said 'I'm gay'."

Luke drew a deep breath and exhaled hard. "Up to this point, was there any indication he wasn't responding to you in the moment?" Noa stared at him with squinted eyes. "Noa, did he have trouble getting or keeping it up?"

The things one has to admit to when your life, and the lives of others are in danger.

Noa withdrew her hands from Luke's and covered her face. "No. There was a big wet spot on the bed where he had, uhm, lain. I barely noticed it. My friend had just told me his life's secret, so I focused on him."

"Have you ever seen him with a guy?"

"No, but I haven't gone out with him or any of my friends. The night I met you was the first time in two-and-a-half years."

"Did he ever bring a guy to meet you?"

Noa shook her head. "Foster was a man whore when he pretended to be straight, and it continued into his new life. Luke, it's him, isn't it? He's lied to me for years. I lived with him for a year. I thought he was my friend. We have to stop him."

Luke reached into his pocket for his phone and, as he retrieved it, it rang. He answered, putting it on speaker. "Jamie, we know who he is."

"Eric Foster."

"Foster Ericson, but yes, same person," Noa said.

"Luke, he has Maddie. Footage recorded inside the club shows him in the crowd. I saw him kissing our sister." Luke gripped the phone, listening as fear exploded from Jamie. He hated hearing her cry, even when they were children.

Noa shuddered. "I'll tell your parents. All of this is my fault. I'm so sorry, Jamie."

"Cut the shit, Noa. I told you last night none of this is because of anything you did or didn't do."

"Hey, the baby can hear you," Noa said.

"No, it can't."

"Got you to stop crying."

Jamie sighed. "We will find Maddie and end Eric. I need to talk to my parents. And no, they won't blame you, so stop your self-pity bullshit."

Monday, 28 June, 10:30 a.m.

He helped Madison to her feet. She forced her arms to wrap around his waist. "What's next?" Madison asked.

"Nothing for you to worry about. Soon, the three of us will be a family. Emily needs to come to us. And she will. I know just how to get her to come home." He ran a hand down Madison's stomach and cupped her in his palm.

Madison stepped back, but he moved with her.

"Not in front of him." She looked towards Davenport.

"He won't tell anyone, and I can blindfold him if you're worried about your modesty."

Foster pulled Madison towards the bed. "You have no idea what you make me want to do to you. But first I need to get Emily back. Sit down, Maddie."

Madison obeyed, keeping her eyes on his, fighting the urge to flinch when he touched her.

Foster stepped away from the bed and headed towards the shelves. Leather straps dangled from his hand as he returned to her side. "Remove your clothes and lie down on your back."

With unsteady hands, Madison undressed. Foster strapped her to the bed, kissed her hard and covered her mouth with a strip of the same silver tape that covered Davenport's mouth.

"I'm sorry, my love. This is going to hurt me more than it's going to hurt you."

Madison blinked. Tears slipped down her temples. He, again, walked to the shelves; Madison watched his every move.

Foster slipped his hands into leather gloves. He removed something from the glass case. From Madison's position, she couldn't see the object in his hand.

"Maddie, I love you. I'm doing because I don't have a choice. If I don't, Emily won't come." Foster lifted his hand to her face.

Hairy legs crept over the glove.

Madison shut her eyes, grateful it wasn't a snake. Few people knew about the tarantula she kept in her apartment.

If she survived Foster Ericson, she might never look at the spider the same.

Make him believe you fear the spider, and not him. Forced, muffled screams came from behind the tape covering her mouth. Madison rolled her head from side to side.

Eight legs tapped over her face, or was it sixteen?

Ignoring her curiosity, Madison kept her eyes shut and focused on breathing faster.

Madison's tears were real.

Foster took a step back and yanked on the metal chain, still fastened around her ankle. Hell's umbilical cord.

"Your beautiful, Madison. They're so lucky to touch you like this. Just a bit more and I will have enough to send to her. Are you cold? You have goosebumps all over your delectable skin. Don't worry, my love, I know how to set you on fire."

Chapter 46

Monday, 28 June

Emily, I'm breaking my own rules sending you this, but it's time you came home. Now.

Attached is a reminder of the extents I go to for you. She doesn't know I killed her brother yet, but in time she will understand I did it because of how much I love both of you.
I have a surprise for you! Please hurry, I can't wait to give you the ultimate gift.

Come home, my love. It's time for us to be a family, as we were always meant to be.

I won't bother warning you about the consequences of what will happen if you don't come. Your soul screams out to mine. Don't tell me you can't hear it.

It's time for our bodies to become one, and our beings to bask in our love. For more than a decade every cell in our bodies have ached for each other.
It's time.

Come, my Emily, and be mine as I am yours.
Forever.

Chapter 47

The scent of coffee and ash hung in the room. Noa sat next to Luke, trying to think of the best way to tell his parents their daughter was in the hands of a killer. She clutched Luke's hand, feeling his pain reverberate through her palm. His pain was hers. *My fault.*

"Aaron, Laura, this is my fault." Luke stiffened next to her. Noa stroke her thumb over the back of his hand. Earlier, they had decided she would tell them – Noa demanded and hadn't left Luke any choice in the matter.

"Maddie was abducted by the same man who abducted me two-and-a-half years ago." Noa stared at her knees and inhaled as much air as her lungs allowed. "The same man Jamie's been hunting for the deaths of five people, and the attack on me last Tuesday morning."

Laura whimpered. Luke left Noa's side to comfort his mother.

"I'm sorry for bringing this man into everyone's lives."

Aaron rose and turned his back to the room. He picked up the poker and jabbed it into the ash in the fireplace. "Who is he?"

"A person I thought was my friend. I had no idea he's the devil."

"What is Jamie and the rest of them doing to locate Maddie?" Aaron stabbed again at the remnants of the ravages of fire.

"Jamie has tracked Maddie's last movements. She's been missing since Saturday afternoon, but we believe she went to him willingly, as her roommate said she met someone the previous night. Jamie found footage of them together at the club. Police officers have been sent to his home and office. Officers in Shadow Bay are at the construction site where he's supposed to be overseeing the construction of a new hotel. I believe he doesn't intend to hurt Madison. I realise it isn't comforting to hear, but it buys us time to find him and get Maddie back."

Luke pressed his mother's head to his chest. "We know he's wounded and will require medical attention. All the hospitals, doctors and even vets in a hundred-kilometre radius have been informed to be on the lookout for him. Mom, I promise you we'll bring Maddie home."

Laura lifted her head, wiping her eyes. "You're supposed to be dead. You can't leave the farm without putting yourself at risk. And Jamie's pregnant." Anguish tore through her.

The sound broke Noa's heart.

"I'm sorry, this is all my fault. I should never have come here." Noa pushed to her feet and walked towards the door.

"Where the hell do you think you're going?" Aaron asked, pointing the poker at her back.

"To go find your daughter and keep your other children safe."

"You have so much to learn about being part of a family. When the shit hits the fan, we don't go our separate ways. We stick together and sort it out. Together." Aaron dropped the poker at his feet and marched up to Noa. "Did you invite this man into your life knowing what he is?" He held up a hand. "Did you hide from life for two-and-a-half years because of what he did to you?"

"I didn't invite a psychopath into my life. We were in the same group of friends and I would've killed him had I known what he is. Yes, I hid from life, but I also lived with Foster for a year after moving here."

"Where did you stay?" Luke asked.

"A house he rented not far from here. After I moved out, Foster cancelled the lease and rented a house in town." Noa rubbed her hands over her arms. "To be close to me."

The message alert on the phone Luke had given Noa that morning sounded. She jabbed at the screen with her thumbs and stilled. Her heart lodged in her throat. Noa turned to Luke and nodded. "We need to leave."

She turned her attention to Aaron and Laura. "I'm sorry for all of this. I promise to do whatever I have to and bring Maddie back to you."

As Luke climbed into the SUV, he asked Noa about the message.

"He sent an email with a video attached. Let me watch it first. It might be of Maddie."

"She is my sister. We don't have time to argue about this. Press play."

Noa understood but didn't agree. She played the video anyway.

Her screams filled the SUV.

Spiders walked over Madison's face and chest. As soon as Luke saw Maddie's naked form, he looked away.

Noa read the message for a second time before turning to Luke. She laid a hand on his shoulder, knowing nothing she did could ease his fear. Luke had seen what Foster Ericson, aka Eric Foster, did to his other victims. "There's only one place Foster ever called *home*."

Monday, 28 June, 11:30 a.m.

Foster placed the tray in front of Madison and waited for her to finish the meal, never taking his eyes off her. She forced every bite down her and smiled. "Thank you. It was delicious."

"Not nearly as delicious as you, Maddie." Foster pressed his mouth to hers, licking his lips as he pulled away.

Madison forced concern into her voice. "Perhaps Doctor Davenport should look at your wound again. I don't want you to get an infection."

"It'll hold. Shouldn't be much longer until Emily gets home." Foster lifted his shirt. A brown stain evident on the gauze. "Must've torn a stitch."

"Let me at least change the dressing for you. The last thing I want is for you to get an infection." Madison touched his stomach. He agreed and watched her every move as she removed the gauze, cleaned the wound and put on a new dressing. "You popped a stitch. Please have him look at it."

"I'll be fine as soon as Emily walks through the door. He can fix me up, before I kill him." Foster grinned at Davenport.

Madison bit her tongue, forcing worry into her words again. "Honey, do you really think my brother will let her come to you? Luke hasn't left Noa's side in a week."

"I love it when you call me *honey*. No one has ever called me by a pet name before." Foster lied but wasn't about to tell Madison about the time he'd spent with a cougar. Judge Gallagher. The dead bitch.

Holding Madison's head between his hands, Foster said, "I'm not worried about Super Detective, Luke Taylor. He can't help either of you from where he is. You see, my love, I ensured the three of us will be together. Forever."

Foster pressed his mouth to her forehead, and whispered, "I killed him."

Laughter and pain collided in the dank room.

Monday, 28 June, 11:30 a.m.

Noa waited for Jamie's feedback on the information she'd given her about the house Noa had shared with Foster.

"The house is in his name," Jamie said.

"Thanks, I'm heading there now. Just need to get King first. He'll become suspicious if King isn't with me."

"SWAT is forty-five minutes out. You're *not* going in alone."

Noa heard Jamie's car accelerating. The adrenaline coursing through her did the same.

"Maddie might not have that much time. Let me go in and stall him until SWAT gets there," Noa said as Luke placed a hand on her leg.

"I'll go with her and use the fact that I'm dead to our advantage. Trust me, Jamie, I won't let him hurt Maddie."

Jamie cursed. "I don't like this, but we don't have a choice."

"No matter what happens, you stay outside. Think about the baby," Luke said.

"I can't let you go in alone."

"This isn't my first hostage situation. I'm more experienced than you are, Jamie. Not rubbing it in your face, just stating a fact." Luke turned the key in the ignition.

Monday, 28 June, 11:45 a.m.

Soon Emily would be home and they would be a family. His family. *Mine.* Foster ran his hand over Madison's lower abdomen and smiled.

Foster hated the way Richard Davenport's eyes were glued to his every move. The invasion of his privacy was a small price to pay to give Emily the ultimate gift.

Madison's neck was warm and intoxicating under his mouth. He grinned against her throat when she moaned. Maddie was such a remarkable young woman – and all his.

He hated putting her through the torture of having spiders crawl all over her. Foster had crushed them with his gloved hands as soon as he removed them from Madison's smooth skin. *No one touches her and lives.*

"May I give him water? He's no good to you if he dies of dehydration," Madison whispered as he thumbed her nipple through her shirt.

Foster shook his head hard. "It takes more than a few hours

to die of dehydration and she'll be here soon. I need to get ready."

He left Madison sitting on the edge of the bed and opened his laptop to access the live feed from the cameras outside the house. The scent of copper now tainted the once musty wine smell he'd loved. *If only these walls could talk.*

A black SUV pulled up in front of the garage. All the months. All the wasted time. Finally, it was over. It had been worth it.

"Emily's home where she belongs." For the first time since she had moved out of this house his heart felt full.

His perfect Emily walked up to the front door, their dog by her side. Foster loved King. After all, he had given him to Emily as a gift. "Welcome home, my love," he said to the woman on screen, as he watched her open the front door.

Monday, 28 June, 11:55 a.m.

The cold inside the house mirrored the temperature outside. There was no sign of anyone living here. No trace of the furniture Noa remembered which had stood in the living room or adjoining dining area. She had lived a year under this roof. Noa knew every nook and cranny.

Noa bent down and scratched King's ear. "Find Foster. Like old times when we played hide-and-seek. Go get him." She patted King's back and watched him scurry through the house.

"Foster, we're home! Where are you?" Noa called out. Silence answered.

King rushed past her legs and into the kitchen. His excited barks lead Noa to him; the dog pawed at the pantry door. The smell of fried bacon lingered in the air, and Noa noticed dirty pans in the sink.

Noa's heart began to beat even more violently in her chest.

"Good boy." She ran her hand over King's back and bent

down to hug him. With her face pressed to his neck, Noa whispered, "find squeaky."

King's head lifted, his tail wagged, and he darted through the kitchen. *Good luck.*

Pushing to her feet, Noa opened the door. In the middle of the pantry's floor – a trapdoor. It was propped open. *Was this always here?*

With careful steps Noa descended the stairs, her legs unsteady, her mind focused on Maddie.

Noa tapped on the steel door at the bottom. "Foster, are you down here? King is looking for you all over the house."

"Welcome home, Emily." The sound of his voice made her fists clench.

Noa exhaled slowly, smiled and opened the door.

Monday, 28 June, 12:05 p.m.

The amount of police cars, standing next to the road leading to Foster Ericson's house, looked like a line at a drive-thru. At the end of the road was the house of a serial murderer. A sadistic killer who now had her sister and her best friend. Jamie prayed silently, placing a hand against her stomach.

Captain Johnson marched towards her car, and she rushed to meet him.

"You're not going in. That's an order, Edwards."

"Yes, sir." Jamie gritted her teeth. "My brother should be inside by now."

"We'll discuss Luke being here later. We need to brief SWAT and I see the paramedics are pulling up."

Jamie turned to see the ambulance coming to a halt.

She followed Captain Johnson and relayed the only information she had – a trapdoor in the pantry. A SWAT officer placed a box on the mobile operations table and Commander Voight stepped up behind him. Jamie knew Voight's record; it was as long as both her arms combined.

"Butch, get the drone up. I need eyes. Fucking old houses with no blueprints," Commander Voight barked.

Jamie walked up to him and extended a hand. "Commander, as I told you earlier, I believe the suspect is holding three hostages. The first is Noa Morgan. She entered the house of her own free will to stall him and buy us time."

Commander Voight shook Jamie's hand and returned his focus to the screen now lighting up inside the carry case. Not a box as Jamie had first thought.

"Who is that?" Voight pointed at a form running towards the house.

"Former Homicide Detective, Luke Taylor. Brother of Madison Taylor, the second hostage, and boyfriend of Noa Morgan." Jamie still couldn't believe Noa and Luke were living together. This wasn't the time to ponder their life decisions.

"Taylor? Good to know he's inside. Heard nothing but good things about the work he did while in Narcotics."

They watched Luke disappear under the roof covering the porch via the screen.

"Who is the third civilian? I've only been briefed on Madison Taylor and Noa Morgan."

"We have reason to believe the suspect lured Doctor Richard Davenport here. The suspect was shot last night when he tried to kill Luke and needs medical attention. Davenport's phone records show he received a call originating from this area shortly after the shooting. Davenport isn't at work or his home and his phone is switched off." Jamie kept her eyes on the screen. "The suspect has used surveillance cameras in the past, we can expect him to have the same setup here. He's good at keeping them out of sight." Jamie knew there wasn't time to elaborate on the cameras found in Noa's home and her own.

"Rose, Cornwell and Brown, you round the house and set up position on the south. Use the tree line to your advantage. Spindler, east. Harris, west. Slay, Duke and the rest of you with me. We're going in. I don't care if he comes out in a bag but we won't have a civilian casualty. Am I clear?" Commander Voight's team nodded in unison. They checked their rifles one last time, and headed for Foster Ericson's house.

Chapter 48

Monday, 28 June, 12:05 p.m.

Foster waited for her to step through the door. Today she'd see *him* for the first time. How often had he fantasised about this very moment? Never more so than when the cricket bat had pulverized a fake Emily's ugly face.

His perfect Emily walked into the room, shaking her head. "So, after all these years of being in love with you, you expect me to share you with this *child*? Emily doesn't share her toys. You know me, Foster."

She loves me. "You're in love with me?"

Emily pressed her hands in her sides, rolling her eyes. "Of course, I'm in love with you. I always knew but when then you said you were gay … When I read the emails you drafted for me, I realised you love me too. And yes, it's romantic. But there's no way I'm sharing you. If you think a ménage à trois is in your future, I can assure you, it isn't."

Emily stepped closer. Foster caught a whiff of her scent. She might've changed her hair, her name, but her smell remained unique. Emily had always smelled like a sweet, delectable, forbidden fruit.

She glanced towards Davenport, who stared at her wide-eyed.

"Why the hell is *he* here?" Emily jerked her head towards Davenport.

"My ultimate gift to you. I'm going to kill him for deserting you and turning you into a slut with daddy issues."

"Now, now, Foster." Emily shook her head and smiled at

him. "I didn't have sex with countless men because of daddy issues. I did it because I liked it. Having all that control over another person, to know it was for my pleasure and I wouldn't see them again – what a rush. But you know that rush better than I do. You killed those girls. Naughty, naughty, Foster. You had too much fun without me."

Emily's hand was warm against Foster's chest. She rubbed her palm over his heart. "You're not going to kill him. I am."

Foster grabbed the back of Emily's neck and pulled her closer. "Fuck. You are my soul."

His hand moved from her neck down her back, stopping at the spot just above her mouth-watering ass. Foster slipped his hand under Emily's coat and removed the gun, placing it on the table behind him. "You're safe with me, my love. No need for you to ever carry a gun again."

Emily trailed a finger over his lips. "I'm angry with you," she said, lifting her mouth to his. "You could've told me years ago how you felt. We could've been together. We wasted so much time. You better make it up to me."

An alert tone on Foster's phone sounded. Emily placed a hand on his as he gripped the phone, her fingers caressing his, teasing him, reminding him. The second Emily had walked through the door he was ready to be inside her.

"It's just King, looking for Squeaky." Emily grinned.

They both laughed.

Monday, 28 June, 12:07 p.m.

Acid swirled in Luke's stomach as he heard Noa speak those words. The thought of *him* touching Noa made his nostrils flare and jaw muscles twitch.

Luke counted the remaining steps and knew, the moment he stepped through the door, the time to think was over.

He steeled himself, trying to forget that it was Noa and Madison inside the room.

Lifting the gun to his chest, Luke took a deep breath.

He stepped through the door, extending the gun in the direction of the man holding Noa against his chest, Noa's own gun pressed against her temple.

"Zombie!" Foster Ericson chuckled and pushed the barrel harder against Noa's head.

"Let. Her. Go."

"Fuck no." Foster laughed. "She's mine. Drop the gun, Taylor or I will kill her. If you force me to kill *my* Emily, I'll still have your delicious sister to play with."

From the corner of his eye, Luke saw Madison sitting on the bed. She swayed. Her eyes bigger than usual as she focused on him.

Noa tapped Foster's arm and tried to pull it away from her neck. "Don't be so bloody dramatic, Foster. Let me go. I came home to you."

A feral sound emanated from deep inside him. "Do you really think I'm dumb enough to believe you love me? You fucking whore! Him standing here is proof of what a lying bitch you are. You betrayed me, Emily. For that, you will die. Put the gun down, Taylor. I'd much rather bash Emily's head in than put a bullet through her."

Luke kept his eyes on Foster, but noticed Noa's slow blink.

The barrel of Luke's gun remained pointing at Foster's snarling face. "Okay, I'll put it down." Luke bent his knees, aware of Noa's gun now pointing at his head.

Foster squeezed the trigger.

The only sound from the gun – a click.

"Why won't you die, you damn cat?" Foster pulled the trigger again and again, pronouncing each word.

Noa twisted her body. Luke's heart stilled.

A guttural sound filled the room.

A deafening bang.

Noa fell to the floor, Foster's arm wound tight around her neck.

Chapter 49

Monday, 28 June, 12:15 p.m.

The pain in his gut didn't compare to the searing pain of her betrayal. Emily's face transformed into the one he had seen before. In the cabin. If hatred had a face, it would be this one of hers.

Foster tried to lift the gun. A blinding pain scorched through his shoulder and down to the tips of his fingers.

Emily's screams amused him until a blade penetrated his chest.

Time stood still.

He stared up at Emily. The blade didn't stop piercing his body.

The Neanderthal grabbed Emily and pulled her away, out of his reach. Foster lifted his head and stared at the handle protruding from his gut. Warmth spread across his chest, running down his ribs.

Fire burned in his lungs, which were unable to fill with enough oxygen.

Darkness came for its master.

Monday, 28 June, 12:20 p.m.

Black figures stormed into the room. Noa became aware of Luke's voice behind her. Noa lifted her trembling hands in front of her. Blood covered her palms and dripped to the floor.

Paramedics rushed to those injured while Luke tended to Madison. He held his sister, her cries drowned out by the other sounds. Noa turned to where a paramedic was hunched over Davenport.

From the cold concrete floor, Noa watched the surrounding mayhem. She wiped her hands on her jeans and waited – waited for reality to sink in, for strength to return to her body.

Noa tried to stand and fell forward, the remnants of two arachnoids between her hands as she braced herself against the floor.

Strong arms lifted and carried her out of hell. The paramedics still tended to the devil.

Luke lowered Noa down onto the porch. He held her, and rocked with her.

A man with an assault rifle over his shoulder carried Madison past them to an ambulance. A jacket with the letters SWAT on it covered Madison's naked body.

Jamie stood next to the ambulance.

"You're both okay," Luke murmured.

Noa shook her head.

"I'm so proud of you, Noa. My heart stopped when you started moving."

She turned to face him. Fear, loathing and relief flooded out of Noa and she pressed her face to Luke's chest. *It's over.*

"Move." A voice ordered from behind them. Luke pulled Noa out of the way.

Foster Ericson passed them; his body strapped to the gurney.

His face uncovered.

Monday, 28 June, 4:00 p.m.

Noa was safe and in his arms where she belonged.

Madison was at home with their parents. Safe and where she belonged.

Foster Ericson was in ICU. Not where anyone wanted him to be.

"I didn't kill him." Noa's body jerked against him. "Why didn't he die, Luke?"

Noa pushed against his chest and found the sledgehammer standing next to the wall. She picked it up. It slipped from her hands and dropped to the floor. Her legs failed her, and Noa sank down, kneeling with her face to the ground.

Anger pulsed through Noa. It echoed out of her, and filled the house.

"It will never be over for as long as he breathes." Her fists pounded the floor. "He deserves to die!" Noa sobered, her face ravaged by fury. She bared her teeth.

"Don't go there, honey." With his back against the wall, Luke eased down onto the floor. He wrapped Noa in his arms and pressed his mouth to her wet cheek. "If Foster survives, he'll go to prison. He can't get to you or Maddie ever again. And he can never ever hurt anyone else."

"But he can be hurt. I can kill him while he's in hospital. Or I can pay some punk to take him out in the joint."

Luke roared with laughter.

Noa glared at him. "Why are you laughing?"

"Punk? Joint?" Luke kissed her and kept doing so until Noa responded.

Out of breath, Noa pulled her mouth away. "I wanted to vomit when he kissed me."

"I know. You saved Maddie and your father. And you kept yourself safe." Luke touched Noa's face and removed the clip from her hair, letting it fall to her shoulders. The way he liked it. "I've never been so scared in my entire life. *Now* we get to live a normal life." Luke smiled. "A boring life."

"Life with you won't be boring. But it will never be normal, not as long as he breathes." Noa's fists slammed against Luke's chest. "I should've killed him."

"You almost did. You did enough damage that he'll remember his last encounter with you for the rest of his life."

"That's the problem. He will always have his memories. About Maddie, the people he killed. They will always be with him."

"Before you stand up, you need to let it go. Stop giving him control over you. You fought him every day of the forty he held you, yet you allowed yourself to be his captive for two-and-a-half years. Not in our home, Noa. It ends *today*."

Noa wrapped her arms around his neck and moved to straddle him. "We need to go check on Maddie."

"We can go in the morning. My parents are with her. Jamie and Spencer are also over there. I need to take care of you."

Noa dropped her head against his and whispered, "I want to make love to you. Not because I need another victory, but because I need you."

Luke lifted his chin, letting his mouth find hers. He stood with Noa's legs wrapped around him and carried her up to their bedroom.

Noa slid down his body and closed the door. For a few seconds she stood with her back to him. When she turned, she noticed the unshed tears in his eyes.

She closed the distance between them and cupped Luke's face in her hands. "I'm safe. I promise I won't give him any more control over me. Luke Taylor, I'm yours for as long as you want me."

Luke's hands glided up Noa's sides and he pulled her top over her head. He brushed his mouth against her stomach. "Forever."

Noa undressed him, taking her time to admire every part of him she bared. With her eyes on his, she unclasped her bra, letting it fall to the floor. She stepped closer, traced the strong line of his jaw and smiled as his stubble tickled her fingers. Still his eyes held unshed tears.

She pressed her lips to his eyes. "Let me love you. I want you to know how much you mean to me. We've been through so much. Now, we focus on the good. Be here with me. Please." Noa brought his mouth to hers and followed him down onto the bed. She trailed the lines of his six-pack with her tongue, smiling against his skin as his body shivered under her touch.

Tears slipped onto Luke's skin as she made her way down his body.

Noa had never before made love. Had never been with a man like Luke.

Raw. Real. Breath-taking. Simple.

Noa forgot the horrors, her mother's rejection and cruel words, her absent father. Not until meeting Luke, had she experienced anything even close to this. Love.

Their bodies became one, their gazes locked, smiling against each other's mouths. Noa slid her fingers between his.

Long after their breathing calmed, their bodies still joined, they kissed. Soft, luscious kisses which left them both aching for more. To have *this* every day – acceptance.

Chapter 50

Tuesday, 29 June, 4:00 a.m.

Foster focused on a spot on the ceiling. The light above his bed was too faint for him to see the exact colour of the spot. He ignored the dark screen of the overhead television.

The irritating, constant beep remained.

I will make you hurt for this, bitch.

He shut his eyes, remembering a man in dark clothing had taken his Maddie away from him. Madison had wrapped her arms around another man's neck and didn't even have the decency to look at him as he'd bled for her. Literally.

Foster tried to move, but his body didn't respond, and his throat burned. He tried to touch his face, but his right arm ignored the cues from his brain.

There was a clacking sound when Foster tried to raise his left hand. Metal encircled his wrist.

"Hurry up and realise you'll never be a free man again. I don't have all day."

Foster attempted to turn his head in the direction of the voice, but whatever was stuck down his throat kept his neck in place.

"Oh, my bad." The voice became louder. "You're not even capable of breathing for yourself."

The owner of the voice came into view and Foster stared at them, unblinking.

"Never imagined you'd wake up to my face, did you?" A predatory smile spread across his visitor's face.

"Don't try to talk now. There will be time for that later. I ook forward to standing on your grave. No one touches my family. Rest, you're going to need all your strength for what I have planned for you."

The person stepped out of Foster's field of vision, and he never heard the voice again.

Vengeful laughter echoed in his ears.

Tuesday, 29 June, 8:00 a.m.

River Valley had never experienced such a terrible winter. Global warming had made it warmer than previous years, but death had brought his cold hands over the quaint town.

Jamie gripped the take-away cup of tea. Her mother had pushed it into her hand before she left the house. Jamie had slept in Madison's room and held her sister as she cried, and again when the nightmares came.

She hoped it wouldn't last but knew better. Jamie had her own demons, and the events of the past week would no doubt give her more.

She stared at the open graves and the bodies next to each. Four graves. Four women in various stages of decomposition. Jamie reached into her pocket and rubbed the menthol-based salve under her nose.

Doctor Burger touched her shoulder. "How are you holding up?"

"Are you asking me as a detective, Madison's sister, Noa's friend or the friend of a serial killer?" The carnage on the other side of the crime scene tape held her attention.

"I'm asking *my* friend." Burger squeezed Jamie's shoulder and placed his arm around her. "If you need to come cry in my office, my door is always open."

"Thank you, Burger. I don't know how I would've gotten through this week without you." She rested her head on his shoulder.

A unique bond is formed between those who, side by side fight evil.

"Do you think there will be more?" Jamie asked.

"I hope not. They've scanned the ground, and that area seems to be his burial ground. Officers are searching the forest."

"When will you start the autopsies?" Jamie crushed the cup and placed it inside her coat pocket. She ducked under the yellow tape and walked to the first body.

Burger came up beside her and squatted next to the body. "No pink dildo. No signs of blunt force trauma to the skull. Different hair colours. It's strange."

Jamie shrugged. "He could've evolved; found his signature."

"He wrapped them in these plastic sheets. It looks like the drop-sheets painters often use. Maybe we got lucky and it's helped preserve evidence. This victim seems more recent than the others. I'll start with the first victim – based on the rate of decomposition – and work my way up to her. Do you want to attend the autopsies?"

"No, but yes. This is still my case, unless Captain Johnson removes me. I spoke to Doctor Davenport yesterday. He was adamant that we keep sending all evidence in this case to his laboratory, as long as it doesn't create a problem when this goes to trial. The state prosecutor said it might, but they'll send someone from our lab to oversee the handling and processing of the evidence. Don't want to give a defence attorney any leg to stand on to have evidence thrown out or not admitted. Problem is, the Ericson's are old money. They can afford the best team of criminal defence attorneys for their son. He should've died in that room." Jamie jerked her head back towards the house.

Burger whipped his head around and smiled at Jamie. "You're tired. Go home. I'll call you before I start. It will either be late this afternoon, or tomorrow morning, depending on how long we take here. There's nothing you can do here, Jamie. Go home."

She didn't leave. Instead, Jamie walked to each body and

took her own photos, made notes, and saw the bodies as the women they once were. "I'll get you justice," Jamie whispered to each as the pressure on her chest pressed harder.

As she closed her car door, Jamie allowed the pressure to consume her. Without making a sound, Detective Edwards cried.

Tuesday, 29 June, 8:15 a.m.

Noa opened the front door. King rushed in ahead of her, sending her stumbling into the foyer. She looked up to find Luke smiling at her. Noa ran to him and jumped into his arms.

"Why did I wake up without you?" Luke nuzzled her neck.

"You were exhausted after round two last night, so I let you sleep, old man. You needed your beauty rest, and I needed a run to clear my head."

He released his grip, and Noa slid down to the floor. Luke took her hand and led her to the kitchen.

Noa thanked Luke for the mug of coffee he held out to her. "I told you I would make you coffee every morning."

"I remember you promised to do much more than make coffee." Noa wrapped her arms around Luke's waist. "You made good on your other promise last night. But you better leave the kitchen if you want breakfast."

Luke playfully pushed Noa away and opened the oven door, retrieving two plates. "I knew you'd be hungry, so I made breakfast. We need to head to my parents. Jamie wants to talk to you."

"Thank you." Noa took the plate he held out to her and carried it into the dining room. "I want to talk to Madison. I need to. How she is?"

"Not good. I can't imagine what she's going through." Luke took a seat next to her.

"I can. That's why I should talk to her. The things you said last night are true, and I need to say the same to Maddie. If you'd been there for me, or if anyone had said what you had last night, things might've been different for me. I might have never killed Emily."

Luke turned to her. "Who do you want to be? Emily or Noa?"

Chapter 51

Tuesday, 29 June, 10:00 a.m.

Madison pressed her face into the jacket and took a deep breath. Every muscle in her body relaxed. She kept her face submersed in the calm and darkness the jacket offered. On the bedside table, the coffee and food Laura had brought her earlier had gone cold.

A knock on the door made Madison stiffen. Her head jerked towards the sound. The familiar voice eased the tension in her shoulders.

"Maddie, it's me, Noa. May I come in? It's just me, I'm not bringing food or anything. If you want to snuggle with King, I can call him. Nobody cuddles like he does. Don't tell your brother I said that."

A faint smile appeared but quickly disappeared as Madison remembered the last time she'd seen Noa. *Or Emily.*

"Okay, Mads, I'll go but I *will* be back later. I won't let you go through this alone. We can do it together. I need you Maddie, and you need me. No one else understands."

Maddie pushed herself up on the bed, clutching the jacket to her chest. "Come in."

Noa eased the door open and as she stepped into the room, a rush of gratitude overcame Madison. Not because Noa had saved her life, but because Noa didn't plaster a concerned smile on her face, which Maddie had come to hate in the last day.

"May I sit?" Noa asked, pointing at the wicker chair in the corner.

"Please sit with me."

Noa climbed on the bed and touched Madison's arm. "I know Maddie."

Madison fell onto Noa's lap. All the emotions she was bottling up burst through her. Madison screamed, cried, and beat Noa's legs with her fists.

Noa didn't utter a single word, neither did she pull away. Silently, she cried with Madison.

Madison took a breath. "I thought I was falling in love with him. He treated me like I was special, precious and he made me feel like a woman. No one has ever treated me like that before."

Running her fingers through Madison's curls, Noa sighed. "I understand. He was the first *man* you were with. A man should treat you with respect, kindness and reverence. Minus the psychopath, abductor, serial killer part."

Madison lifted her head and moved to sit next to Noa, taking her hand. "I'll need to be more specific with the requirements stipulated in my online dating profile."

Noa tried not to laugh, but her shoulders shook. She glanced at Madison to see a faint smile. "I understand, Maddie. For over a decade I considered him my friend. I lived with him for a year. And I loved him. Not once did I suspect him of being the devil." Noa rubbed circles on Madison's back, which was soothing to them both.

Together, they survived in silence. Each grasping the extent of the lies they'd been fed.

Madison pulled her legs under her.

Noa turned and held Madison's face between her hands. "Maddie, what I'm about to say to you, I wish someone had said to me hours after I was rescued. It would've changed the course of the past two-and-a-half years of my life. A wise man told me I have a choice to remain his captive, even though I'm now free. I decide whether I give him more control. Please don't make the same mistakes I did. You have family and friends who love you. Don't shut them out and create your own prison. He can never hurt you again."

Madison threw her arms around Noa's neck. "Will you help me? And how can I help you?"

"Isn't that what sisters do for each other? Oh, and I'm going to help you write songs, angry songs, songs where you can scream and claim victory."

"I can't go back on stage. That's how he found me."

"He didn't find you because of your music. Don't let him take it from you." Noa stroke her hand down Madison's back. "You need to get out of this room as soon as possible and carry on with your life. Yes, you'll be more cautious and going to therapy is a good idea. Don't give him power over all the things in your life like I did. Don't let him take your studies, work, friends, family or your music. Go see a therapist to deal with all of it. *All* of it."

"This is so screwed up. He can't be charged for raping me. I slept with him because I wanted to. I left with him of my own free will on Friday night and went back to him on Saturday afternoon. At most, he *abducted* me." Madison released Noa and lifted the jacket to her face.

"And this is exactly why you need to speak to a professional and deal with *all* of it. I also had a sexual encounter with him, years ago, to which I consented. It's messed up, but Maddie, we *will* get through this. Together."

"Why did he do this to you?" Madison looked at Noa with tired, burning eyes.

"I have no idea. I might never have the answers to all my questions. And I need to live with it."

"I don't want to be a *victim*."

"Something horrible and traumatic happened to you. And, unfortunately, there's no way to undo the past. However, you Madison Taylor, hold the power to survive and see yourself as a *survivor*. By the way, the SWAT jacket makes you look badass." Noa's smile reached her eyes.

"I want a gun."

"Okay, I'll take you shooting later today. But you won't be

able to carry it around campus, or when you go to clubs. Wha
about a knife, like the one I had on me yesterday? I have :
spare. Luke can teach you to use it and the best ways to concea
it."

"Thank you, Noa, for saving my life. How can I ever repa*
you?"

Noa squeezed Madison's hand. "You kept yourself aliv*
and don't you ever forget that. Whatever you did to stay aliv*
is testament of *your* strength. There's only one thing I want yo*
to do, for both of us – *live*. Take it one day at a time but focu
on living with intention. If you need me, no matter the time
I'm here for you and I'll visit you in Shadow Bay."

"I can't go back there, and I can't stay here. I'll always b*
the woman who slept with a serial killer."

"There are ways around being *labelled*. I'll do everythin*
humanly possible to ensure your name stays out of the paper
and the trial. It has been done before for other survivors, an*
I promise to protect you. Don't let him win. Don't make th*
same mistakes I did. To run from your support network i
the last thing you need. When you're ready, I want you to joi*
the online groups I run. It's a place for survivors, and other
affected by crime, to share their stories and also their victories
You're not alone, Maddie." Noa kissed Madison's head an*
held her, for both their sakes.

***

Stepping out of Madison's room Noa sent a text message.

Noa: We need to keep Maddie's name out of the papers an*
the trial.

Jamie: I've already spoken to Captain Johnson and the stat*
prosecutor.

Noa: Thank you.

Jamie: What about your name?

Noa: Use Emily Gallagher. She was his victim. Will the*
charge me for faking my suicide?

Jamie: No. Noa Morgan is free.

Noa stared at Jamie's words. Not yet, she thought.

Jamie: Are you at my parents? We need to talk. I'll be there in thirty minutes.

Chapter 52

Jamie waited for Noa in the living room. She hugged Noa the moment she stepped through the doorway. "Thank you for saving my sister."

Noa patted Jamie's back. "I didn't do anything. I bought some time for SWAT. That's all."

"You did much more than that. Please sit down. We need to talk."

The tone of Jamie's voice told Noa that whatever followed wouldn't be good. "I wanted to discuss this with you, without Luke hovering around. Foster's awake and told Captain Johnson he'll confess, but only if you're in the room. Well, he wrote his request as he still has a tube down his throat."

Noa dropped her head into her hands. "I'll do it. For the families of the people Foster murdered."

"He wants to see Madison too." Jamie's hands balled into fists.

"No. He doesn't get to see her. Ever." Noa placed a hand over Jamie's fist.

Jamie met Noa's stare. "Will *you* be okay facing him?"

"For two-and-a-half years I dreamt of the day I'd come face to face with the monster who held me in that cabin. I don't need closure anymore. I know who Foster is. And he has no remorse for the hell he put me through. But, if it can bring some form of closure or answers to the murdered women's families, I'll face him."

"I'm proud of you, Noa. You're a remarkable person. I've liked you since the day we met. It's easy to see why my brother is in love with you – you're brave and compassionate. We'll never have the same surname, the whole I'm-an-Edwards-now-thing, but I'm proud to have you as my sister."

Noa bumped her shoulder against Jamie's. "Have you booked the wedding venue yet? Set the date? Told your brother he's marrying me?"

"Oh, he knows he is." A male voice came from behind them. "Come, it's time for lunch. Whatever the two of you were talking about can wait."

Jamie and Noa followed Aaron to the dining room.

Tuesday, 29 June, 12:24 p.m.

Noa glanced at the people around the table and wondered how they spent their family meals, when a shadow wasn't hanging over them. Laura's eyes were red. Aaron kept rubbing the bald spot at the back of his head. Jamie leaned her head on Spencer's shoulder while he stared at the plate in front of him. Luke held her hand but was uncharacteristically quiet.

A chair remained empty – Madison's.

"She'll be back at the table as soon as she's ready. You just need to give her some space," Noa said with a hint of a smile.

"Who?" A soft voice emanated from the doorway.

Noa turned to see Madison clutching the jacket to her chest. Luke stood and pulled out a chair for his sister, kissing the top of her head as she sat.

"I'm proud of you," Noa whispered as she squeezed Madison's hand, keeping it firm in her own.

With her eyes closed Jamie said, "Officer Davis is going to need that jacket back."

"Why can't I keep it? *Someone* mentioned it makes me look like a badass."

Noa sniffed the jacket.

"Like dog, like owner?" Madison pushed Noa away.

"Hey, I offered to let you cuddle with King. Damn, that jacket smells good. Mind if I borrow it?"

Luke shook his head. "I thought you liked the way *I* smell."

"Calm down, Taylor, I do. But this jacket carries the scent of protection, strength and the sexy man who wore it. Maybe Maddie needs the man more than the jacket," Noa snickered.

"Dammit, Noa, not you as well. What is it with the women in this house?" Aaron removed his hand from the back of his head.

"It's a family affliction. I believe it rubs off on people." Noa placed her other hand on Luke's thigh, moving it high enough to make him blush.

"He was kind," Madison said, reaching for a glass of orange juice.

"And hot." Added Noa. From the corner of her eye she noticed Luke shake his head. "What? He had an assault rifle over his shoulder, handguns strapped to his thighs and carried Maddie past us without showing a sign of strain. I'm not saying you're overweight, little sister. Sorry, *youngest* sister. And to top it all, he gave Maddie his jacket. Hero, right there."

"His has a soothing voice and kind eyes. I'm willing to bet he can make you lose sleep. A lot of sleep." Madison darted a glance at her parents as she bit her bottom lip.

"Who?" Jamie asked. "Slay?"

Noa and Madison burst out laughing. In unison they asked, "Slay?"

"Yes, it's his nickname. And I'm serious about him wanting his jacket back. He called me earlier to ask when he could stop by to fetch it. He also asked to see you Maddie, if you're up to it. If not, I'll give it back to him."

Laura wiped her eyes and slammed a hand on the table. "Enough. Stop it. You can't sit here and talk as if nothing happened."

Madison looked at Noa and nodded. She pushed the chair back and stood. One by one she made eye contact with her family sitting around the table. "Mom, please look at me." She waited for Laura to meet her eyes. "A wise man once told Noa that we're in control of how long we allow our captors to have power over us. I choose to live without fear. And take it one day at a time. Don't get me wrong, I understand the severity of what happened, and I'll go see a therapist in Shadow Bay. But please, I beg you, don't treat me as if I'm broken. You're my safe place, my support. And I need this, the banter, teasing, all of it. Noa and I have decided not to let him control our lives for another second. You need to do the same. What happened affects all of us. By the way, I'm getting a gun."

Madison held up a hand as her mother opened her mouth to protest. "I'm going to do what I need to do in order to feel safe and move on from this."

Noa wrapped an arm around Madison's waist, making no attempt to hide her tears. "I'm in awe of you. You're much stronger than I was."

Laura's chair fell backwards onto the carpet with a hard thud. Madison met her mother halfway around the table and walked into Laura's open arms. "I love you, Maddie. Do whatever you feel is best for you. Dad and I will support you every step of the way. As you said, what happened affects all of us. It's going to take us some time as well."

"One day at a time, Mom."

Laura tilted Madison's head down and kissed her forehead. "One day at a time."

They ate. They laughed. For the first time in her life, Noa's heart was full and at peace.

The kind of fullness that only the unconditional love of a family can give.

Noa thought back to the crushing loneliness she had experienced after her rescue and realised the effect a loving family can have on a person's recovery. Never again would she have to face anything alone, not after she saw Foster for the last time.

She savoured the moment. Noa knew how Luke would

react when he heard she was going to be in the same room as the clown demon. *Minus the mask.*

Tuesday, 29 June, 1:00 p.m.

This is hell. Foster couldn't believe no one had come to visit him, except for his early morning visitor and the police captain. Surely, by now, his family and friends should've heard of his hospitalisation. Why did no one rush to see him? It couldn't be because of the things the captain had mentioned.

Over the years, he'd been a good friend to many people who didn't deserve his time. Foster often gave money to charities under the name Eric Foster. He'd even sacrificed his old life to help Emily get back on her feet in this small town.

When will Emily come? Foster stared at the overhead television. No one bothered to turn it on for him. He knew someone was standing outside the door; the captain had spoken to someone on his way out.

Where are all the female nurses? The hospital surely employed female staff.

Foster was looking forward to seeing Emily again. While he waited, he thought of ways to get himself out of this predicament.

No way in hell was he going to prison. The police didn't have any evidence linking him to the crimes Captain Johnson had mentioned. Apart from his blood found next to the road close to Luke Taylor's farm, the police didn't have a thing. Foster had made sure of it. Blood next to the road didn't prove he'd shot the muscle monkey.

Before long, Foster Ericson would be a free man and then he'd find Madison. *She's mine.*

Chapter 53

Jamie recorded Noa's testimony. She listened as a detective, not as a friend. Noa explained how she had entered the house, King had searched for Foster and described the scene upon entering the cellar. Luke had listened as Noa made her way through the house; her phone was in her coat pocket.

"He had your gun to your head?" Jamie asked.

"Yes, but I'd emptied the magazine and ejected the chambered bullet before we drove up to the house. It served as a decoy as my baby Glock was in my pocket."

"And you had the knife down the front of your pants? There's a question I never expected to ask to you."

Noa gave a weary shrug. "I didn't care about my safety. To get Maddie out was all I thought about."

"And your father?"

"Maddie said he kept her calm and told her to do whatever was needed to stay alive. How is he?"

"Richard will be released from the hospital later today. He wants to see you."

Noa stood and walked to the window. "Why?"

"He received a photo and thought it was you. Richard didn't even stop to tell anyone where he was going. Noa, he's your father, and cares about you."

Noa stifled a laugh. "Where was he when I was growing up and I had to listen to my mother bitch and moan about him every day my of life?"

"He needs to explain to you what happened between them."

Noa turned around to face Jamie. "He told you?"

Jamie nodded. "Yes, when I spoke with him yesterday."

"When do you want me to see Foster?" Movement behind Jamie caught Noa's eye.

Luke stood in the doorway with his arms crossed over his chest. "You're not seeing him." His face was red and contorted with rage.

Noa moved closer and reached for his arm. Luke stepped around her and marched towards Jamie. "Noa can't be in the same room as that psychopath."

"Luke, this isn't your call. If Noa decides to go and gets him to confess …" Jamie shrugged. "It's up to her."

"I don't like the idea of Noa being in the same building, never mind confined room, as Foster."

Noa's arms wrapped around Luke and she rested her cheek against his leather jacket. "He'll only confess if I'm there. The families of the people Foster murdered deserve closure. I'm not doing this for me. I'm doing it for them."

"Have you told her yet?" Luke asked Jamie.

"No, was about to when you stormed in."

Noa stepped around Luke, resting her forehead against his chest. This was the only way she could think of to calm his breathing and ease the tension in his shoulders. "Told me what?"

Jamie slumped down on the couch and waited for Luke and Noa to do the same. Luke pulled Noa onto his lap and buried his face in her neck. She stroked his hair and felt his body relax.

Jamie waited for Luke to calm down before telling Noa about the bodies of the four women they had found behind the house. She didn't divulge any details about their murders.

"Four?" Noa pressed a fist to her forehead. "Four. More."

"I'm heading to the morgue later today for the autopsies. Doctor Burger will contact me when he's ready to start."

"How many people did he kill?"

"We're not sure yet. I'm on my way back to the house, and I need to speak to Detective Davidson about unsolved cases in Marcel. He sends his regards and is ecstatic that after all these years we've arrested your abductor."

"Thank you. I should call him. He did so much for me during the six months before I left Marcel."

"I don't want Foster close to you." Luke murmured against her ear. "Please promise me that you won't go."

"I can't. I have to do this for every person he's murdered, their families, for Kim, you, Maddie, and myself."

Jamie placed a hand on Luke's arm. "You can observe. I'll clear it with Captain Johnson. It won't be for a couple of weeks. Noa cut Foster pretty good."

"He is to be chained to the chair and the second she gets uncomfortable it ends."

Noa pushed away from Luke, keeping a hand on his shoulder. "*She* can talk for herself. Luke, I appreciate you trying to protect me, but I have to do this. I am doing it. For now, let's focus on finishing the remodelling at home and I need to go to my house and pack. I don't know what furniture you want to keep, or even what I want to keep. So, let's head over there, together, and sort out what we can. I've already contacted a realtor and put the house on the market. Whatever we don't want or need, I'll donate."

"I want your couch. I've had fantasies about you on that couch."

"Hello, I'm right here." Jamie lifted her arms above her head. "And with that disturbing mental image, it's time I leave."

"It's not like you haven't seen me have sex," Noa snickered.

"True, but not with my brother. Bye."

Luke grabbed the back of Noa's neck and brought her mouth down hard on his. He kissed her with an intensity he never had before.

Noa pulled away from him, pressing her fingers to her chin. "Not liking the stubble very much at the moment, but I love seeing your chin dimple." She ran a finger over the newest thing she loved about him. Noa hadn't known Luke had a dimple until he walked out of the bathroom that morning. "Let's go pack up my old life. Then we can start our new life."

Luke's head tilted to the left. "You're stalling on seeing your father."

"I know smartass. Do you mind if I invite Madison to come stay with us tonight? I promised to take her shooting later this afternoon."

"Only if you promise to be quiet tonight. You know what it does to me seeing you handle a gun."

Tuesday, 29 June, 2:45 p.m.

The sealed fridge doors in the mortuary gave no indication as to which victim was laying behind them. Jamie wondered how it was possible a mortuary, as small as this one, had enough space for the number of bodies which had been brought in during the past week.

At least Kim didn't end up here. Kim's recovery would be long, but recovering is better than being dead.

Luke had also dodged a bullet, without dodging it. Jamie didn't doubt that ballistics would match the bullet to the one extracted from a wall in Kori Sheridan's house.

The one person who deserved to be in the morgue was lying in a hospital bed.

Jamie rubbed her lower abdomen. "I'm seeing you tomorrow baby, Mommy can't wait. You're safe, your family is safe, and I'll figure out what I'm going to do. Soon. I promise."

An assistant helped Doctor Burger lift a body bag onto the steel table. Jamie remained out of their way. She knew their choreographed dance as they prepared to listen to the bodies of the dead. The ones who shouldn't be here.

The assistant left before Doctor Burger unzipped the bag, exposing the body of a woman ravaged by death. "We haven't prepared her for autopsy; the past few days have been busy. I believe this woman is the first victim – based on the advanced stage of decomposition. We'll need DNA samples from relatives or friends for identification. Has any of these women been reported missing?"

"No." Jamie opened a case file on the desk in the corner of the room. She spread out the photos and placed four personal identification cards next to each other.

Jamie cleared her throat. "He kept these as trophies. The crime scene investigators found an envelope hidden inside the fireplace in a guest bedroom. I sent photos to Shadow Bay's Missing Persons office. They don't have records of anyone filing a report for any of these women. I also sent it to other stations in the area. It appears our women were ladies of the night."

"No pimp will admit to losing his product." Burger braced himself against the steel table. "No matter how or why they ended up on the street, no one deserves to die like this."

Jamie nodded. "Any ideas on cause of death?"

"You won't see it as well on her neck, but strangulation marks are visible on some of the more recent victims. I'll check her hyoid bone to see if there's damage consistent with manual strangulation."

"He strangles four, then bludgeons three. Stages a suicide for Clarke. Shoots Officer Sheridan. Tries to kill Kim by running her over with a car, and shoots Luke. Not forgetting Judge Gallagher, who was also bludgeoned. Foster's one twisted SOB."

As Jamie listed the victims, Doctor Burger removed his glasses and began inspecting the body. Jamie knew he'd take his time with each victim, giving them the care, no one had showed them in life.

Happy, loved little girls don't grow up to earn a living on their backs or knees by choice.

"You don't need to be here while I conduct the autopsy. My wife wasn't great with smells while pregnant, and trust me, once I open our victim up ..." Burger's eyes filled with compassion. "When I'm done with all four victims, I'll contac you."

Jamie was grateful Burger didn't expect her to stick around "Is there anything you noticed that stands out about the wa he murdered these women? Anything different from the othe three, except the obvious?"

"There's no visible evidence he bit any of them. At least no with the two most recent victims. Not sure about the othe two, but I'll let you know."

Jamie pushed her fingers through her hair. "Why th sudden oral fixation with the three victims he bludgeoned?"

"Your guess is as good as mine, Jamie. It's as if I'm lookin at the work of two different killers. But killers evolve, fin what they like and don't. I don't think anyone, except th actual killer, will be able to tell you."

"If only he could talk. At least Foster's family is refusing t pay for a defence attorney, and they won't be here for the tria They severed all ties with him." Jamie failed to hide her smile

Chapter 54

If he was to remain confined to the bed, with no means to contact his beloved Madison, he could at least draft her a letter in his mind. Foster committed it to memory and decided to recite it to Maddie when she lay snug in his arms, after making love to her.

My Darling Maddie,

I'm sorry they took you away from me. This isn't how I intended our life together. We're supposed to be a family. Me, you and Emily. Fucking Emily who thought she could kill me. I told her she's my soulmate – it's impossible for her to kill me. I blame her for the time you and I spent apart. And I promise you, my love, I'll make Emily pay.

Darling, I don't blame you for not looking at me. The sight of me must have pained you greatly as I lay fighting for my life, and for you.

Because you're my life.

I promise we'll never spend another day without each other.

You're mine. Forever.

Chapter 55

Tuesday, 29 June, 5:30 p.m.

Their age difference baffled Noa – twelve years. Having an instant sibling for Jamie, and two five-year-olds in the house, couldn't have been easy for Aaron and Laura. Noa leaned against the wall, gazing at Luke with his arms around Madison. King hadn't left Madison's side since she arrived and lay with his head on her lap.

The silence between the siblings spoke volumes. Madison had decided to get a Glock 43 after shooting with Noa's. Luke had agreed to help her with the paperwork.

"Are you joining us or are you going to keep staring at us?" Luke asked with his back to her.

"I'm hungry. What do you guys want for dinner?"

"She's beautiful, sexy, knows how to handle a gun, not to mention a knife and she cooks. I understand why you're keeping her. Is she as good in bed as I suspect?" Madison whispered loud enough for Noa to hear.

"I heard that." Noa stepped closer and ruffled Madison's hair.

"I wanted you to. Thank you for asking me to stay here tonight. I needed to get out of that house. Mom's constant crying was driving me nuts."

"Give her time. You're her baby and she's probably thinking about what could've happened. And blaming herself for letting you out of her womb." Noa walked towards the kitchen, turning around halfway. "I think we can all do with some pizza, red wine and binge-watching a comedy series. Question, why is there such a big age gap between you guys?"

Luke met her eyes over Madison's head. "Our parents were twenty-one when they fell pregnant with Jamie and back then they didn't live on the farm. Even now social workers and police officers don't earn a lot of money and then they had me to take care of as well. My grandfather passed away a year after they adopted me, and we all moved in here to live with my grandmother. I inherited the farm from her. My mother's parents left Lamont Estate to her with specific terms in their will that it one day be passed onto Jamie and Madison. They never accepted me as part of their family. But my paternal grandmother always made sure I knew how much she loved me."

"They were assholes. I'm glad they're dead." Madison said.

Noa agreed but kept her opinion to herself.

"What's done is done. I love this place and now I love it even more." Luke winked at Noa.

"When are you two going to make babies?"

Noa stifled a laugh and rushed for the safety of the kitchen. "You're on your own with your sister, Taylor."

Luke cleared his throat. "Well, Maddie, that isn't any of your business."

"I just want to know if I should sleep down here tonight. I don't want to hear anything my young, innocent ears can never un-hear."

An alarm tone sounded on Luke's phone. Madison stiffened in his arms. "It's okay. It's just Slay coming to fetch his jacket."

Luke rose and walked to the front door. King leapt off the couch and ran outside.

Noa peeked around the corner. "You do realise he'll know you've been wearing it if you're still wearing it when he walks through the door, right?"

Madison unzipped the jacket and shrugged out of it, pushing her bottom lip out. "I want to keep it."

"Maybe he'll let you keep it when he realises you've been wearing it."

"He won't know." Madison rolled her eyes.

"Hey, Sherlock, it smells like you." Noa grinned.

Madison cursed.

Tuesday, 29 June, 5:45 p.m.

Footsteps on the porch signalled their guest's arrival. Madison's heart lodged in her throat, and she drew in an unsteady breath. Noa peeked around the corner again, giving her a wicked smile.

"I don't like you very much. I'll take my brother back. Don't push me." Madison smiled as Noa stuck her tongue out. "You're the childish one, middle daughter."

"I never had siblings. I have a lot of time to make up for and learn. Suck it up if you want my help writing songs."

"You've got the sibling blackmail down. Who would've guessed the bitch in the kitchen was the infamous lead singer and occasional drummer of Slay?"

"Yes?" came a familiar voice.

Madison turned to face the man who had carried her in his arms the previous day when she could've easily walked. The man who had stayed with her until Jamie had taken her to hospital. The man whose jacket Madison hadn't taken off except when she showered, and it had been a coin toss about wearing it in the shower.

"I'm glad to find you up and about." He extended a hand. "I'm Clay Davis. My friends call me Slay."

Madison shook his hand and moved closer. She stood on tiptoes and wrapped her arms around his neck. "Thank you for taking care of me. Damn, you smell good. What is it?" She pulled away.

The corners of Clay's mouth lifted. His light blue eyes were full of laughter.

Luke patted Clay on the back as he walked to the kitchen. "Welcome to the rollercoaster which is Madison Taylor. Do you want a beer?"

"Thanks, Luke, a beer sounds good. Your brother told me

you went shooting today and you're getting a Glock 43. I'm impressed. If you ever want to go target shooting in Shadow Bay, I can go with you. I go to a private shooting range whenever I can."

Madison's heart clenched, and she took a step back.

Clay's eyes dropped to his feet. "If you want. Whenever. Doesn't have to be tomorrow or next week."

Luke returned and pushed a beer into Clay's hand. "I'd prefer it if you went shooting every week. It's not something you do once a year. And who better to help you than a member of SWAT. I'm, of course, the best option, but I've seen Slay in action. He can hold his own."

Madison frowned. "You two know each other?"

"Yes. All SWAT officers go through training in Marcel. Slay was part of the team when we took down the syndicate I'd spent years infiltrating."

"I'll drink to that. Not a bad first time out with the team." The men clanked their bottles together.

Noa joined them and asked Clay if he wanted to stay for dinner. He said he would as long as he wasn't imposing. After dinner, Luke and Noa busied themselves in the kitchen.

Madison and Clay sat on the couch. King nestled between them with his head on Madison's lap. She rhythmically stroked King's back and smiled when he sighed.

"Is he yours?" Clay asked.

"No, but I want to keep him. He hasn't left my side since I got here. It's as if he knows." Madison trailed her fingers over King's head.

"I wish I could get one, but dogs aren't allowed in my apartment complex. And it's cruel to keep a dog inside for hours at a time."

Madison kept her focus on the dog. "Where do you live?"

"In Shadow Bay, a complex called The Gables."

"No way, which block?"

Clay studied Madison, his arm resting on his jacket laying on the armrest. "Number four."

"I'm in block one. Small world." Madison dragged her eye from Clay's and looked at her hand gliding over King's back.

"Listen, Madison." Clay shifted to face her, aware of the dog keeping a protective eye on him. "If you need anything someone to talk to or run errands with, let me know."

"I'll be okay. Thanks for offering, but I can't take you up on it." Madison made an attempt to smile.

"The offer stands. Your friends might not understand when you get anxious in public places. It helps to have someone who does. I brought you the contact details of the department appointed psychiatrist we all see when we need to. I like her Doesn't feel like going to see a shrink, more as if you're talking to the cool aunt your parents say is a bad influence on you." Clay's smile was warm and honest.

Madison took the card he held out to her. "Is this part of your duty, taking care of women you carry out of cellars where serial killers held them hostage?"

Clay shook his head and looked away. "No, it's not. But keep in contact with some of the people who've come across my path over the years. I just want to help. I'll go now." Clay pushed to his feet as Luke and Noa came into the living room both glaring at Madison.

"I'm sorry. It's very kind of you. I'm just new to the whole being a victim thing. I'm not yet sure how to act or react."

"You survived, Madison," Clay said, turning to her. "No everyone is that lucky. Luke has my number. If you need a shoulder, a friend, whatever, call me. Thanks for dinner, Noa Good seeing you again, Taylor. Wish it was under different circumstances."

Madison's eyes followed Clay as he headed towards the front door. She realised that Clay didn't take his jacket. "You jacket." Madison held it out to him.

"Keep it. It smells like you. Call me any time, Madison. Day or night. You don't have to go through this alone."

Madison didn't know how to respond to Clay's kindness.

"Thanks, Slay. It means the world to me that you're willing

to keep an eye on Maddie," Luke said, walking Clay out the door.

Madison inhaled as much air as her lungs allowed, and as she exhaled, tears dripped onto her chest.

Noa hugged her and rubbed the same soothing circles on her back she had done earlier in the day. "One day at a time, Mads. One day at a time. Just don't shut people out who are trying to help you. You don't have to take Clay up on his offer, but don't make the same mistakes I did. Please."

"I felt calmer while he was here. I don't know if it was petting King or Clay's presence and scent, but I didn't want him to leave. How screwed up am I?" Madison buried her face in Noa's shoulder.

"It's completely normal after what happened yesterday. You see Clay as a protector, and you need to feel safe."

"Yes, but does his eyes, smile, voice, compassion and the way he smells add to the feeling of being safe?"

Noa laughed. "You're going to be fine, Madison Taylor. Give yourself time and go see the psychiatrist Clay told you about. And promise me, if you feel unsafe, you'll call him?"

Madison lowered her voice. "I'm not feeling very safe now with the way my brother is looking at me."

Luke sighed. "Dammit, Maddie, Slay was just being nice to you. He lost his sister a few years back after an ex-boyfriend took her hostage. Boyfriend shot her, and a SWAT sniper took him out before he could kill anyone else in the building. Slay was there at the scene. He didn't realise his sister was the target as the hostage taker refused to talk to the negotiator. Clay isn't the type of guy who will hold it against you, so please, call him if you need anything."

Chapter 56

With a grateful smile, Noa returned her phone to the kitchen island and switched on the kettle. Emily's ex-boyfriend, Justin, was safe. He had checked himself into rehab for his gambling addiction. Justin confessed to Noa that he wanted to address his addiction before getting married, if his fiancée still wanted him after learning the truth.

It was pointless to ask Justin what he remembered about the night before Emily had broken up with him. After seeing a photo of the lingerie Officer Kori Sheridan had worn at the time of her death, it left no doubt in Noa's mind – Foster had orchestrated it.

The devil had ruined enough lives. Noa wasn't going to tell Justin about his involvement in their break-up. When Justin had asked, she didn't lie when she said she had realised they were not a lifetime fit. Noa didn't mention she'd realised this while they were still dating.

A sense of calm surrounded Noa now that the refurbishment was complete, her boxes unpacked, and their home created. Noa smiled every time she walked into the kitchen, grateful Luke had agreed to break down the wall.

She drank her coffee, watching the sway of the willow trees on the riverbank. King ran past the window. Luke walked not far behind him and winked when he caught her watching him.

Here she had found everything a person should want in life. This life, this peace, the passion she and Luke shared.

This is what it's all about.

Noa glanced at the photo Jamie had sent the previous day. She ran her thumb over her phone's screen. "One day we will give you a cousin," she said at the sonogram photo.

Everyone in the family was grateful for the twins growing inside Jamie. It would be weeks before they learned the gender of the babies. Luke had been adamant they be named Lucas and James if they were both boys, or Luca and Jamie for girls. Luke and Luca for a brother and sister. None of the other family members approved.

"How about we work on that cousin as soon as we get home?" Luke hugged Noa from behind, resting his chin on her head. "Does life get any better than this?"

"I can't imagine it could."

"Are you ready to go?" Luke increased his hold on her. "I feel sick."

"Big, strong you, scared of me being in the same room as a chained man? Jamie will be right next to me, and there will be two guards in the room." Noa turned in his embrace and stood on tiptoes to press her lips to his chin.

Luke bent his head and kissed her hard, making her stomach flip. For a moment Noa considered staying at home and working on a cousin for the Edwards twins.

"Have you decided whether you want to be Noa or Emily?"

"I'll tell you later. Let's go. I want this over with. I believe you mentioned you're cooking tonight and I'm dying for your pasta. The one with the Vodka, cream and tomatoes. And the very special dessert you serve afterwards. Oh, and you're going to be the plate, again." The memory flashed in Luke's eyes. Noa's breath caught as she felt his body respond.

"I believe it's your turn to be the plate. We're having dinner with my parents tonight. Our special dinner will have to be tomorrow night. How did you get the strawberry stains out of the bed sheet?" Luke smacked Noa's bum as they headed out the door. "Maddie, Slay and Richard are also joining us tonight."

"You can call him my father." Noa would be forever grateful that Luke had invited Richard over for coffee. At the time she hadn't been, but after hearing the truth, Noa realised her mother had destroyed Richard's life as well. She'd been the reason Noa never had a relationship with her father by lying to both of them. And in the end, life is too short to carry a grudge. Especially when the person to blame was dead.

Noa turned to Luke as he closed the front door. "I'm so happy that Maddie is spending time with Clay. It's good to know she has someone to look out for her. The last time we spoke she told me she has been hitting the bull's-eye every week. Why are we all having dinner tonight? I don't remember it being someone's birthday."

Luke reached for Noa's hand. "We always have something to celebrate."

Wednesday, 28 July, 9:00 a.m.

The anticipation of seeing them sent Foster's pulse racing. He bided his time in the holding cell. *A fucking cage.* He didn't have to rehearse what he planned to say to Emily. Since the day she had gutted him, Foster fantasised about putting the cricket bat to work on her face.

The police still didn't have much on him – for which Foster was grateful. He didn't have much confidence in his defence attorney.

On the day of Foster's arrest, the Ericson's had turned their backs on their son. Foster didn't need them. He'd never cared about Father and Mother Ericson. At least he'd made something of himself, on his own. Without their inherited money, they'd be nothing.

As soon as he was free, Foster planned to start drawing again. He missed designing buildings.

Perhaps he'd change his name, seeing he had gained some notoriety in the media over the past month. The names Foster

Ericson and Eric Foster were now that of a serial killer, and not a man deeply in love.

Nothing mattered except Maddie being naked next to him. And Emily? Smashed to pieces. In the literal sense. Foster had designed a very specific instrument for Emily; the drawing was laying on his cot. The dumb guards who searched his cell every morning thought it was a picture of a medieval wheel. *Idiots.*

The metal door opened, and the guards strode towards him. It was time to see his girls again. Foster smiled when his body responded to the memory of their taste. He didn't try to hide his excitement from the guards.

A guard yanked down his pants while the other took photos.

"Send it to Captain Johnson and Detective Edwards. Got you, you sonofabitch."

Foster's adrenaline spiked. "That constitutes police brutality, and is a form of sexual assault. You will lose your jobs."

The guards looked at each other and laughed.

The younger guard slammed handcuffs around Foster's wrists. "Not the first man to be taken down by his own dick."

Chapter 57

Wednesday, 28 July, 9:15 a.m.

Luke's knuckles turned white as he gripped the back of a chair in the observation room. He hated the idea of Noa and Foster being in the same room.

This would be Jamie's last case for the foreseeable future.

The previous week Luke had offered her a job. He needed help as the shooting range had proved to be a good business decision. After news broke of a serial killer in their quaint valley, even residents in the surrounding towns started taking self-protection seriously.

Foster's smug smile grated on Luke's nerves. Since being brought in, he stared at the two-way mirror. The fact that Foster's hands and legs were chained did nothing to calm the hatred boiling in Luke's blood.

Luke watched the guards' every move as they secured the chain to the floor. *I hate this.*

Jamie entered the interrogation room with Noa on her heels. Jamie focused on Foster. Noa's eyes were trained on the back of Jamie's shoes.

Captain Johnson joined Luke and crossed his arms over his chest. The guards stood with their backs against the wall, one on either side of Foster.

"Well, *Detective*, aren't you the picture of radiance? Pregnancy suits you. How is the precious bundle of joy growing inside you? I hope your morning sickness is gone by now. You poor thing."

There wasn't a room in Jamie's house the crime scene

investigators hadn't found a hidden camera.

Foster shifted in his seat, the chains clanking eerily against the metal of his chair. "It was a marvellous conception. Thank you for sharing it with me."

Jamie opened the folder laying on the table. "Let the record state that Foster Ericson, aka Eric Foster, has admitted to installing surveillances cameras inside the house of Detective Jamie Edwards." Her eyes lifted towards the ceiling in the right corner. "This conversation is being recorded. Anything you say *will* be used against you in court."

Foster gave a single nod. "Noted, Jamie. Voyeurism is a misdemeanour. As for the charges of breaking and entering, you invited me into your home, as your friend. You should be careful who you allow close to that precious child you're carrying."

Foster leaned back in the chair and turned his attention to Noa, who was still keeping her head bowed. "My darling, Emily. It's wonderful to see you again. Why are you afraid of me, my love? There's no need for fear here. We're family. And families love each other, take care of each other, keep each other safe. All those things I did for you. Why are you here, if you won't even look at me?"

Jamie stood and walked to the two-way mirror, leaving a clear view for those on the other side of the glass, when she turned around. "Cut the bullshit, Foster. Noa's here. Start talking. You agreed to confess to the murders of the four women found buried behind your house. Tell me why you killed them?"

"Are you sure there are only four? I could've sworn there were more."

"How many people did you kill?"

"Are you sure *I* killed them, Detective?" He smiled, placing his cuffed hands on the table.

Jamie kept emotion from her voice. "Stop wasting your time and confess. I'm sure you're eager to get back to your cell."

"Speaking of my cell, I wish to lay a complaint against these two guards for sexual harassment and production of pornographic material. Distribution of said material, I believe, should also be added."

Jamie walked to the table and laid her hands on the back of the chair she had vacated. "Do you remember having your cheek swabbed? When the forensic dentist took a mould of your teeth? Or when your fingerprints were taken?"

"Of course, I do. I felt like a lab rat." Foster faked a shudder.

"Mr Ericson, the guards didn't touch you, as per the judge's instruction. Therefore, taking a photo of your erect penis does not constitute harassment. It's gathering evidence."

Foster chewed the inside of his cheek. "No court will allow it."

"Ted Bundy's teeth impression matched the bite mark found on one of his victims. Fingerprints and DNA have aided to convict murderers for decades. Even ear, palm, knee and footprints have been submitted as evidence. As we speak, the photo of your penis, including its length, girth, veins and the distinct ridge which formed because of your botched circumcision, is being compared to the DIY dildos you left inside three of your victims. So is the one found in Benjamin Clarke's house, as well as the one retrieved from the duffel bag you left at Noa Morgan's house when you assaulted her. Also, those found in the cabin where you held Emily Gallagher captive for forty days. It's all evidence, Mr Ericson, or Mr Foster, whichever you prefer." Jamie moved around the chair and sat, pulling the file closer.

"The dildos were gifts I made for my lovers. Someone stole them from my house." Foster grinned. "Did it bring you pleasure, Emily?"

"Why did you stab my mother to death?" Noa asked, keeping her hands on her lap.

Foster bent forward to scratch his nose with the back of his right hand. "Your mother? She wasn't stabbed to death dear, precious, *Emily*. As I recall, she had her skull bashed in.

She deserved far worse for not loving you. If memory serves me right, her case has never been solved. The police suspect a disgruntled family member of a person she convicted was responsible. Why mention her now? In all the years we've been friends we rarely spoke about her."

Noa's head lifted and she leaned back in the chair, her hands remaining on her lap. "The police never made her cause of death public. Only the killer knows how she died."

Laughter filled the room.

Luke wanted to wrap his hands around Foster's neck and squeeze until his eyes bulged out of his head.

"Tell me, how is my delicious Madison?" Foster leered at the two-way mirror. "Maddie, my love, are you back there? Come, sit with us. I miss you." His eyes shifted to Jamie. "I said I'd talk if *both* Emily and Madison were in the room."

"Madison gave me a message to give to you," Noa said and then remained silent.

Foster's head bobbed. "Well, out with it."

"That was her message to you. Nothing. See, Foster, you think spending two nights with her created an eternal bond." Noa's shoulder's shook, joy bubbled from deep within her. "Madison felt nothing for you. You're nothing more than a hangover to her. Remember how we were at her age? You promise yourself you'll never drink again, or have another one-night stand, yet before you know it, you do. Madison's in a committed relationship now. I guess she learned something after wasting a weekend of her life with you."

Foster tried to stand up. "Fucking whore! You're lying." The guards pushed him back down.

"No. I'm not. I should thank you for *everything* I have in my life now – a family, a relationship with my father and the love of the most incredible man. Thanks to you, Madison realised what she's worth and that she deserves love. Remember the SWAT officer who took her away from you? Well, he didn't need to take her away from you emotionally. Madison never cared for you past her orgasm."

Foster grinned. "Tell me, does she glow like Detective Edwards here? Does she know my child is growing inside her? I'll always be a part of her life, through my child. I could smell and taste her ovulation."

"Wow. You're a walking, talking, ovulation stick. Did she have to pee on you? No?" Noa lowered her voice. "Madison isn't pregnant. She's on the injection and they gave her the morning-after pill at the hospital, just to be safe. Guess there aren't any Father's Day gifts in your future."

Luke's chest wanted to explode as he watched Noa.

"I think we're done here. Guards, take him back to his cell." Jamie pushed her chair back.

"We haven't spoken about the eight women you found. Isn't that why you came?"

"Eight? I remember saying four."

"Elementary, my dear Edwards."

Jamie shrugged. "We don't have to talk about them. You didn't kill them. You had knowledge of their murders and will be charged as an accessory. Someone was a bigger, badder wolf than you – Benjamin Clarke. We found Clarke's DNA inside the victims and his fingerprints on the envelope containing their identification cards. You murdered Clarke because of his fascination with Noa."

Foster threw his head back in exasperation. "Clarke didn't study Emily. He studied me through her. Yes, he killed them because he wanted to be like me. I'm the one sitting here, not him."

Noa leaned forward. "And you think you're better off than him?"

"I have my entire life to look forward to. I'll be found innocent by reason of insanity. Didn't you see the papers my attorney filed?"

Noa and Jamie both laughed.

"You're a malignant narcissist, not insane," Noa said. "Detective Edwards, we're done here." Noa stood, holding her right hand over her left.

"I will always remember your taste, Emily." Foster licked his lips.

Luke headed for the door. Captain Johnson grabbed his shoulder. "She's doing well. He knows you're in here. Don't give him the satisfaction." Captain Johnson removed his hand, after giving Luke's shoulder a hard and reassuring slap.

Noa kept her back rigid. "Hold on to the way Emily tasted. Remember it when you're giving blowjobs for protection inside the joint."

"Me need protection? I'm a serial killer. You don't get worse than me. I'm at the top of the food chain."

"You only murdered three women. Your supposed student, Benjamin Clarke, did better than you. Don't you think the big guys will find it interesting that you, Eric Foster, a gay man, enjoyed sticking things inside your female victims? To them, you'll be nothing but a plaything, something to keep them warm at night."

"I'm not gay. I've never been with a man." Foster pursed his lips.

"Well, Eric Foster is, and you'll be tried and convicted as Eric Foster."

Foster snorted a laugh. "No plaything kills four women, one man and let's not forget the well-matured Judge Gallagher. Mommy tried so hard to please me, but I considered her an appetiser to you, my main course."

Jamie looked at Noa and nodded. "The fourth women being Officer Sheridan?" Jamie asked.

"Someone who kills a police officer is considered the highest on the food chain inside," Foster smirked.

Jamie opened the file and scanned through the pages. "I don't see her name listed as one of your victims. Her case remains unsolved, as we believe the suspect to be a man called Rick, last name unknown. No mention of you."

Luke felt the same pride towards his sister as he uncrossed his arms.

Foster stared at Jamie. "Did you, or did you not, find a pink dildo next to her body?"

"No mention of it in her case file."

"Bullshit, Jamie. It was in her mouth when she took a bulle
between her eyes."

Luke turned to Captain Johnson. "His desire for recognitio
is working in our favour. Typical."

"You admit to shooting and killing Officer Kori Sheridan?"
Jamie asked.

"No." Foster pressed his lips together.

"Only the killer would know about the *pink* dildo. W
found it intact and compared it to the others. Your dick real
is your nemesis."

"Top of the food chain, bitch. I'll be out before you go fo
your next sonogram appointment."

Foster turned to Noa. "Any parting words for the love o
your life? It won't be forever; I will taste you again." He flicke
his tongue at her.

"Some advice … don't drop anything. A pretty guy lik
you is prime meat in prison. Oh, and don't sleep. One of you
victims' brother is in the same penitentiary." Noa tapped he
right pointer finger against her forehead. "I can't recall he
name. Jamie, can you?"

"No, but it's definitely one of the three innocent youn
women he tortured, mutilated and murdered."

Noa continued with a smile. "Don't show them the sca
I gave you. Doesn't make you very badass that your victi
gutted you like a fish."

"Your taste, Emily, will get me through all of it."

Noa placed her palms flat on the table and leaned forward
"Emily's taste. Me? Noa Morgan? I taste of Luke. Thanks t
you, I have such an aversion to condoms I can't stand the sigh
of them. And who needs condoms when you're making lov
to your fiancé."

Foster glanced at Noa's left hand. "You're mine, Emily
Mine!"

Noa headed towards the door. "Goodbye, Eric, Foste

soon to be bubba's bitch. Enjoy the few days you have left on this earth. Someone will finish what I started."

Foster called after her. "Thank the Neanderthal for visiting me in hospital."

Chapter 58

Wednesday, 28 July, 10:30 a.m.

A few doors down from the interrogation room, Noa sank to the floor. Her body trembled. Luke ran down the passage and joined her on the floor. "I'm so proud of you, honey."

"Noa. I want to be Noa."

Luke helped Noa to her feet and they walked out of the prison.

In the bright winter sun, Noa stopped, closed her eyes, and lifted her face towards the sky. "I haven't felt free in years. I've missed this feeling."

Luke pressed his mouth to her hair, drawing her into his arms.

Noa placed her hands on his leather jacket, staring at the ring. She tried to remove it from her finger. "I swear your grandmother's ring didn't fit this snug two days ago when we first got the idea to throw Foster off."

Luke took her hands in his. "I had it resized." He smiled and bent down on one knee. "Noa Morgan, I love you. I've been infatuated with you since the night we met. Please don't ever remove this ring. Will you marry me?"

"Guess I need to change my name again." Noa touched the stubble on his cheeks. "Noa Taylor? I like the sound of that."

"You need to say *yes*." Luke stood and cupped her face in his hands, bending down until their lips almost touched.

"Yes, Luke Taylor. I love you." Noa pressed her mouth to his, wrapping her arms around his neck. Luke lifted her up and hugged her tight against his body.

"Hey, you two, this is a prison parking lot. Take it home," Jamie said as she strode past them.

Luke eased Noa down and she held her left hand out to Jamie. "We're engaged for real. Luke asked me to marry him."

Jamie stared at her brother and frowned. "Outside a prison? How romantic." She rolled her eyes. "Thought you were going to ask her tonight before the hush-hush engagement party."

Luke ran his thumb across Noa's bottom lip. His smile matched hers. "It doesn't matter. She's mine."

Acknowledgements

My fellow Thriller Babes. Your support and encouragement are unmatched. I'm forever grateful to share the highs and lows that come with being an author with you. Each of you inspire me more than you'll ever know.

My utmost gratitude to you, the reader. Without your support, I wouldn't be able to keep doing what I love most – sharing my imaginary friends with you.

To my first-pass readers – Holly, Jen, Maricka, Nicolina, Tania, and Yolanda. As always, your feedback is invaluable. Thank you.

A special shoutout to Nicolina Pieterse for always ensuring the medical information is correct. And to Jen Peterson, for reading it again after the last round of editing.

Every ARC reader. I know your time is valuable and your to-be-read list never-ending. Thank you for making the time to read and review Death Isn't Enough.

Jessica Huntley, my editor. Your help is greatly appreciated, and even more so, your time and dedication to ensure that my work is the best it can be. The comments you made in certain scenes made me laugh out loud. Thank you.

Jana and Marc Barclay, for the cover design. Your patience is commendable. I'm beyond grateful to share the pre-release journey with both of you. Marc, thank you for giving me permission to use your name. You're a phenomenal drummer; Noa has nothing on you.

Kori Sheridan, your enthusiasm at the idea of having your name in one of my books was incredible.

Thank you, Doctor JJ Odendaal, for sharing your knowledge of medicine with me. Hopefully I'll never need to use it for anything other than my writing.

To my family and friends. There are no words to thank you for what you do for me behind the page.

Most of all, to God. May I always use the talent You gave me

All mistakes are my own.

About the author

Mariëtte Whitcomb studied Criminology and Psychology at the University of Pretoria. Writing allows her to pursue her childhood dream to hunt criminals, albeit fictional and born in the darkest corners of her imagination.

When Mariëtte isn't writing, she loves reading psychological thrillers and true crime books or spends time with her family, friends, and two miniature schnauzers.

Connect with Mariëtte:
Sign up for her newsletter on her website:
https://mariettewhitcomb.com
Email: mariette@mariettewhitcomb.com
Facebook: @mariettewhitcombauthor
Instagram: @mariettewhitcomb
Goodreads: https://www.goodreads.com/
goodsreadscommariettewhitcomb
Bookbub: https://www.bookbub.com/authors/mariette-whitcomb

Also by Mariëtte Whitcomb

FINLEY SERIES

Orca / Book One

Deception / Book Two

Binding Lies / Book Three

Fortius / Book Four

STANDALONE THRILLERS

The Skull Keeper

9 781991 202932